THE SKELETON FLUTE

THE SKELETON FLUTE

DAMARA ALLEN

ALADDIN

New York • London • Toronto
Sydney • New Delhi

ALADDIN

An imprint of Simon & Schuster Children's Publishing Division
1230 Avenue of the Americas, New York, New York 10020
First Aladdin hardcover edition August 2024
Text copyright © 2024 by Damara Allen
Jacket illustration copyright © 2024 by Nipuni
Simon & Schuster: Celebrating 100 Years of Publishing in 2024
For information about special discounts for bulk purchases, please contact
Simon & Schuster Special Sales at 1-866-506-1949 or business@simonandschuster.com.
The Simon & Schuster Speakers Bureau can bring authors to your live event. For more
information or to book an event contact the Simon & Schuster Speakers Bureau
at 1-866-248-3049 or visit our website at www.simonspeakers.com.
Designed by Tiara Iandiorio
The text of this book was set in Tisa OT.
Manufactured in the United States of America 0724 BVG
2 4 6 8 10 9 7 5 3 1
Library of Congress Cataloging-in-Publication Data
Names: Allen, Damara, author.
Title: The skeleton flute / Damara Allen.
Description: First Aladdin hardcover edition August 2024. |
New York : Aladdin, 2024. | Audience: Ages 8 to 12. | Summary: As Sam learns his
parents are separating, a stranger offers him a magic flute that will grant his greatest
desire, but soon Sam discovers that while it worked on his parents, his two siblings
have disappeared, as if they never existed.
Identifiers: LCCN 2023059650 (print) | LCCN 2023059651 (ebook) |
ISBN 9781665946605 (hardcover) | ISBN 9781665946629 (ebook)
Subjects: LCSH: Magic—Juvenile fiction. | Flute—Juvenile fiction. |
Wishes—Juvenile fiction. | Siblings—Juvenile fiction. | Separated parents—Juvenile
fiction. | Families—Juvenile fiction. | CYAC: Magic—Fiction. | Flute—Fiction. |
Wishes—Fiction. | Siblings—Fiction. | Separation—Fiction. | Family life—Fiction.
Classification: LCC PZ7.1.A43838 Sk 2024 (print) | LCC PZ7.1.A43838 (ebook) |
DDC 813.6 [Fic]—dc23/eng/20240408
LC record available at https://lccn.loc.gov/2023059650
LC ebook record available at https://lccn.loc.gov/2023059651

To my husband, Hugh, and to my daughter, Avery—
it's never too late to chase your dreams,
and you both helped me see that

Chapter 1

HEIGHTS AREN'T MY THING. BEING UP high makes my head spin and butterflies surge into my stomach. The high dive at Lake Ingershall stretches out over the blue-green water, twenty feet above the glittery surface.

Taunting me.

Everyone else in the seventh grade can make the jump. Heck, even most of the sixth graders have done it.

But not me.

My nine-year-old brother, Grayson—who says I'm a chicken and that's why I won't jump—plops down on the beach blanket. His curly black hair is dusted with sand, and his light brown skin is shiny from the sunscreen Mom made him put on when we got here.

He turns to me and frowns. "This is weird. Why did Mom and Dad let us skip school and come to the beach?"

"Who cares?" I say, watching our parents chase our three-year-old sister, Addie, across the sand. "We're at the beach on a school day. Derek's gonna freak when I tell him."

What I don't tell Grayson is that he's right. This *is* weird. Of all the things I was expecting when I woke up this morning, a beach day wasn't one of them. Math? Social studies? Embarrassing myself in gym class? All possibilities.

But lounging on the beach at eleven o'clock on a Tuesday morning? Totally weird. I wasn't gonna argue, though. It's giving me one last chance to prove I'm not a chicken.

"But, Sam," Grayson says. "Don't you think Mom and Dad are being strange?"

I shake my head. "Let it go, Gray. Just have fun. Who knows if we'll get this chance again?"

It's just like Grayson to try to ruin an epic day at the beach by being grumpy. Dude takes life *way* too seriously. I, on the other hand, have big plans for today—hot dogs from the concession stand, sunbathing in the last rays of sun before autumn sets in, making sandcastles with Addie.

And finally, once and for all, jumping off the high dive.

"Are you gonna do it?" Grayson asks, following my gaze across the lake.

"What?"

"The high dive. Are you gonna jump?"

I swallow hard and nod, but I can tell he doesn't believe me. I've been saying I'm gonna jump for weeks now. I spent the entire summer trying to work up the nerve, and now, on our very last trip to the beach before it closes for the rest of the year, I'm not sure it's gonna happen. The butterflies are already fluttering around in my stomach.

"Go on, then," he says, almost like he's challenging me. "Do it."

"Shush, Grayson. Don't rush me."

He frowns and pulls a bright yellow bag of potato chips from the picnic basket. I scowl at him as he eats them—like some kind of *monster*—with his mouth open. The wet crunching sound makes the dark hairs on my arms curl up in disgust.

"Ugh," I say, snatching the bag away from him. "Were you raised in a barn?"

He tosses a chip at me, and it hits me in the cheek, one sharp edge stinging my skin.

"Yes."

I scrunch up my nose. "I knew it. The smell was a dead giveaway."

"Hey!" Grayson shoots me a dirty look as Mom crosses the sand to the blanket, her sun hat flopping lazily around her face.

"Sam, be nice," she says, even though I'm sure she didn't hear what I said. Her mom radar is on point.

"He can't be nice," Grayson says. "He was raised in a barn too."

Mom sinks down in her beach chair and shakes her head. "You two are something else."

Grayson breaks into a fit of giggles. I peel off my T-shirt, and Mom hands me the sunscreen. I roll my eyes but rub it on anyway, because winning this fight would be like winning a pie-eating contest against a bear after hibernation.

Mom glances at the lifeguard stations. "Stay close and make sure you check in once in a while."

"Okay, I will."

She gives me a smile, but there's something behind it. Sadness? Exhaustion? I never know anymore. This morning at breakfast her eyes were puffy and red-rimmed. Now they're just sort of empty.

Something's going on, but I've known that for a

while. There've been lots of hushed conversations behind closed doors, super-awkward family dinners, and a feeling of *wrongness*. I'd have to be completely clueless not to have noticed.

A little shiver shakes through me. I don't wanna think about that. Not today, not on beach day.

All buttered up, I wade out into the water toward the deep end. It's gloriously warm. I move toward the high dive with purpose. *This is it, Sam. It's your moment to shine.* On the other side of the lake, the ladder with peeling green paint thrusts out of the water, leading straight up to the high dive. The sun-warmed rungs smell tangy and sharp.

At least the beach is empty. The usual gang of boys from Stapleton Middle School is stuck in class today, so there's no one here to laugh at me when I freeze up. Unless you count Grayson, and I rarely do.

I look up at the pale blue board hanging above me. It's high. *Too* high. I place one hand on the rung in front of me, then another. My stomach clenches and I swallow hard.

I can do this. I can do this.

Sweat breaks out on my forehead—little quivering beads of cowardice. If the guys from school were here, now's when they would be laughing at me and pointing.

I can do this. I can—

I can't do it.

I let go of the rungs and drift backward through the water. This was supposed to be my moment. But I choked. Again. I sink into the water and roll onto my back.

Maybe next summer.

The sky is clear and bright blue. I stare up at it and it stares back, the sun warming my skin from the top as the water warms it from below. Small ripples float across the surface from Addie and Grayson playing in the shallow end.

Addie squeals and I sit up, watching them. She grabs a handful of sand and chases Grayson down the beach. Her black curls bounce around her head like a wild halo. Grayson runs away from her, his head thrown back. Addie catches up, ready to nail him with sand, but he tickles her before she gets a chance.

I scowl.

If I hadn't chickened out, I'd be watching them from the top of the high dive right now. I sigh and wade back through the deeper water to the shallow end. When I plop down in the sand, Addie joins me, bucket and shovel in hand.

"Sammy, help?" she asks, looking up at me with big brown eyes.

I smile. "Yes, I'll help you, Addie."

We pile the wet sand into the bucket and pat it down tight with the shovel. She sits close to me, one chubby little hand resting on my leg. Every couple of minutes she looks up at me and smiles. At least *she* doesn't know what a chicken her brother is.

"I thought you were gonna jump," Grayson says, coming up behind us. He smirks, and I consider dumping the bucket of sand over his head.

"I changed my mind."

Grayson opens his mouth to say something rude—I'm sure of it—when Dad sits down in the sand. "You'll get it eventually, bud—don't stress about it. I believe in you."

My cheeks burn a little. "Thanks, Dad."

"I didn't like heights when I was your age, either."

He winks and Grayson closes his mouth. *Ha, got you there.* He can't tease me without teasing Dad, too. I smile. Dad might be telling the truth, or he might be telling a little white lie. Either way, I'm grateful for the save.

Grayson shrugs and turns to me. "Will you help me with my model later?"

I roll my eyes and sigh, pretending to be annoyed. "I guess."

He grins. "Thanks, Sam."

"Sandcastle!" Addie says as I tip the bucket over and pull it free of the sand.

I rub her back. "Yeah, good job, Addie."

Addie stomps on the castle we just created, and my stomach growls loudly—that means it's hot dog time. I leave Addie and Grayson with Dad by the water and wander up to the blanket. Mom has a book in her hand, but her eyes are focused on the sand in front of her. She jumps when I grab my T-shirt from the ground.

"Oh, Sam, you scared me!"

I frown. Mom's not usually this jumpy. "Sorry. Can I get a hot dog from the concession stand?"

She reaches into her purse and pulls out a ten-dollar bill. "Get one for Grayson, too."

I snag the money. "What about Addie?"

Mom glances at the beach bag. "I packed her some snacks. She's way too busy to sit down and eat a hot dog."

I shrug and wrap my towel around my waist, then jog off toward the bathhouse on the other side of the lake. For the first time in like forever, I don't have to wait in a line at the concession stand. I order two hot dogs, fork over my money, and wait while the guy behind the counter puts them in buns.

Spiderwebs hang from the rafters above the window. I eye them, making sure none of the little eight-legged creeps up there decide to drop down on top of my head while I wait. I *hate* spiders.

Something rustles behind me.

On edge, I nearly jump out of my skin, then spin around. There's a flash of movement between the leaves and branches of the tall bushes that line the walkway around the lake. They shiver and shake, like someone's behind them, moving slowly.

I tilt my head. "H-hello? Is someone there?"

There's no answer except for the rustling of leaves. I frown. Who'd be hanging out in the bushes? A creepy-crawly sensation inches across my arms. I glance at the spiders again, but it's not them making my skin tingle. It's the feeling of being watched.

"Two hot dogs!"

The guy at the counter hands the hot dogs through the window. Heart thrashing, I grab them and turn back to the bushes. The movement's gone, but the feeling of being watched follows me as I balance the hot dogs in my hands and step onto the walkway.

Halfway around the lake, I stop and look behind me. A man's lurking in the shadows next to the bath-house. He's dressed in a full suit and brown dress shoes. His dark eyes peer out at me, but when I notice him, the man slips away and disappears from view.

An uneasy feeling slides into my stomach.

I turn back toward our blanket, meaning to tell Mom and Dad about the creepy dude in the bushes, when Grayson spots me coming. He runs down the beach and practically tackles me, snatching a hot dog from my hands.

We eat them sitting cross-legged on the blanket while Dad chases Addie down the beach. That girl has more energy than a Chihuahua.

"Hey, Gray, I think you got some ketchup on your shirt."

Grayson looks down at where I'm pointing, and I poke my finger into the tip of his nose.

"Hey!"

"You're not even wearing a shirt, you goof."

He narrows his eyes and goes back to eating his hot dog. I lean back, prop myself up on my elbows, and smile. If I could, I'd freeze this moment in time—the warm breeze blowing off the lake, Grayson with ketchup and mustard smeared across his mouth, the sound of Addie laughing. Except for the weird dude watching me from the bushes, it's been an epically perfect morning.

The good mood follows me through the rest of the day, all the way home, and into the evening. A day at the beach is tiring in the best way possible, and Grayson and

I lounge on the couch watching TV until dinner. Mom's making spaghetti and meatballs. Everything is right with the world.

I've completely forgotten about Mom's puffy red eyes and the sad smile on Dad's face as he carried the beach chairs to the car this morning. Nothing can ruin my good mood.

That is, until Mom sets her fork down during dinner and clears her throat. Her eyes are red again. She pushes her plate away and laces her fingers in front of her. Dad runs a hand over his short, curly black hair.

"Your dad and I need to talk to you both about something," Mom says quietly.

An uncomfortable feeling surges into my meatball-filled stomach, chasing away the happy memories of the beach.

I *knew* something wasn't right.

The ticktock of the clock in the kitchen is a hundred times louder than normal. The silence stretches, and stretches some more until I'm sure I'll explode. Whatever's going on, someone needs to spit it out. Now.

I swallow a lump in my throat. "What's wrong?"

Mom looks down at her hands. "Dad and I are separating."

Chapter 2

SHE FLINGS THE WORDS INTO THE AIR like she can't stand to have them inside her a minute longer. I flinch as they tumble from her mouth. *Ah, there it is.* It's all clicking into place. The last-minute trip to the beach on a school day to soften the blow.

Well played, Mom and Dad, well played.

Heat rises into my cheeks, spreading into my neck. Grayson's next to me, twirling spaghetti around with his fork, while Addie's using her fingers to make a masterpiece in the sauce on her plate. I turn my head and stare out through the thin curtains, trying to focus on the shapes beyond.

Anything not to think about what Mom just said.

"What does that mean?" Grayson asks, frowning. There's panic in his voice. The poor kid doesn't know "separation" is code for "divorce."

Dad shifts in his seat. "It means I'm going to move out, and you kids will stay here with Mom."

I squeeze my eyes shut. Separation? This is like a baseball bat upside the head when you're not expecting it. Not that you're ever expecting a baseball bat upside the head, but that's beside the point.

The space in my chest fills with fluttering.

I'm breathless, my heart thudding now. "You're getting a divorce?"

"No, sweetheart. We're taking a break. To work things out." Mom's voice wavers, and something inside me begins to unravel, like a spool of thread in the pit of my stomach slowly coming undone. If I'm not careful, it'll unwind into a tangled mess all over the floor.

Grayson's chin trembles, his brown eyes filling with tears. I know what he's thinking. There are too many kids at school whose parents "took a break," and now they've got two rooms, separate birthdays and Christmases, and a shiny new stepmom or stepdad trying to be best friends with them.

I swallow, scared of the answer, but needing to ask anyway. "When are you moving out?"

My question hangs in the air until Dad finally says, "The day after tomorrow."

I bite down on my bottom lip, trying to hold back the next question that jumps into my head. I don't wanna say it, I mean really don't wanna say it, but the words just kinda pop out. "Can't we live with you?"

Mom sucks in a sharp breath. There. That's why I didn't wanna say it. Her blue eyes cloud with hurt as she looks down at her hands. I love both my parents, but Dad and I are closer. I can't even think about not seeing him every day.

He shakes his head, and my cheeks sting like someone slapped them. How can he just leave us like this? That's like child abandonment or something.

"I'm staying with Uncle Chris for now, in his guest room," he says, his eyes going misty. "It's just temporary, Sam. I'll visit on the weekends."

Visit on the weekends? Dads aren't supposed to visit. A wild laugh bubbles up in my throat. Do they even hear themselves? The ridiculousness of it makes me uncomfortable. And when I'm uncomfortable, I make jokes. But I can't think of a single thing to lighten the mood right now. Besides, there's nothing funny about any of this.

My eyes dart back and forth between my parents' faces. They can't be serious. Can they? I never thought anything like this would happen to us. Maybe other people did, because Mom's white and Dad's Black, and people sometimes look at our family like we're a puzzle they can't put together. But we've always been happy.

Well, until recently.

Addie points at the spaghetti-sauce drawing on her plate. "Look, Dada. I make it for you."

He smiles and pats the top of her head. "Thanks, peanut."

I scowl at Addie, then instantly feel the sting of guilt. It's not her fault, but I am kinda jealous. What I wouldn't give to be that clueless. She has no idea what's happening right now. No idea that everything's about to change.

"Do you have to go?" A big tear rolls down Grayson's cheek, the question quivering on his lips. He grabs my hand under the table. I squeeze it back and fight my own tears, anger sparking to life in my chest. He might be my annoying little brother, but I hate seeing him cry.

Mom shifts off her chair and around to Grayson's side. She tucks her dirty-blond hair behind her ears, pulls him into her arms, and smooths his curls off his forehead. "It'll be okay, sweet pea."

I scowl. "Why don't *we* have a say in this?"

"I know this is going to be hard, guys," Mom says, ignoring my question. "Change isn't easy."

"But why does Dad have to go?" I ask, sounding whinier than I mean to. "Can't you work things out *here*?"

"We need a break," Dad says. "It's hard for you to understand at your age. Trust me, bud, if we thought there was a way around this, I wouldn't be leaving."

I press my lips together, the little spark of anger spreading like wildfire. What does my age have to do with anything? I don't have to be an adult to know this isn't fair. Parents shouldn't get to make big decisions like this without giving the kids a choice. We're part of this family too.

But they've made up their minds, and now my life is crumbling around me like a soggy cookie left in a cup of milk for way too long. If you're not careful, you get a pile of mush in the bottom of your cup. And that's what this feels like. Cold, yucky mush.

Dad stands, pats me on the back like that's supposed to make me feel better, and walks away, mumbling something about needing to start packing.

I'm trembling in my seat now, the heat inside my chest spreading through my body, into my arms and legs, a fire about to send me up in flames.

"Sam?" Mom asks quietly. "You okay?"

I shake my head, tears stinging my eyes and blurring my vision. Is she serious right now? How could I possibly be okay? Our family's splitting up. There's nothing okay about that. In fact, it's the most not-okay thing that's ever happened to me.

What are we gonna do without Dad?

I push away from the table. The longer I sit here staring at Grayson's pitiful face, the more the heat will build. I wanna scream and yell at them, tell them they have no idea what they're doing to us, how *hurt* I am. But I can't, because I know it won't come out right. I'll start crying and trip over my words, and they won't take me seriously.

So instead, I grab my backpack, walk through the kitchen, and step out into the backyard. My bike is against the house where I left it yesterday. I gaze up at the sun, low in the sky but not down yet. I still have time. I need some air. I need to get away from the heavy sadness in the house. I need to think, just for a minute, before I suffocate.

I yank my bike from the bushes and swing onto the seat.

Mom's voice carries out to me through an open window. "Sam! Sam, come back here!"

I should go back. I shouldn't ignore her. But my feet push hard against the pedals, carrying me down the driveway and left onto the sidewalk instead.

The neighborhood goes by in a blur, and the clickety-clack of the playing cards in the spokes of my back wheel rises up around me. It's a trick Dad taught me. The sound of the stiff cards smacking against the spokes of the wheel as I pedal helps take my mind off what just happened.

Sweat drips down my forehead and soaks the neckline of my shirt. I've never pedaled so fast or so hard in my life. It's calming in a weird way—the speed, the burning in my legs. But no matter how much distance I put between myself and home, I can't change the fact that Dad's moving out. If my bike was a time machine, I could ride it right back to the beach, back to the last moments before everything went wrong.

A tear slips from my eye. I can't stop it, no matter how bad I want to. I thought our family was safe. Mom and Dad are always telling the story about when they met in college, how it was love at first sight.

How did it go from love at first sight to *this*?

Dad's a science teacher, so you'd think this would be a formula he could work out—how to keep Mom happy. It can't be *that* hard, can it? I mean, they argue sometimes, but everyone does. Dad must've forgotten how to fix things—some dark chocolate, a bouquet of flowers, maybe a foot massage. He's done it before.

So there has to be something I missed. Something so big, it worked itself between them, prying them apart. Am I just as clueless as Grayson?

At the end of the street, I turn left toward the park, still within the limits of where I'm allowed to go on my own. Weird how you think about things like that even when your life is crashing down around you.

I pedal straight under the stone arches, past the parking lot and the playground, onto an overgrown trail Derek and I ride our bikes on sometimes. Branches and leaves slap at my ankles, stinging my skin. I put my head down and push forward.

The wind whipping across my face makes me feel alive. Its sharp teeth bite into the soft skin of my cheeks and chase away some of the numbness. The trail loops around behind the playground, barely wider than my bike tires. Trees and bushes thrust out of the dry earth on both sides, a blur of green and brown.

My vision clouds as more tears slip from my eyes. The ache in the center of my chest gets sharper, the hurt smoldering inside me. I turn my face toward the sky, and the words burst out of my mouth.

"I wish they'd just stay together! It's not fair!"

Up ahead, the trail curves sharply to the right. A weird, thick fog clings to the ground, swirling across the trail like a living creature. I don't remember seeing fog here before. The smell of cigar smoke curls into my nostrils.

What the heck?

Fog or no fog, I know the trail like the back of my hand, and I'm going way too fast to make the turn safely. I can't count the number of times Derek and I have wiped out in that very spot. A dark, shiny scar on my right knee is proof of that. I need to slow down before I—

A man appears on the path.

One minute there's no one there; the next, he's right in front of me. My heart jumps into my throat and I slam on the brakes. My wheels shudder against the hard-packed dirt, and the brakes squeal like a dying animal.

"Gah!"

My rear tire slides sideways, tilting me dangerously to the right. I throw myself to the left to keep from toppling over, and the bike comes to a stop inches from the man. He doesn't even flinch. The smell of cigar smoke and something else, something sickly sweet and *wrong*, gets stronger.

Chest heaving, I let my eyes travel upward from the man's dusty brown shoes. The dude's huge. His clothes are worn and tattered, some strange getup that kinda looks like the suit Dad wears for special occasions. Only it's not at all like Dad's. *Dad's* is charcoal gray and has creases running down the legs.

This guy's suit looks like it was patched together from a bunch of different suits in all different colors. Blue, green, yellow, purple, deep red. A blue-ticket special from the thrift store if I've ever seen one. There's something familiar about it I can't quite put my finger on. But I'd remember seeing a suit like this.

I stumble off my bike and thrust it between myself and this strange man. Just in case he gets any ideas. "Sorry, mister."

The man has black locs kinda like Derek's, only they're long and bunched up on top of his head, flowing down over his shoulders. His skin is dark and pitted with scars. He smiles, revealing a gold tooth that glints in the dying sunlight. He runs the tip of his tongue across it.

"Hey, son, you okay?" His voice rumbles in his chest, deep like distant thunder.

"Yeah, I'm fine. Sorry, I didn't see you there."

"No harm done." He smiles again, but this time a shadow passes over his face.

I shift my backpack on my shoulders, grab my handlebars, and go to step around him. He raises a hand to stop me. Something's not right with this guy. Goose bumps prickle across my arms, my Spidey senses activated.

"Hey, not so fast, son. It's almost dark," he says. "You shouldn't be out here by yourself."

"Oh, I'm not by myself." My eyes dart toward the park. "My parents are over at the playground, waiting for me. I told them I'd be right back."

The lie comes out so easily, so smoothly, even I believe it. *Not bad.*

The man grins. "Okay, just looking out for you."

I know I should go—I definitely should *not* stay and talk to this guy—but curiosity gets the better of me. Derek and I are always out here on this trail, and we never see anyone. It's why we like it so much. We can be as loud as we want without getting yelled at.

I tilt my head. "What are you doing out here on this old bike trail anyway?"

"Taking an evening stroll," the man says. "It's good to clear the mind."

I shrug. "Yeah, I guess."

The man narrows his eyes. "Something on *your* mind, son? You look troubled."

"No, I'm fine."

There's a flash of something white in his hand. I narrow my eyes, squinting to see what it is. It's long and straight, with dark circles down the front of it, like some kind of musical instrument. A flute, maybe? He glances up at the darkening sky, then back at me, moving the instrument from one hand to the other. A half smile pulls at one corner of his lips as he slips it into an inside pocket of his jacket.

"There's nothing worse than family troubles," he says.

His dark eyes pin me to the trail, and a block of ice plops down in my stomach. I didn't say anything about family troubles. Who is this guy and how does he know I'm having family troubles?

"I'm good, really, mister."

I need to get out of here, but I weigh my options first. I could turn around and go back where I came from, but I'm not so sure about turning my back on this guy. I could go around him, but then I'll be within arm's reach. Neither is a great option.

"Okay, okay. I gotcha. But old Bones here is a good listener if you need to talk. Sometimes it's hard to know who to trust. I'm *always* here if you need me."

Bones? That's not a name.

I take a step backward. "I really have to go before my parents get worried."

"Not so fast. I have something for you. Something that might help." The man reaches into his jacket pocket again and pulls out the flute I just saw him playing with.

"I don't need any help—I—"

"Old Bones has the sight," he says, tapping a finger against his temple.

I shake my head. "What does that mean?"

"It means I can see into your heart. Your hopes, your dreams, what you want most in this world. I can see what troubles you."

My legs start to tremble. This is getting weird—I mean weird*er*. Why am I still standing here talking to this guy?

He holds out the flute and nods at it. "Go on, take it. It might be useful."

"Useful? For what?"

I can't help but feel completely ridiculous, reaching out to take the flute from him. I turn it over in my hand. The man grins in a way that makes my insides quiver, his mouth spreading wide to reveal that gold tooth again. His tongue darts out of his mouth and moves across it, almost like he's caressing it.

"It's a very special flute. I think you can use what it has to offer."

I narrow my eyes. "And what's that?"

"Your greatest desire, of course," the man says. "All you have to do is play it and make a wish, and so it will be."

Is this guy for real? I can't just blow into a flute and get whatever I want. This isn't a movie or a tale in some storybook. Real life doesn't work that way. I wish it did, but it doesn't. Still, I play along.

"What's the catch?"

The man laughs. "Catch? Who said anything about a catch?"

"I—I just—"

He squints at me. "What wouldn't you give to have your greatest desire?"

I can't think of a single thing, but I don't tell *him* that. Nothing about this feels right. The skin on my hand is even starting to tingle. Tiny shock waves of static electricity travel up my wrist, crackling and fizzing into my fingertips.

I thrust the flute out. "I don't think I need it. Here."

The man shakes his head. "Tell you what. Why don't you think it over? If you change your mind, you can bring it back."

"No, I can't—"

"Think about your parents," he says sharply. "If you could keep them together with nothing more than a wish, don't you owe it to them?"

I swallow the lump in my throat. How does he know about my parents?

The man smiles again, and my grip tightens around the flute. If what he says is true, if it's as simple as playing this thing and wishing for my parents to stay together, how can I say no?

I grab my bag and slip the flute into the side pocket. I'm not gonna make a decision now. I'll think about it, like the man said. No promises.

I look up to tell him that, but the trail is empty. He's gone. Something about the way he disappeared causes my heart to skip a beat. A memory from this morning at the beach washes over me: a man in a suit wearing brown dress shoes, watching me from the shadows.

It was him.

Chapter 3

I **SHOOT INTO THE DRIVEWAY JUST AS THE** streetlights come on, and let out a breath. That was close. Mom and Dad would kill me if I was out past dark. As it is, I'll probably be grounded for a month for ignoring Mom when she called me. I lean my bike against the house.

"Hey, Sam!"

I jump and spin around, still spooked from the encounter with the stranger in the park. Derek's poking his head through his bedroom window, which looks out over our driveway.

I let out a breath. "Oh hey, Derek."

A line of concern creases the smooth brown skin of his forehead, and he runs a hand over his short black locs. "Where were you today? You weren't in school."

"Mom and Dad let us skip. We had a beach day."

His dark eyes widen. "Lucky! Thought you were coming over to play video games."

"Shoot, I forgot." We made plans over the weekend, but Mom and Dad dropped a bomb and it slipped my mind. "Sorry, D."

"It's all good. Maybe another night." He tilts his head. "You okay?"

I stare down at the driveway, tracing a line of cracks with my eyes. I have to tell him. He's my best friend. He'll know if I'm lying.

"My parents are separating," I say. "They told us after dinner."

"Oh man." Derek frowns. "They did it after beach day?"

"Yup."

He shakes his head. "That's harsh."

"My dad's moving out on Thursday."

"I'm sorry, Sam."

"It's okay."

I bite down on my bottom lip, unsure what else to say. My mind is spinning, filled with thoughts of Dad packing boxes, loading them in the car, and driving off down the road without looking back.

Derek sighs, awkwardness hanging between us

like a third person. "I don't know what to say. . . ."

"It's all right. I gotta go."

"See you tomorrow, Sam."

Mom and Dad are waiting in the kitchen. They shoot up from the table when I walk in the door. And they don't look happy. I can feel the tension in the air, as heavy and as suffocating as when I left.

"Samuel Jacob Windsor!" Mom's voice rises so high, I expect the glass on the counter to shatter. Surprisingly, it doesn't.

"What were you thinking, taking off like that?" Dad asks, frowning.

I look down at the floor, anger flaring in my chest. *They* don't have a right to be angry. "I just went for a bike ride."

"Didn't you hear me calling you?" Mom slaps her hands down on her hips and glares at me. I shrivel a little. She can be scary when she wants to be.

"I'm sorry," I mumble. "I went to the park . . . to clear my mind."

The stranger's words come out of my mouth without me even realizing it. I blink, remembering the glint in his eyes and the way he smiled at me. I might not have meant to echo his words, but they hit home. Mom's eyes soften. Dad bites down on his lip. Good. They owe me one after the bomb they dropped tonight. Giving me a pass for this is the *least* they can do.

"All right," Mom sighs. "Get upstairs and get your studying done. Lights out at nine thirty."

I climb the steps with my backpack slung over one shoulder and step through the baby gate at the top. In the upstairs hall, tinny twinkling music floats through the air. I pause beside Addie's bedroom door. It's open a crack, and through it I can see her narwhal-shaped night-light projecting a rotating scene of stars and moons on the ceiling.

She's beneath her covers, reaching her little hand up toward the lights, humming softly. She's so little, she won't remember this. Any of it—the good *or* the bad. She won't remember how happy our parents used to be, and she'll forget all about our perfect day at the beach . . . and how Mom and Dad ruined it.

"Where'd you go?" Grayson is in his doorway, a sour look on his face. He takes a page out of Mom's book when it comes to scary facial expressions.

"To the park."

"You said you'd help me with my model," he says, his voice breaking.

Guilt tugs at my insides. "I'm sorry, Gray."

"Can we do it now?"

I shrug and follow him to his room. He's already found out his parents are separating. I can't let him down too. Besides, I could use something to take my mind off everything. Even if it's just for a little while.

The model of a robot sits on his desk, so close to being done. We've been working on it for ages. Sheets of pressed metal sit beside the model, along with a small tin snipper and a pair of pliers. Grayson picks up the tools and plops down on the rug in the middle of his room. I grab the robot and the final sheet of metal and sit next to him.

I examine the sheet. "These last pieces are gonna be hard. We have to be careful with them."

Grayson hands me the snippers. I clip the tabs on the next piece and hold it out to him so he can bend the sides inward. Once the piece is formed, I hold the robot still while he fits it into place. I watch his face as he works, his tongue poking out of the side of his mouth. I can't help but wonder what he's thinking. Is he as angry, frustrated, and confused as I am?

"Hey, Gray?"

He looks up. "Yeah?"

"You okay?"

I snip the next piece out and pass it to him.

His eyes shift to the floor. "I dunno."

"Me either," I sigh.

He raises an eyebrow. "Really?"

I shrug. "I mean, I know I'm pretty awesome, but I don't know *everything*."

"Coulda fooled me," he says, a smile pulling at his lips.

I nudge his shoulder with my fist. "You know you can talk to me about stuff, right?"

He nods. "Yeah, I guess."

"Okay, good."

He pauses, fitting another piece into the model. "I don't want Dad to leave," he whispers. "I want us to stay together."

"Me too."

"Do you think they're gonna get a divorce?"

The word flashes in my head like the title screen of a video game. *Divorce! Divorce! Divorce!* I squeeze my eyes shut, my breath catching in my throat. "I don't know that either."

"Today was fun, wasn't it?" Grayson asks, a sad smile revealing a gap where his two front teeth should be.

I nod. "Yeah, it was."

"What if we never go to the beach all together again?"

I clear my throat and suck in a breath to stop the tears burning behind my eyes. Can't let Grayson see me cry. I have to be strong. The truth is, I wanna tell him everything's gonna be okay, that *of course* we'll go to the beach together again. But I can't.

He bends the tabs on the final piece around the holes in the model. "Done!"

We stand, and he lifts the robot onto the shelf above his bed, then steps back and admires it with his hands on his hips.

"That looks awesome," I say, and for a moment the pain fades from Grayson's eyes. "Good job, dude."

He grins. "Thanks for helping me, Sam."

"Welcome. Night, Gray."

A lump forms in my throat as I close his door behind me. I was serious when I told him he can talk to me about anything. I don't have all the answers, but the least I can do is be there for him. That's what big brothers are for, right?

I push open my bedroom door and launch my bag across the room onto the bed. It hits the mattress with a solid thump, but another noise catches my attention. I flip on the lights, and my breath catches in my throat. The stranger's flute stares up at me from the floor.

I crouch down to get a better look at it in the light. It's not like any flute I've ever seen. It's pale and shiny in places, dull in others. The mouthpiece is worn, and five finger holes line the body of it. Strange symbols and shapes are carved into it, dark against the ivory-colored instrument.

I nudge it with my foot, then pick it up from the floor, my hand trembling. I suck in a quick breath. *Dude.* It's made out of bone. I tilt my head. What kind of bone could it be? Maybe the better question is, *Whose* bone could it be? The image of a smiling skeleton missing one of its arm bones swims in front of me. Gross.

I never should've gone to the park alone so close to dark. I shouldn't have talked to the stranger. And I *definitely* shouldn't have taken the flute from him. I wasn't thinking straight. If I'd had any sense, I would've turned my bike around and left him there in the middle of the trail. Especially after he went from strange-but-mostly-friendly to strange-and-definitely-creepy.

I turn the flute over in my hand and study the carvings. The rough image of a snake twists up from the mouthpiece. Each finger hole has some weird tribal-looking symbol above it. It might actually be kinda cool—if it hadn't come from some creep in the park.

A voice in the back of my head shouts at me to tell Mom and Dad about it. But I can only imagine the lecture I'd get if I told them about the stranger on the bike trail. They'd rake me over the coals for talking to him *and* for not telling them right away that he gave me the flute. That's a special sort of torture I don't wish on my worst enemy.

I shiver again and drop the flute onto my desk. I have a unit test tomorrow in social studies. If I don't get some studying in before bed, I'll be in deep doo-doo. Things might be weird right now with Mom and Dad, but that won't get me out of schoolwork. If I flunk this test, I'll get grounded. That's the last thing I need right now.

I pull out my social studies book and a sheet of paper to takes notes on, then plop down in my wooden desk chair. But focusing is almost impossible. The words on the page swim in front of me as my mind drifts back to the conversation at the dining room table.

There's a knock on my door.

I shove the flute under a pile of papers and turn around. "Come in."

Dad pushes the door open and pops his head in. "Hey, bud. Studying done?"

I wave my paper in the air. "Yep."

He takes a step into the room. "You want to talk?"

I shrug. Earlier, I wanted that. Now what's there to say? He's moving out and there's nothing I can do about it. All the talking in the world won't fix that.

Visions of Christmas at two houses instead of one crowd into my head. What will happen to our tradition of picking out a tree and decorating it as a family? And Christmas Day? The thought of splitting the time between my parents, instead of having one gloriously lazy day playing with toys and eating until I feel like exploding, looms over me.

"No," I finally say. "I'm just gonna go to bed."

"All right, well, I'm here if you need me. Night, bud, love you."

"Love you, too, Dad."

No, talking will only make it worse. Worse than worse. It'll make it *real*. If we don't talk about it, I can pretend it's not really happening. An ache starts deep in my chest and spreads down into my stomach. It flutters like I'm standing at the top of the high dive looking down at the water twenty feet below me. Only it's not heights filling my stomach with butterflies this time.

Chapter 4

THAT NIGHT I DREAM OF SKELETONS. Ones in all different shapes and sizes chase me through the woods, bony hands reaching out to grab me. One is missing an arm bone, another a finger. The decaying skeleton of a dog limps after me, one of its four legs completely gone. I wake up drenched in sweat, my bedsheets twisted around my feet. I almost fall face-first onto the hardwood floor trying to untangle myself. *Smooth, real smooth.*

I get dressed for the day, then snag the skeleton flute—after *that* dream what else could I call it—from my desk and shove it in the side pocket of my backpack. I wanna show it to Derek on the bus. I haven't decided yet if I'll tell him where it came from. Maybe I'll just say I found it.

After stepping through the baby gate at the top of the stairs, I tiptoe down to the kitchen, careful not to wake Addie up. Once the little terror's awake, there's no peace for any of us. She's lucky she's so cute.

Grayson's already at the table, chewing silently on a Pop-Tart. His eyes follow Dad as he moves through the downstairs rooms, picking things up and putting them into cardboard boxes on the dining room table—his coffee mug, a notebook, his favorite pair of slippers.

He's taking an awful lot of things with him. Seems less temporary—like he said it would be—and more like moving out for good. My stomach flip-flops. How can he do this to us?

I slide into a chair across from Grayson, and he passes me the box of Pop-Tarts. Cherry. My favorite.

"Morning, Sam," Mom says. She runs a hand over my tangled black hair. "Make sure you comb this before the bus comes."

She pours herself an extra-large cup of coffee and drinks it with her back resting against the counter. Her eyes dart back and forth, joining Grayson and me in following Dad's chaotic tour through the downstairs. Pick up an item, drop it in the box, pick up another item, drop it in the box.

My stomach churns again and I shove the Pop-Tarts

away from me. Appetite ruined. A sleepy cry floats down the stairs, and Mom drops her chin to her chest, muttering something about never having time to finish a cup of coffee.

I stand quickly, pushing myself away from the table. "I'll get her."

I'd do just about anything to get away from what's happening in the dining room. I climb the stairs and stop at the gate, where Addie has her arms stretched into the air. She squeals when she sees me. "Sammy!"

I pick Addie up and cuddle her for a second, breathing in the flowery scent of her shampoo, then plop her down at the bottom of the stairs. She takes off running toward the kitchen. I step into the downstairs bathroom to brush my teeth and comb my hair. In the mirror above the sink, I gaze at my dark brown eyes and tan skin. In a lot of ways, I look like Mom, but with darker skin and eyes.

Today we even have matching frowns.

I take a shuddering breath. Seeing Dad gathering up his things and packing them into boxes made my stomach feel like there was some sort of creature inside it trying to claw its way out—sharp fangs and talons ripping at my insides. It's a pain like nothing I've ever felt before.

He's actually moving out.

They're separating and there's nothing I can do about it. I could stomp my feet and scream at the top of my lungs, and nothing would change. I'm just along for the ride. The awful, messed-up ride. It isn't fair.

"Sam!" Dad calls. "Bus is coming!"

I flip off the light, grab my backpack off the hook, and run out of the house without looking into the dining room. I don't wanna see those boxes *ever* again. I jog down the driveway and up the steps of the bus just as the driver, Mr. Bennett, is starting to look annoyed. His green eyes narrow at me.

What's he have to be so grumpy about, anyway? At least *he* doesn't have seventh-grade math to deal with the day after finding out his whole life is falling apart.

Derek saved a seat for me halfway down the bus. He scoots over, and I flop down onto the fake leather seat. As always, he looks flawless. His short, neat locs, collared shirt, wrinkle-free shorts, and spotless sneakers make me feel out of place. I look down at myself, thinking about how I grabbed my own shorts and T-shirt from a pile on the floor, sniffing them first to see how dirty they were.

He fist bumps me. "Hey, Sam."

"Hey, D."

"How's it going?"

I shrug. "Okay."

"For real?" Derek asks, tilting his head.

Busted. We've been best friends since kindergarten. We ride the bus together every day. We have the same classes, go to the same summer camp, and have sleepovers on the weekends. There's no way he's buying that things are okay after what I told him yesterday.

I sigh. "No, but I don't wanna talk about it."

"Okay, that's cool."

I stare through the window, watching the streets pass by in a blur of shapes and colors. I know Derek's just trying to be a good friend. I'd do the same for him. I'm just not ready to talk about it. Not yet. Besides, he doesn't understand what this feels like.

His face brightens. "Wanna come over later and play video games?"

"Maybe," I say. "I'll have to ask my mom."

I swallow hard, thinking about how tonight will be our last night together as a family. No one is gonna be in a good mood. Mom will probably cry. Heck, Grayson'll probably cry too. Maybe I *should* go to Derek's. Playing video games would be loads better than watching Dad pack up moving boxes.

I shift my backpack from my lap to the floor between my feet and catch a glimpse of the skeleton flute sticking out of the side pocket. I reach down and wrap my fingers around it, then look around to see if anyone's watching. I slide it out of the pocket and hold it out to Derek.

His eyes widen. "What's *that*?"

"It's a flute."

Derek takes it from me and spins it around in his hand. "Yeah, but where'd it come from?"

I tell him about the stranger in the park. The words feel silly—childish—coming out of my mouth. Greatest desire and all that.

Deep lines etch into Derek's forehead. "Dude, that's a wild story."

I nod. "I know."

"Do you think he's legit?"

"Like, actually magic or something?" I frown. "No. I think he was just some weirdo in the park."

"But what if—now hear me out—what if he was telling the truth?" Derek asks, handing the flute to me. I slip it back into the pocket of my bag.

"No way," I say. "He was just messing with me."

Derek smirks. "There's only one way to find out."

"I'm *not* putting my mouth on that thing. First of all, it's made out of bone and that's gross. Who knows where that thing came from?"

Derek lets out a laugh. "Valid point."

"Second of all, it's not magic. Magic isn't real."

"I don't know," Derek says. "If my parents were splitting and I could do something that might keep them together . . ."

He pulls out his phone, dropping the subject, but I can feel the judgment radiating from him. I sit back against the seat and cross my arms over my chest. What does he know, anyway? His parents aren't splitting up.

Besides, he's wrong. Playing the flute wouldn't just be a bad idea; it would be pointless. The stranger at the park must've heard me crying and thought it'd be funny to mess with me. There's no way this thing is actually magic.

Chapter 5

WHEN THE BUS DROPS US OFF after school, I wave goodbye to Derek, then plop down on the front steps. I pull the skeleton flute from my bag, studying it for, like, the millionth time. Derek's voice pops into my head.

If my parents were splitting and I could do something that might keep them together...

"Whatever," I mutter. "There's no such thing as magic."

In the sun, the shiny parts of the flute catch the light and reflect it outward. I turn it around in my hand, then upend it and stare down the hole. Nothing about it screams magic. It's just some weird old flute that's probably made out of deer bone or something. The dude in the park probably carved it himself.

The front door opens and Mom sticks her head out. "Sam? Oh good, you're home."

I jam the flute back into my bag before she can see it, then jump up and follow her into the house. Addie comes running into the entryway and throws her arms around my legs. She squeezes tight, like I've been gone for days instead of hours.

I guess to a three-year-old, it might seem like I have been.

Her excitement at seeing me fills me with warmth—a feeling I've been missing ever since Mom and Dad made their announcement last night. It makes me remember how happy I was when they told us we were getting a baby sister. Grayson is great and all, but Addie completes our family. She's silly and fun, and way less serious than Grayson. Any time I need cheering up, I can always count on her to help.

I drop my bag and sweep her off the ground, pulling her into my arms. "Hey, Addie."

She pats my cheeks. "Kiss, Sammy?"

I plant a kiss on her round little nose, and she giggles and pushes me away. I set her down and wander into the kitchen. Mom's stirring something on the stove. I sniff the air, the earthy scent of cumin and chili powder drifting under my nose. "What's that smell?"

"Homemade chili," Mom says.

I sit at the table and pull out my homework, looking up every once in a while to watch her work. She adds a spice and stirs the chili, tastes it, then shakes her head and adds a little more. My mouth waters as the smell coming from the pot intensifies.

I finish my math problems and glance at the clock. Dad and Grayson will be home soon. Grayson's after-school program ended a few minutes ago. A squirmy sensation wriggles in my stomach at the thought of us all being together again.

"Can I go to Derek's to play video games?"

Mom brushes the hair out of her eyes. "Not tonight, Sam. I thought we could have a nice meal together."

I freeze, my stomach flip-flopping. *A nice meal together.* One last nice meal before Dad moves out and nothing's the same ever again. My eyes dart to the stack of boxes on the dining room table, then back to Mom standing at the stove, a half smile painted on her face.

"Sam, I—"

The front door slams, interrupting whatever she was about to say. Grayson comes down the hall, followed by

Dad. He stops short in the doorway, his eyebrows knitting down over his eyes.

"What's this?" he asks. "Smells amazing."

"Dinner," Mom says. "I thought it would be nice before you . . ."

Dad nods and sets his shoulder bag down on the counter. He moves to the cupboard and pulls out some bowls and hands them to Grayson, who takes them to the dining room table. Mom fills a jug with lemonade, and Dad carries the pot of chili into the other room.

When we sit down to eat, it's obvious they're trying to make this meal seem normal, like everything isn't about to change. They smile and ask about school, but a feeling of wrongness hangs over us, like the staticky feeling in the air before a storm. It's like an uninvited guest at the table.

"Let's have a game night!" Grayson says suddenly, his eyes lighting up. "That'd be fun, wouldn't it?"

A shadow of doubt passes over Mom's face. She looks at Dad, who frowns before setting down his spoon. "I don't know, buddy. I've still got some packing to do."

The smile fades from Grayson's face, and his lower lip trembles. "But I thought we could have one more game night."

"I'm sorry, honey," Mom says. "We—"

"I hate this," Grayson mumbles, kicking the leg of the table. "This sucks."

Mom opens her mouth to scold him, and the muscles in my body tighten. I won't let her yell at him for this. It's not his fault. It's *theirs*. I'll go down for being disrespectful before I let Grayson take the fall.

But I don't have to come to the rescue, because he jumps up and runs upstairs before she can say anything. A minute later his bedroom door slams, rattling the picture frames on the dining room wall.

"Mama, Gray sad?" Addie asks, her little lips forming into a pout. She sniffles, and tears gather in her eyes.

I clench my jaw. All Grayson wanted was one last night of pretending like everything's okay. Pretending we're a happy family instead of a broken one. The least they could do is play along. This isn't fair. Not to Grayson, not to Addie, and not to me.

This has been the worst meal ever.

I perch on the edge of my bed, the skeleton flute grasped in my hand. I turn it over and over, twisting it so that the snake carving looks like it's slithering across the pale bone. The conversation with the stranger replays in my mind, his deep rolling-thunder voice ping-ponging around my head.

All you have to do is play it and make a wish, and so it will be.

An uncomfortable, squirmy feeling slides into my stomach. There's no way this thing'll give me my greatest desire. How could it? But . . . what if Derek was right? If there's any chance at all that I can do something to keep our family together, I should do it.

Shouldn't I?

I lift the flute to my mouth and put my lips around the mouthpiece, trying not to think about where it came from, what kind of bone it's made out of, and how many germs might be crawling around the surface. How do I even play this thing? Do I put my fingers over the holes or just blow into it?

I'm scrunching up my face, trying to figure it out, when a soft yellow glow pulses beneath my fingers. I gasp and yank the flute from my mouth, an icy shiver dancing down my spine. Warm against my skin, the flute brightens and darkens with an eerie yellow light.

I tilt it and hold it up to my eye, looking down through the mouthpiece like it's some kind of morbid spyglass. There's nothing inside. So how is it glowing? And what does this weird, freaky glow even mean?

When I took the flute from the stranger, I didn't believe it would give me my greatest desire. Not really.

But sitting here holding it, feeling the glowing warmth against my skin, I'm not so sure.

Maybe it *is* magic.

I get up and set the flute down on my desk, then slip out of my room into the hall. Voices float up the stairs from the kitchen. Mom and Dad are arguing but trying to be quiet about it. I can tell Mom's crying and Dad is frustrated, just by the tone of their voices. Hers is high-pitched and strained; his is snappy and short.

I blow out a breath and knock on Grayson's door. "Gray?"

Silence, then a muffled "What?"

I push open the door. Grayson's lying on his bed, his face shoved into his pillow. He looks up when I come into the room, tears staining his cheeks. He sucks in a shuddering breath as I sit down beside him.

"You okay?"

He shakes his head. "No."

"I'm sorry about game night."

"I just wanted us to have fun together. . . ."

The unspoken *one last time* hangs in the air between us. A tear rolls down Grayson's flushed cheek, making my heart thrash in my chest. I wanna curl up beside him and cry too, but I can't. I'm the big brother. I have to be strong. And I have to fix this.

"I have a plan," I say quietly.

Grayson lifts up on one elbow. "You do? What?"

"I can't tell you about it now, but if it works, I'll explain everything. Okay?"

He nods, no trace of doubt in his eyes. "Okay."

"Good night, Gray."

"Night, Sam."

Back in my room, I grab the skeleton flute from my desk before I can change my mind. I have to do this. Not just for me, but for Grayson and Mom. For Dad and Addie. If there's any chance this thing is magic, I don't have a choice. I have to keep our family together. No one else is gonna do it. It's up to me to fix things.

I slip the flute between my lips, puff out my cheeks, and blow into the mouthpiece. It gives a long, slow, warbling note, then fades. As it does, I say the words—my greatest desire—out loud.

"I wish my parents would stay together."

When my words fade, nothing happens. No genie floats from the end of it to grant me three wishes; no magical elf appears to do my bidding. Nothing happens at all. I'm frozen, waiting for a sign that this thing worked.

But it doesn't come.

I cross the room and poke my head out of my bedroom

door. Mom and Dad's raised voices float up from down-stairs, even louder than before. *It didn't work.* I shut my door again, scowling, and toss the flute onto my desk. It hits the wooden surface with a thunk.

Here I was, hoping the thing really *was* magic. Turns out it's a dud. I cover it with a T-shirt to block out the yellow light. I don't know what kind of trick the stranger used to make it glow, but I do know one thing: this freaky thing isn't gonna keep *me* awake all night.

I climb into bed and stare up at the ceiling, dis-appointment settling in my stomach like a heavy stone. Magic flute. How ridiculous. I'm about as gullible as they come. No. That's not true. I'm not gullible; I'm des-perate. Desperate to keep my family together, even if it means believing in magic.

Well, the joke's on me.

Chapter 6

THE ALARM CLOCK BLARES FROM the table beside my bed, pulling me from a dream where I was in the middle of landing a sweet trick on my bike. I sit up and frown, looking down at the glowing red numbers. *What's that doing there?* I put it across the room ages ago so I couldn't reach it to hit snooze a million times. Mom threatened to make me walk to school if I missed the bus one more time.

This morning it's sitting right next to me on my bedside table. I wipe a line of drool off my cheek and reach for the button to turn it off. My hand freezes, hovering over the clock. Seven o'clock? That's not right.

I usually have it set for precisely 7:35, exactly

twenty-five minutes before the bus pulls up in front of the house. I gotta maximize every last minute of sleep I can get. I push the button to stop the beeping. Grayson must've come in here and moved it on me, then changed the alarm while he was at it. His idea of a joke. That kid has a weird sense of humor.

"I could've gotten an extra half hour of sleep," I grumble, throwing my bedroom door open. I step into the hall, head for the bathroom, then stop short. Music drifts up the stairs from the kitchen.

I run my hand through my sleep-tangled hair and go downstairs, where I hesitate outside the kitchen. I pull in a deep breath, imagining Dad listening to music while he loads boxes of his stuff into his car.

The breath catches in my chest, hitching and shuddering inside me. I can't do this. I can't face him packing up and leaving. But what choice do I have? I stand a little straighter, take a deep breath, and give myself a pep talk. *You got this. Whatever today throws at you, you can handle it. You're strong. You* have *to be.* It works, giving me just enough strength to step through the doorway.

Mom looks up from the table and smiles. "Morning, Sammy."

"Morning, Mom."

Wait, what did she just call me? No one but Addie calls me Sammy. Mom doesn't seem to notice the look of confusion on my face, though. She's busy scrolling through an app on her phone and chuckling about something.

My eyes dart away to Dad, standing in front of the stove, stirring something in a pot. A wireless speaker sits beside him on the counter, an upbeat jazzy number tap dancing through the air.

He turns from the pot. "Morning, champ. Oatmeal for breakfast, grab a bowl."

I ignore the fact that he just called me champ, and scrunch up my face. "Oatmeal? You cooked?"

"Why do you look so surprised? Come on, get a bowl before it gets cold."

He must be in shock. This moving-out thing is messing with his head. I mean, Dad isn't a bad cook. He and Mom trade dinner duties, and he usually comes up with some decent recipes. But breakfast? No one cooks breakfast on a weekday. Everyone's too busy.

I reach for a bowl in the cupboard and carry it over to the stove, my eyebrows slanted down over my eyes. Okay, I'll bite. I don't know where this is going, but I guess I'll find out. Dad dips a spoon into the pot and scoops some oatmeal into my bowl, then drops a pat of butter in the center and sprinkles it with brown sugar.

"Thanks . . ."

"Welcome, champ!"

I carry the bowl to the table and sit, my brain doing cartwheels inside my head. Dad sets a bowl down in front of Mom, and she smiles and pats his hand. "Thanks, honey."

Honey? What is going on? Why is Dad calling me champ? Why did Mom call me Sammy? Why are they acting like this isn't the worst morning of my life?

"Is Grayson up yet?" I ask, spooning the steaming oatmeal into my mouth.

Mom frowns. "What's that, sweetie?"

"Hey, Sammy! What do you say I give you a ride to school this morning?"

Dad swoops across the room and slides into the chair across from me. A smile spreads across his face, deep dimples dotting his smooth, brown cheeks.

I freeze, spoon hovering over my bowl. "Aren't you leaving today?"

"Leaving?" Dad's smile flickers. "What're you talking about?"

Okay, something weird is definitely going on. Are they messing with me right now? If they are, it's not very funny. In fact, it's kinda messed up.

Mom glances up from her phone. "Are you okay, Sammy? You look a little off."

She leans over and presses the back of her hand to my forehead. I shrug but don't answer. I mean, who tells their kids their dad's moving out, then the next morning pretends it never happened?

"Well, finish up and go get ready for school. Also, remind me to schedule you for a haircut. You're looking a little shaggy."

I glance at the clock.

By now, Addie's usually screaming her head off for Mom to rescue her from behind the baby gate. *Wait a minute....* I set my bowl down, stand up, and cross to the doorway. I don't remember stepping through the gate when I came down for breakfast.

I glance up the stairs. It's not there.

"What's going on?" I scrunch my face up and press my hands to my forehead. My brain has moved from cartwheels to full-blown acrobatics.

"Hurry up, champ! I've got a massage scheduled for eight fifteen sharp!"

A what? Did he just say what I think he said? *Massage?* Dad doesn't get massages. Besides, he's supposed to be moving out today! Did everyone but me forget about that?

"Oh, and Sammy?" Mom calls.

I stick my head around the door frame. "Yeah?"

"Tonight's date night, so you're solo for dinner. There's leftovers in the fridge for after soccer practice."

Date night? Solo? Leftovers? *Soccer?* What in the actual—

I sprint up the stairs, heat rising in my cheeks. Beads of sweat break out on my forehead, and a sour taste surges into my mouth. At the top, I slam into the door to Addie's bedroom, and what I see sends a scream clawing up my throat. Well, actually, it's what I *don't* see.

Her toddler bed, toy chest, and favorite rocking chair are gone. The night-light that projects stars onto the ceiling, gone. There's nothing in the room except for a desk, a chair, and a filing cabinet holding a printer. A gold plaque on the desk reads DAD'S OFFICE.

I stumble out of the room. Where are Addie's things? Where is Addie? I turn toward Grayson's room, my heart thrashing against my rib cage. I knock on the door.

"Grayson?" My voice is trembling now. "Are you in there? It's time to get up for school."

Silence.

My hand hovers over the doorknob. I turn it slowly and push the door inward. It swings open and slams against the wall. In the center of the room, where

Grayson's wooden treasure chest normally sits at the end of his bed, there's no bed, and no chest—just a table covered in fabric and scissors. Shelves line the walls, stuffed full of bins and baskets instead of metal models and vinyl figures.

My eyes dart wildly from side to side. The light blue walls are covered in flowery framed pictures and weird signs with sayings on them like I CRAFT SO HARD, I SWEAT GLITTER. The spot where Grayson's bed should be has a sewing machine and a rack with a half-sewn quilt hanging from it.

"Sammy? What're you doing in my craft room? Do you need something, sweetie?"

I spin around. Mom's behind me, her head tilted to the side. Craft room? Mom doesn't craft. I mean, she always said she wanted to get into it but could never find the time.

"Where's Grayson?" I ask in a rush of breath.

Mom's eyebrows raise. "Where's who?"

"Grayson, Mom! Where's Grayson? And Addie?"

"Sammy," she says, taking a step forward. "Are you sure you're feeling okay?"

"Why do you keep calling me that?"

I shake my head and back away into the room. This has gone too far. How did Mom and Dad pull this off while I was sleeping, anyway? I'm a heavy sleeper, but not *that* heavy. Where are they hiding my brother and sister? Or are Grayson and Addie in on it too? What did I do to deserve this?

The questions spin around my head like a windstorm. Maybe they're still upset about me taking off the other night without telling them where I was going. I mean, it's not the first time I've taken my bike to the park alone, but I know they were worried.

"Sammy, you're scaring me. Maybe I should call the doctor."

I pull in a breath and hold it, closing my eyes for a moment to steady myself. Okay. Maybe this deranged joke they're playing will end quicker if I play along with it. If I don't let them see how much it's messing with my head, maybe they'll give it up.

I force a smile. "No, no doctor. I'm fine, Mom. Really."

"Okay . . . Dad's waiting for you. Get dressed."

"Yeah, sorry. I'll be quick."

I step into the hallway, and Mom follows behind, muttering to herself. "Grayson and Addie. Do I know a Grayson and Addie?"

In my room, I strip off my pj's and turn to the pile of clothes on my floor, where I usually make my daily selection. Only there's no pile there. The floor in front of the closet is spotless. I frown and open the dresser, then pull a clean pair of shorts from a neatly folded stack inside.

Looking for my shirts next, I slide open the closet and find them all on hangers, organized by color. I recoil at the sight, snatch a T-shirt off a hanger, and start to close the closet as quickly as possible. I stop, my mouth dropping open. On the floor, neatly lined up against the back wall, are two pairs of cleats. Where did *those* come from?

Mom said there were leftovers for after soccer practice. I don't play soccer. In fact, I don't play *any* sports. That's totally not my thing. Running, sweating, getting hit with flying balls. No thanks. I slide the closet door closed, the T-shirt trembling in my hands.

I pull it over my head and slip on my shorts, then reach across my desk to grab my homework. My hand freezes. Sitting on the desk, on top of a notebook, is a brand-new cell phone. I tap the screen and it lights up, the words SAMMY'S PHONE displaying across the top.

"A phone?" I murmur.

All the other kids in school have phones, even Derek. I've been begging Mom and Dad for one for years. They always tell me I don't need one and to wait until I'm older. I'm not sure why—or *when*—they changed their minds, but I grab it and shove it into the pocket of my shorts. I'm not one to turn down a gift, even if it's a weird one.

I turn to leave the room, then remember the skeleton flute. If Mom comes in here to put away clean clothes or pick up my hamper, she might see it sitting on the desk. The last thing I need is for her to ask me where I got it. I spin around and reach for the spot where I left it last night.

It's gone.

Chapter 7

MAYBE MOM'S RIGHT. MAYBE THERE *is* something wrong with me. I left the flute right on the edge of my desk underneath an old T-shirt, I'm sure of it. But both the flute *and* the shirt are gone. If all these weird things weren't happening, I'd suspect Grayson of coming into my room and taking it. It wouldn't be the first time he's taken something of mine. But there's no Grayson, or his sticky fingers, to pin this on.

With Dad downstairs yelling at me to get a move on, I don't have time to search for it. I give the desk one last quick scan. It's completely and totally gone.

"Sammy!"

"Coming!"

Downstairs, Mom kisses me goodbye and reminds me again about the leftovers. Dad practically shoves me out the door. I stop short on the brick walk in front of the house.

Someone else's car is in the driveway.

Dad's car is an old beater, something to get him back and forth between home and school. The car in the driveway is shiny and silver. It looks expensive and new.

Dad walks around to the driver's side and pulls open the door. "Coming, champ?"

"Whose car is this?" I blurt the words out, forgetting I'm supposed to be playing along with their weird little joke.

Dad stares back at me with a blank look on his face, then gives a hearty laugh. "Good one, Sammy. Get in, you're going to be late."

I climb into the passenger side of the strange car, stunned into silence. Normally I have to shove papers and empty energy drink cans off the front seat to ride with Dad. I can't count the number of times I've wondered if he might be able to grow a new life form in the back seat. Mom's always on him to clean it out.

The interior of *this* car is black leather, shiny, and spotless. Dad shuts his door and pats the steering wheel affectionately, then pulls out of the driveway.

"Hey, champ, I'm glad we got a moment alone," he says. "There's something I want to talk to you about."

I sit forward in my seat. Is he finally gonna admit this is all one big, elaborate joke? If he is, there'd better be an apology coming, because this is not cool. Not cool at all.

"Okay."

"You know how Mom and I are going on a date tonight?"

"Yeah . . ."

"Well, I've got a surprise for her, but I wanted to tell you about it first. I'm taking Mom on a trip to Hawaii."

I swear I'm trying to hide the look of shock that twists my face and makes my mouth drop open. I really, truly am. I just can't anymore.

"A trip to *Hawaii*? Dad, isn't that expensive?"

He looks at me like I've grown a second head. I pat my neck, just to be sure I haven't. Nope, still just one confused, curly-haired head there.

"Sammy—"

"I mean, for all of us to go to Hawaii, that's gotta be, like, thousands of dollars."

"Well, that's the thing, champ. This trip is just for Mom and me. You'll stay with Grandma while we're gone."

"I—what?"

"You know, like the last time, when we went to Tahiti."

"Tahiti?"

"Yeah. Sammy, what's going on with you this morning? You're acting really strange."

What's going on with *me*? What's going on with *him*? Hawaii, Tahiti, massages, *Grandma*. I can't remember the last time I even saw Grandma, let alone spent the night with her. Ever since Grandpa died, she spends most of her time traveling. Besides, just last night he was packing up his things and planning to move out.

How am I the one acting strange?

"Nothing," I mutter. "I'm fine."

I sink back into the soft leather seat and stare out the window. For once, I can't wait to get to school. I need to talk to Derek. Everyone in my house has been body-snatched or something, and he's the only one I can talk to about it. Maybe he can make sense of what's happening.

Dad pulls up in front of the school and turns to me, his eyebrows all scrunched up. "If you're upset we're not taking you with us—"

"No, that's not it. It's fine. Grandma and I will have a grand old time."

"Don't let Grandma hear you use the *O* word," Dad chuckles.

I push open the door and grab my backpack.

"Have a good day!"

"Enjoy your massage," I mutter, slamming the door.

I turn and jog up the walk toward the main doors of the school, hoping I'm not too late to catch Derek by the vending machines. Every morning we hang out there before first bell, then walk to homeroom together.

Pushing through the crowded entranceway, I dodge elbows and backpacks, eager to find Derek. He's leaning against a vending machine, his arms crossed over his chest.

I smile and wave, then stop short. Something's off about him. No, not just off. Something's *different* about him. His hair. Derek's had short locs as long as I've known him. They're just about the coolest thing about him, if you forget that he always has the latest Nikes and they're always spotless.

His locs are gone. His black hair is cut close to his head, faded on the sides, with a zigzagging pattern shaved into the hair above his temples.

I stop in front of him, my mouth dropping open. "Derek, dude, what happened to your locs?"

"What?" he asks, his eyes narrowing.

"Your hair, you cut it."

"I don't know what you're talking about, man."

Oh no. No, no, no. We've been best friends since the beginning of time, but now he's looking at me like a stranger. Has Derek been body-snatched too?

My words catch in my throat, clinging to it like a wad of chewed bubble gum. "I . . . your locs . . . I thought you said you'd never cut them."

Derek glances around, then repeats in a low voice, "Dude, I don't know what you're talking about."

"Sammy!"

My name rings out across the entranceway. A short, thin kid with mousy brown hair is shouldering his way through the crowd, heading right for me. I think he's in my homeroom, but I don't remember his name. Amos? Aiden? School only started a couple weeks ago, and middle school is a mix of kids from a couple different elementary schools. He clearly knows my name, though.

"Sammy, I was waiting for you over there," he says, jerking his thumb behind him. "Ready to go to homeroom?"

"Uh . . ." I glance at Derek, who turned away to talk to someone else. I hesitate, unable to move. My feet are cemented to the floor.

"C'mon, Sammy."

I hesitate a moment longer, then fall in line beside

this strange kid. Am I the only one in this town who hasn't been kidnapped by aliens? Or brainwashed? Or whatever's going on?

"What were you doing talking to Derek James?"

I shove my hands in the pocket of my shorts. I'd be lying if I said there wasn't a stabbing pain in the center of my chest, that I'm not fighting back tears because my best friend in the whole world looked through me like I was invisible.

"Sammy?"

"Huh?"

"I said, what were you doing talking to Derek James?"

I shrug. "Um, I just needed to get into the vending machine, and he was in my way."

"Ohhh. You had me worried for a minute. Thought you were going over to the dark side."

I stop walking. "The dark side?"

"Yeah, you know . . . trying to get in with the cool kids."

"No, uh, totally not going to the dark side, or whatever."

The kid squints at me, his brown eyes magnified behind his glasses. "You okay?"

I wish everyone would stop asking me that. I'm not the one who isn't okay. It's everyone else. Who is this little dude who thinks he knows me, anyway? Things are gonna get real awkward real fast if I don't figure out what to call him.

We step into homeroom as the room is filling up. The teacher, Mr. Briggs, mumbles our names as we pass his desk, throwing me a lifeline. "Sammy Windsor . . . Alex Morales . . ."

Score.

"Listen, Alex . . ."

"Yeah?"

"You ever wake up feeling like everything's wrong? Like, changed somehow?"

Alex stares back at me, and I can almost see the wheels turning in his head. He pushes his glasses up on his slender nose. "What do you mean by changed?"

There's no way I can even begin to explain all the weird things that've happened to me since I woke up this morning. Especially not to this kid I only met three minutes ago. I need to talk to someone who knows me, someone like Derek. Only that's not possible.

I sigh. "Forget it."

I slide into my desk by the window, and Alex takes the one next to it. He looks at me sideways, but I ignore him until the bell rings for the start of class. I tap a pencil against my open notebook, staring out through the window next to me.

The classroom overlooks a courtyard that's surrounded on all sides by the three-story brick walls of the school. There's a stone fountain and benches, picnic tables, and a grassy area where kids hang out. It's where Derek and I usually eat lunch.

My eyes widen, and I lean forward in my seat. Just yesterday I was at this exact same desk, watching a pair of robins splash around in the fountain. It's the same view I've been staring at for the last two weeks, ever since school started.

Only it isn't.

There's no fountain out there. Instead, there's a huge metal sculpture of an eagle where the fountain should be, with the words STAPLETON EAGLES etched into it. The metal wings catch the sunlight, throwing a glare back at me through the window.

No way.

I'm willing to consider the idea that aliens came down from outer space in the middle of the night and replaced everyone I know with some weird alien version of themselves, but I'm *not* willing to believe they also replaced the fountain in the courtyard at my school with a sculpture of an eagle. That would be pointless.

My ears start to ring. I turn from the window and stare down at my desk, my eyes darting back and forth.

What is going on? Why are Mom and Dad acting so strange? Just two days ago they made a big production of telling us that they were separating and Dad was moving out, and last night they refused to have a game night because *Dad had to pack*. But this morning they were talking about date nights and vacations to Hawaii like nothing's changed. Or like *everything's* changed.

And Derek. Why doesn't he know who I am? The friend I share everything with looked at me like I was a piece of gum stuck to the bottom of his shoe.

The ringing in my ears gets louder. A vision of Grayson's and Addie's empty bedrooms swims in front of me. They're gone. Like *gone* gone. No one remembers them. How is this possible?

A lump forms in my throat. All these things started happening after I met the stranger in the park. *Bones.* He told me that playing the skeleton flute would give me my greatest desire—for my parents to stay together. Maybe it worked after all.

Chapter 8

THERE'S NO OTHER EXPLANATION for it. Aliens wouldn't come here, snatch everyone in town, and leave me behind. So it has to be the skeleton flute, right? It *changed* things. Was the stranger in the park an alien? Did I somehow summon his alien buddies to come down from outer space when I played the flute?

I shake my head. *I have to get it together. I'm getting everything all mixed up.*

Magic. It has to be magic, then. I took the skeleton flute because I wanted so badly to believe there was something that could stop my parents from separating, something that could keep my family together. And it worked. My parents are together. But my brother and sister are gone. At least with Dad moving out, we would've seen him on the weekends. It's like Grayson and Addie don't exist—like they never existed at all.

What have I done?

My stomach churns—all angry and acidy like when I eat too many salt-and-vinegar chips—just as the bell rings for first period. I grab my things and bolt across the room, nearly running into a girl making her way out of the classroom. She whips around and glares at me.

I shrug past her. "Sorry."

Alex is calling my name, but I keep walking. In the bathroom, I stare into the mirror above the sink, pretty sure I'm gonna hurl. The white tile walls feel like they're closing in, the room getting smaller and smaller every second. Chaotic fluttering fills my chest, and my head crackles and pops with static, reminding me of the moment I first held the skeleton flute. My stomach flip-flops. Definitely gonna hurl.

I turn the faucet on and thrust my hands under it, gasping at the coolness of the water. I splash it across my face, then use a paper towel to dry off. My stomach settles. The nausea passes. I take a deep breath and steady myself on the sink. What am I gonna do?

The warning bell rings out from the speaker above

me, shrill and urgent. I'm gonna be late for my first class, but I don't care. How can I go to class, knowing what I know . . . or don't know? I have to figure out what's happening. But how? There's a hall monitor stationed by the school's front doors, so there's no way to leave without getting caught.

I let out a strangled cry.

Having my parents together and going on date nights is great, but trading that for Grayson and Addie? For Derek? It's not worth it. If the skeleton flute is to blame, I need to find it and bring it back to the stranger. I have to get him to make things right, at least with my brother and sister and Derek. I wanted Mom and Dad together. I didn't want everyone else *gone*.

The hinges on the bathroom door squeak.

"Sammy?" Alex pokes his head inside. "What're you doing? You're gonna be late for science."

"I just needed a minute. I felt sick."

He frowns. "You okay?"

"Yeah, I think so."

A grin replaces his frown. "Good, let's go!"

I follow him through the door and down the hallway to science class, the whole way trying to figure out how to get back home to look for the flute. Between Alex babysitting me and the hall monitors watching the exits, it'll be impossible. I could fake sick, but then Mom or Dad would have to come pick me up, and I'd be stuck in bed all day. That won't do either.

By lunchtime I've given up hope. It'll have to wait until after school. If I go right home, I should have some time to search for the flute before Mom and Dad get home from work . . . if they even *have* jobs. Dad's massage appointment this morning makes me wonder, but how could he afford that fancy car without a job? Maybe I'll even have time to go back to the park and look for the stranger.

"Hey, Sammy, you gonna eat that?" Alex asks from across the table.

I look down at my tray. I haven't touched my burger. I push it across the table to Alex. I'm not hungry anyway. The lunchroom is loud, conversations rising and falling around me like buzzing insects. Two tables over, a group of kids breaks out in laughter. It's the popular table, reserved for only the coolest kids at Stapleton Middle School.

Derek's in the center of the group, telling a very animated story while the others look on and laugh. The Derek I know wouldn't be caught dead sitting with those kids.

When the bus pulls onto our street after school, Derek jumps up from his spot at the back and pushes past me. I let out a breath as I climb down the steps behind him, thinking about all the times I'd go straight to his house after school so we could play video games. This strange version of Derek doesn't even look in my direction. A stab of sadness pokes at me.

I step onto the sidewalk and glance at the driveway. It's empty. Mom and Dad aren't home. Perfect. I need to search my room for the skeleton flute and try to get to the park without them knowing about it.

I hurry up the front walk, then take the front steps in one leap. I slide my key into the lock and ease the door open a few inches before sticking my head inside. Silence—except for the ticktock of the clock in the kitchen.

I step through the door. "Mom? Dad? Are you home?"

No answer.

I race upstairs, pausing outside Grayson's bedroom. I press my palm against the door and close my eyes. Pain pulses in my chest, like a hole's been opened up and it's getting bigger by the minute. He can be annoying, but that's kinda his job. Next to Derek, Grayson's the best friend I have. He doesn't deserve to be erased like he never existed and replaced with craft supplies.

I have to make this right.

In my room, the first place I check is my hamper. Maybe it got swept in there along with the old T-shirt. But there's nothing in there except for a pair of shorts and a hoodie. I move to my desk and shove papers and books around, searching frantically. The flute was right here on the corner, a T-shirt draped over it to block out the glow. How did it just disappear? With every second that goes by, I'm more and more convinced the flute really was magic, but I'm pretty sure it didn't grow legs and walk away.

"Where is it?"

I turn over the garbage can beside my desk, scattering balled-up pieces of paper and pencil shavings across the floor. Frustration builds as I sift through piles of papers and open every single drawer in my desk. I drop down onto my hands and knees, pull my phone from my pocket, and tap the flashlight icon at the top. I direct the beam under the bed, then scramble across the room and search under my dresser.

It's useless. It's not here.

I sit up and shift to sit cross-legged with my back against my dresser. How can it be gone? How can my brother and sister be gone? Objects and people don't just disappear. I drop my head into my hands. A warm tear escapes from one eye, sliding down my cheek.

My chest tightens. Everything is so messed up, and the thing that's probably responsible for it all has vanished. I inhale and hold my breath, then let it out slowly. I need to calm down. Panicking won't do me any good.

As I sit there on the floor, my mind spins ideas around so fast, it's dizzying. *Think, think, think.* The stranger's rumbling voice rushes into my head.

Old Bones here is a good listener if you need to talk. Sometimes it's hard to know who to trust. I'm always here if you need me.

Always *here if you need me.* That's it. I have to go back to the park and find Bones. It's his flute. He's the one who told me to play it and make a wish. This is all happening because of him.

I pull myself to my feet, slip my phone back into my pocket, and step out into the hall. The wall running down the right side of the staircase is lined with picture frames. I study them as I make my way out of the house.

There's my kindergarten school picture. And me in my Halloween costume from when I was seven—I was a taco that year. At the bottom of the steps, a jolt of shock buzzes through me. The last picture on the wall is the one we took as a family four years ago when we were on vacation in Maine. The frozen images of Mom and

Dad smile down at me, buried up to my neck in sand. I remember this picture well.

I remember the vacation well too. Grayson was five, and Mom was pregnant with Addie. Only . . . in this picture she isn't. Her smooth stomach peeks out from beneath a beach cover-up, tanned from days of sunbathing. It should be big and round and covered in the stretch marks she hated so much, just like I remember.

Grayson worked for over an hour to bury me in the sand. When Dad snagged a guy walking by to snap the picture, he was right beside me, smiling proudly at his hard work. In the picture nailed to the wall, it's just Mom, Dad, and me.

No Grayson, no Addie.

Tears gather in my eyes again and I press my palms into them, stopping them before they can fall. I need to keep it together. I take a shuddering breath and open the front door. This is fine; everything's fine. I just need to find Bones and get him to make things right.

Outside, I discover that my bike—which I'm positive I left leaning up against the garage—is gone. Either someone took it, or this is one more twisted part of this whole twisted situation. I'll just have to get to the park the old-fashioned way.

I start walking, and a block from home, a sign that

reads STAPLETON TOWN PARK catches the light from the sun, shining like a beacon. I turn left, walking with purpose, my chest heaving in and out.

That little annoying voice in my head returns, telling me that finding the stranger again, alone, is a terrible idea. Finding him *is* what got me into this mess. But I don't have a choice this time. I need to get him to fix everything he turned upside down.

The park is almost empty except for a couple of little kids on the playground. I step onto the narrow bike trail and my stomach tightens. If things go south once I find Bones—*if* I find him—there's no one to hear me scream.

A light breeze blows, rustling the trees and bushes around me. Every little movement makes me jump. The granola bar I had on the bus gurgles around in my stomach, threatening to make a reappearance. *Not today, granola bar.* I'd like to talk to this guy with clean shoes.

Up ahead, the sharp curve in the trail comes into view. Of all the things that could've changed in my life, *of course* this awful section of the trail is still here. I guess I should be relieved because it's where I first met Bones, and it's where I'll hopefully find him again. I come to a stop, my eyes searching the forest. Birds flit from tree to tree, but other than that, I'm completely alone.

I spin in a circle. "Hello?"

My voice echoes and fades. No one answers.

"Hello? Is anyone there?"

Nothing. I must look ridiculous standing here yelling at the trees. It was silly of me to think I'd be able to find him again so easily. I set my mouth in a line. I can't give up. Not yet.

"Hello! Mr. Bones? Are you here? I need to talk to you!"

A twig snaps behind me. I spin around as a familiar smell drifts on the breeze. Cigar smoke. Earthy, with a hint of vanilla. Just like the day I met him. The trail is empty, but the smell creeps along, slow and strong, slithering into my nose. I flare my nostrils. Tendrils of fog inch across the ground, drifting out of the woods like reaching hands. They surge forward, swirling around my feet.

My stomach flutters. "H-hello?"

"Hello, son."

Chapter 9

HE STEPS OUT FROM BEHIND A TREE like he's been there all along, watching me. I yelp and jump back, my heart leaping into my throat. He's wearing the same patchwork suit he had on when I saw him before. The same dusty brown shoes. And the same freaky smile plastered on his face. His bubble-gum-pink tongue swipes across his gold tooth.

I can't look away from his pitted skin and soul-staring dark eyes. They look back at me expectantly, his bushy eyebrows rising to meet his hairline. My skin tingles, and goose bumps rise beneath the hairs on my arms.

"You came," I breathe.

Bones nods. "How can I help, son?"

"You said you were always here if I needed to talk."

"What's on your mind? Old Bones is *always* happy to listen."

Something about the way he says this sounds rehearsed, insincere. It makes my skin crawl, like he's done this before and is just repeating lines.

"The flute," I say. "The one you gave me—"

"Ah," Bones sighs. "Yes."

There's a twinkle in his eyes now, a look like he knows exactly why I came back to the park to find him. Anger sparks to life inside my chest, fueled by the memory of my brother's room filled with craft supplies and by the blank look on Derek's face as he stared through me.

I ball my hands into fists. "Whatever you did, you need to fix it."

Bones blinks. "What do you mean, son?"

"The flute. You told me to play it and wish for my greatest desire."

"That's correct." He reaches into his jacket pocket and pulls out the skeleton flute, spins it around in his hand, then slips it back inside his jacket.

My jaw drops. "How'd you get it back?"

"It served its purpose, so it returned to me."

"You need to fix things," I say again. The burning in my chest is getting hotter by the second. "Everything's changed."

Bones shrugs. "That was the point, wasn't it? You made a wish, and it came true."

"This isn't what I wished for."

He leans in close. "Isn't it, though? You wanted your parents to stay together, yes?"

I blink in surprise. How does he know what I wished for? "Y-yes, but—"

"You were troubled, so I helped you."

"But how did you help? What is even happening?"

"I gave you your greatest desire."

A wide smile spreads across Bones's face, revealing a mouthful of pearly white teeth, all except for the gold one. A shiver races down my spine. Yesterday there was nothing I wanted more than for my parents to stay together, to be happy.

My greatest desire.

I shake my head. "I never asked you for help in the first place. And you didn't tell me that playing the flute would mess everything up. You changed things without asking."

"Look, son," Bones says, his voice close to a growl. "I gave you a choice. This was *your* decision."

"But—"

"Are your parents together?"

"Yeah, but—"

"Are they happy?"

"Yes, but—"

A shadow flashes across Bones's face. "Then what's the problem?"

"You fixed the problem with my parents, but my brother and sister are gone." The words come out shaky, my voice cracking slightly. "My best friend doesn't know me. Everything is *wrong*."

"You called to me, and I gave you what you wanted. I don't see how I'm to blame."

"Called to you? I never called to you!"

I frown, thinking back to the moments just before Bones appeared on the trail that night. I was riding my bike and thinking about Dad moving out and how unfair it was. I definitely didn't *ask* Bones for help. I didn't even know he was there.

Bones pulls the skeleton flute from his pocket again. He sticks it in his mouth and blows on it. Instead of a note, the forest fills with the sound of my own anguished voice:

"I wish they'd just stay together! It's not fair!"

I blink and draw back from him. How does he

have my voice? I spoke those words when I was alone. "That wasn't for you! I was just blowing off steam."

Bones holds his hands up in front of him. "Nevertheless . . . I fixed your problem. Just like I did for the others."

I clench my teeth together, glaring at him. "But you created, like, twelve more problems. Take it back. Fix things. I don't want this."

Who does this dude think he is, anyway? Listening in on other people's private moments and changing things without permission. He can't do this. He doesn't have the right.

Bones shakes his head. "No can do, son."

"Why not?"

"You played it already. Your wish came true. It can't be undone. Old Bones only offers his services once." His eyes narrow. "Especially to those who are ungrateful."

"But I never asked for them in the first place!"

"That's the way it works. There are rules, you know."

"I want my brother and sister back, and my best friend. I don't know anything about your rules. You said there was no catch!"

My lower lip quivers. I bite down on it, unwilling to let him see how close to crying I am. I'll eat an entire plate of brussels sprouts before I let him see me cry.

Bones smiles. "Wish I could help, son, I really do. But I'm always here if you need to talk."

I open my mouth; angry, inappropriate words perch on the tip of my tongue. I don't get a chance to unleash them, because the fog returns, rising up from the ground and spinning around him like a miniature cyclone. It picks up fallen leaves and small sticks as it spins, and they twirl around him too. Bones lifts the flute to his mouth, and a familiar note rings out. He waves at me through the fog, and when the air stills, he's gone.

Chapter 10

THE SOUND OF A RINGING PHONE startles me as I walk through the front door. I was expecting Mom and Dad to be home already, wondering where I've been, scolding me for not leaving a note or asking permission before leaving. Then I remember date night. I'm on my own this evening.

I pull the cell phone from my pocket. "Hello?"

"How was school today, Sammy?"

"Hey, Mom. It was okay."

"Are you home?"

"Yep."

"Mrs. Morales will be there soon to take you to soccer practice. Make sure you get your homework done after.

Dad and I will be out late. Don't forget the leftovers."

She ends the call before I can respond, and I freeze, right there in the front hallway.

I forgot something, all right, but it wasn't the leftovers. *Soccer practice.* I slip my phone back into my pocket, dying inside at the thought of having to go to practice. Playing soccer's bad enough, but having to do it when my mind and my life are so jumbled up is gonna be almost impossible. My stomach aches just thinking about it.

All I wanna do is crawl into bed, hide under the covers, and pretend none of this is happening. This day has been a roller coaster, and not the good kind. I don't know how much more I can take.

I find a soccer shirt, black shorts, and shin guards in a bag beside the cleats in my closet. I get dressed, feeling completely and totally like someone else, sprint down the stairs, and step out of the house. A light blue minivan is waiting in the driveway.

A woman with dark brown hair beeps the horn and waves. The back door to the van slides open, and Alex grins at me from the back seat. "I was worried you weren't coming. Ready for soccer?"

I shrug. "I guess so."

He eyes me as I climb into the car. "You feeling better?"

"What?"

"Earlier, this morning, you said you felt sick."

"Oh yeah. I took a nap after school. I'm good to go."

"That's good. With the big game coming up against Cedarville, I'd hate for you to miss practice."

Big game? Great. Not only do I have to fake my way through practice, but there's a game coming up too. I know nothing about soccer—I mean, besides the basics: Kick ball into goal. Stop ball from going into goal. That's it.

This is gonna be epically embarrassing.

Alex's mom turns into the parking lot behind the school and stops beside the soccer field. Alex and I climb out of the back and grab our water bottles and duffel bags from the trunk.

"You think you can help me with my roll and twist today?" Alex asks as we step onto the soccer field.

"Roll and twist?"

"Yeah. I just can't get the hang of it, and you promised you'd help. If I don't get it, Coach won't let me play in the game," Alex says, his cheeks flushing red. "I kinda told Mom I'd be playing this time."

The team is gathered beside one of the soccer goals, dressed from head to toe in red and black. The coach—a tall guy with blond hair and a goatee—waves us over. Uncertainty flutters in my chest. How am I supposed to help Alex with a soccer move when I don't even know what it is?

"Windsor, Morales, shake a leg! You're late."

We jog across the field, dropping our things on the sidelines, and join the rest of the team. Across the circle of players, I lock eyes with Derek. Things really are upside down. The Derek I know wouldn't have anything to do with sports, even if someone paid him.

"Grab a ball and a partner," the coach says, "and get started on drills."

Instinctively, I take a step toward Derek, forgetting he's practically a stranger. He turns without glancing at me and teams up with a stocky kid with short red hair. Hurt pulses in my chest.

"C'mon, Sammy," Alex calls, kicking a ball down the field.

"This is gonna be a disaster," I mutter.

"Windsor!" the coach calls, stopping me.

I turn to him. "Yeah?"

"It's bad form for the team captain to be late to practice. Don't let it happen again."

I swallow hard and ice water slides down my spine. Team captain? This is worse than I thought it was. A captain is someone who leads people. I'm not a leader. I'm a gamer. Need someone to join an online campaign and blast zombies, or tell you where all the spawn points are? I'm your guy! But I know nothing about soccer *or* about leading people.

I stammer an apology and turn to Alex, who's waiting down the field. No wonder he thought I could help him with his moves. Boy, is he gonna be unpleasantly surprised. It'll be all my fault if he doesn't get to play in the big game.

"Ready?" he calls.

I nod and he kicks the ball toward me. He's surprisingly strong for a scrawny kid. When he draws back his foot and makes contact with the ball, it sails toward me through the grass a lot faster than I'm expecting. I panic and do this strange running-in-place, hopping-sort-of move to try to stop it.

The ball rolls past me and I shuffle over to it. Alex frowns. It's my turn to pass the ball back. How hard can it be? Aim, swing, kick. *I got this.* I stop behind the ball, pull my right leg back, and let it swing. Of course, when my leg comes up and over it, I miss completely, lose my balance, and fall flat on my back. Heat creeps into my face as I climb to my feet.

Seriously? I can't even kick a ball twenty feet across a field? I mean, I'm no athlete, but I do go to gym class three times a week. The pressure of trying to be something I'm not is getting to me.

"Dribble it back!" Alex calls.

I glance at the other players. They're taking turns kicking the ball to their partner, then running it back down while kicking it from foot to foot. *Oh no.* I couldn't kick the ball when it was sitting still, right in front of me. How am I going to kick it while it's *moving*?

Alex blinks at me, waiting. *Here goes nothing.* I kick the ball gently and run forward to meet it with the opposite foot. *Okay, not bad. Keep going.* Another gentle kick. As I move forward with my other foot, my ankle twists before it makes contact. I stumble, trip over the rolling ball, and fall right on my butt in the grass.

"Windsor!" the coach yells. "Stop messing around!"

Alex jogs down the field and stops beside me. "Are you sure you're okay, Sammy?"

"Maybe I'm not as good to go as I thought I was."

He reaches out, grabs my hand, and pulls me to my feet. "Maybe you should sit out for the rest of practice."

"Windsor!"

The coach is marching across the field from the sidelines, his hands on his hips. The look on his face says he isn't the least bit impressed with my disaster of a practice. Well, neither am I. Everyone else on the field has stopped to watch what's going on. What a nightmare. I'm supposed to be the team captain.

I run a hand through my hair, picking out a blade of grass that's nestled into my curls. "Sorry, Coach. I'm feeling off today. I think I might hurl."

The coach gives me a disgusted look. "Can't have you hurling on the soccer field."

I clutch my stomach dramatically. "I should probably sit this one out."

He sighs. "We have a big game coming up, Windsor. We *need* our team captain."

"I know, Coach, I'm sorry."

"All right, fine. Sit out for the rest of practice." He leans in close. "But make sure you're tip-top by next week, or you'll be riding the bench."

"Yes, Coach."

I shoot Alex a look of apology and jog over to the bleachers. He trudges off to join another pair of players, disappointment slumping his shoulders. Maybe one of *them* can help him with his roll and twist. Besides, riding the bench sounds like a solid plan. If I don't get out of this, or figure out how to fix things, the whole school will be there to see me make a fool of myself.

I slide onto the bench and drop my head in my hands. Everything is so messed up. None of this would be happening if Mom and Dad hadn't decided to separate. I never would have gone to the park, met Bones, and decided to play that awful flute.

This is all their fault.

Chapter 11

WHEN MRS. MORALES DROPS ME off at home, she notices that the windows in the house are dark. She glances in the rearview mirror. "Sammy, honey, do you want to come back to our house for dinner? We're just having leftovers, but it's your favorite, tamales."

"Oh, no thanks, Mrs. Morales. I'm not feeling very good."

"Oh dear," she says, frowning. "Well, get some rest."

Honestly, tamales sound amazing, but I let out a sigh of relief that she bought my act. Dinner with Alex and his family would be totally awkward. Besides, I need some time to think. Weird as it is that my parents are out on a date, I'm happy to have the house to myself. I need to get serious about figuring out what to do.

I eat the lasagna Mom and Dad left in the fridge while I sit on the couch. I turn the TV on, but barely pay attention to the images flashing across the screen. Leftover lasagna isn't tamales, but it also isn't as bad as it sounds. The microwave makes the cheese nice and gooey, like molten lava. Just the way I like it.

My parents haven't gone on a date night since before Addie was born. My *old* parents anyway. The ones who weren't body-snatched. *These* parents seem to do a lot of things on their own, leaving me with Grandma or a plate of leftovers and unsupervised TV watching. It isn't so bad, I guess, but it definitely isn't what I'm used to.

I click off the TV and set my plate down on the coffee table. It's so quiet, I can hear every creak and groan of the house settling.

I run my hand down my face and sigh. What am I gonna do? How do I fix this if Bones won't help me? I got frustrated at soccer practice and blamed Mom and Dad for what's happening, but I was wrong. It's not their fault. It's mine. *I* played the flute and made a wish, and now everything's messed up.

My blood boils just thinking about it. Bones acted like he did me some big favor, like I should be grateful.

I fixed your problem. Just like I did for the others.

Wait a minute. I sit up straight and bring my hand down on the coffee table. Bones's words slam into my skull like a speeding car. *The others?* What others? Does that mean there are other people like me out there whose lives he turned upside down? Others who can help me figure out how to fix things?

I hurry upstairs to Dad's office—formerly known as my little sister's bedroom—and flip on the overhead light. The computer sits in the middle of the desk, a colorful screen saver of bouncing shapes moving around the screen. I sit in the desk chair and wiggle the mouse. The screen saver disappears, revealing the desktop. I click on the browser and pull up a search page. My fingers hover over the keyboard; I wiggle them and scrunch up my face.

Where do I start? What do I search for? I have to find out if there's someone else who ran into Bones in the park, someone else who played his flute and made a wish. But how?

Keywords!

With a thrill of nervousness I type "body-snatched parents" in the search bar. A whole page of results comes up, but they're all reviews and summaries of some old movie. I frown, then type in "patchwork suit man."

No results.

"Patchwork suit man" and "flute."

Nothing.

"Bone flute" and "gold tooth."

Still no results.

"Bones" and "man" and "flute."

At the top of the page, a link to a message board pops up. I click on it, then wait for the page to load. Tingles race through me, and the lasagna in my stomach turns into a cold, hard lump. There's a post from twelve days ago in a group called Strange, Weird, and Unexplained in Stapleton. I take a deep breath and click on it.

> LenaXXLenore: I need help and I don't know
> where else to turn. Please don't stop reading.
> Has anyone around Stapleton come across
> a tall man who calls himself Bones? He
> has a flute made of bone. Desperate to find
> answers. DM me with info. Thx.

I sit back in my chair and let out an explosive breath. *Oh my God.* This LenaXXLenore person is looking for information on Bones. *My* Bones.

I click the bubble beside LenaXXLenore's name to send them a private message. Blood thunders in my ears. The blinking cursor taunts me as I sit, trying to figure out what to say. *Hey, I know this Bones guy. Did he body-snatch your family and friends too?*

No. Too weird.

> Sam_Wind: Hi, my name is Sam. I've met
> Bones too. Can you help?

Short and sweet.

I click send and bite down on my bottom lip, chewing on a piece of skin. The post isn't super recent, so the person who made it might not even see my reply. I just have to hope they're getting alerts for responses or something. I *need* to talk to them.

Five minutes go by.

I stare at the screen—and the unanswered message—my hope slowly turning into hopelessness. A pendulum toy sits beside the keyboard: four metal orbs suspended by wires connected at the top. I pull one orb back and release it. It slams into the next ball with a clack. That ball slams into the next, and then the next, until a rhythmic clacking fills the air.

Ten minutes.

The feeling of despair inside my stomach is growing with each clack of the pendulum—from a pit to a canyon, from a canyon to an abyss. After thirty minutes without a response, I push back from the computer, shut off the screen, and shuffle back to my room. Looking online was a shot in the dark. Actually finding someone who knows Bones was pure luck. But there's no way of tracking them down if they don't respond to me.

I toss and turn for hours, too excited about finding the post on the message board, and too nervous about whether or not they'll respond. Around midnight the front door opens and clicks shut. Mom and Dad are back from their date. They whisper loudly to each other and giggle all the way up the stairs to their bedroom. I smile to myself—at this carefree version of my parents—then finally drift off.

When my alarm goes off, I shoot out of bed and yank open my bedroom door. Mom and Dad are already downstairs. I can hear them talking. The smell of coffee drifts up from the kitchen. I push open the door to Dad's office, cross the room, and wiggle the mouse.

Please, please let there be a response.

When the page comes up, there's a little red bubble with the number one inside it next to my message to LenaXXLenore. I let out a little whoop. My hand's trembling so bad, I can barely hold on to the mouse as I move it to open the message.

LenaXXLenore: Sam, we need to talk. ASAP.
Meet me at Stapleton Town Park today at
3pm. I'll be wearing a red hat. Come alone.

This almost feels too good to be true. There's someone else out there who knows Bones. After what happened the last time I met a stranger at the park, meeting this person alone seems about as smart an idea as playing the flute was. I have to take the chance, though. If they know anything about Bones, anything at all, I need to talk to them.

I close the browser and go back to my room to get dressed. On the way out of my room, I stop and grab my backpack, then step into the hallway. My stomach is suddenly all fluttery at the thought of meeting LenaXXLenore. I grimace, clutching at it to calm the fluttering. It's gonna be a long day.

Mom looks up from her phone when I walk into the kitchen, and smiles. "Good morning, sweetie."

"Morning, Mom."

"Morning, champ. There's pancakes on the stove. Grab a stack," Dad says. He turns the volume up on the speaker on the counter and does a little dance move across the kitchen in time with the beat.

I smile, pulling a plate from the cupboard. I throw

on a few pancakes and settle down in a chair. Dad pours juice into three glasses and slides them across the table. This breakfast-in-the-morning thing isn't so bad. I could get used to this.

Mom hands me the syrup. "How was your night? Did you manage dinner okay?"

"Yeah, it was fine," I say, drowning the hot pancakes in sticky deliciousness. "How was date night?"

"Amazing," Mom says in a dreamy voice.

She beams across the table at Dad and reaches out to squeeze his hand. The look in her eyes is almost enough to turn my face red. I can't remember the last time they looked at each other like that. It just proves that I haven't been paying attention. I really thought things were okay between them. I thought we were one big, happy family.

Pain blossoms in my chest. They do so much for me and for my brother and sister. They run us around to activities, take us to appointments, and keep on us about homework and grades. They deserve to feel this way. They deserve to be in love.

And here I am, trying to get things back to the way they were. Back to normal, where date night is a distant memory and Dad is moving out.

Chapter 12

MY STOMACH FLUTTERS AS I WALK beneath the stone arches of Stapleton Town Park shortly before three o'clock. I had to ditch Alex after school. He found out where I was going and tried to invite himself along. I kinda feel bad about it, but LenaXXLenore said to come alone.

Besides, Alex doesn't know about Bones, and I'm not ready to answer his questions. Plus, I don't know anything about the person I'm meeting here. They could be a serial killer for all I know. Or Bones trying to trick me again. No, it's better Alex didn't come along. If I'm making another mistake meeting this stranger, it's better I don't involve him.

I cross the grass to the swing set, scanning the park

for someone in a red hat. It's not crowded, but it isn't deserted, either. As long as we stay out in the open, I should be okay. I perch on the edge of a rubber swing, shoving myself backward with both feet. My toes drag in the sand as I sway back and forth, waiting. At exactly three o'clock, a shadow falls over me.

"Are you Sam?"

My head whips up, and a girl about my age stands in front of me, arms crossed over her chest. She has a face full of freckles and fiery red hair that's tucked under a red baseball cap. She looks me up and down with intense brown eyes. I exhale, relieved it's someone my age, since I don't know many kids who are also serial killers. I don't know any serial killers at all, actually, but that's beside the point.

I scramble off the swing, tripping over my own feet. My face burns as I right myself. "Yeah, I'm Sam. Are you LenaXXLenore?"

"Lena," she says.

"I'm Sam."

"I know. You said that already." A smirk pulls at the corners of her mouth.

My face burns. *Get it together, Sam.* "Sorry."

"Let's go over here." Lena motions to a picnic table across from the playground. "We need to talk in private."

I follow her across the grass to the table and slide onto one of the benches. Lena sits across from me and presses her lips into a thin line. I open my mouth and close it. I don't even know where to start.

Lena raises her eyebrows. "You said you knew the patchwork man."

"The patchwork man?"

She stands up suddenly, her face flushing red. "Let me guess, you were just messing with me on the message board. Well, real funny."

"No!" I cry as she turns away. "That's not it. I call him Bones. You must call him the patchwork man because of his—"

"Weird suit jacket. Yeah."

I swallow hard. "Yes, I know the patchwork man. I met him a few days ago. Right here, in this park."

Lena sinks back onto the bench. She narrows her eyes as if she still doesn't trust that I'm telling the truth. My mouth goes dry, and I can't form the words to explain what's happening to me. I haven't told anyone about this. What if she doesn't believe me? What if she hasn't experienced the same thing? There's no taking it back once it's out there.

Lena sighs. "This is new for you, then, so you're still freaked out."

I nod. "Yeah."

"Okay, I'll break the ice." She takes a deep breath and releases it. "A couple weeks ago, I met a man in a colorful suit who changed my life. And I don't mean he did something nice for me. He *changed* my life. Does that mean anything to you?"

"It does," I say quietly. "The same thing happened to me."

"Tell me about it."

There's a glint in her eyes. Like she's been waiting a long time to find someone else who knows what she's going through, someone she can talk to. So I spill the whole pathetic story—my parents' separation and how I met Bones on the bike trail. About how he gave me his flute and told me it would grant me a wish—my greatest desire.

How I woke up and everything was different and my brother and sister were missing.

Lena closes her eyes, and a look of relief washes over her. "I'm not losing it, then."

"Not unless we both are."

"No one believes me. I tried to talk to my parents about it and they sent me to a therapist," she says. "Don't get me wrong, it's nice having someone to talk to, but she doesn't believe me about the patchwork man either."

That's exactly why I didn't tell anyone. "That sucks."

"It's like talking to a wall," Lena says. She makes her voice high-pitched. "What do you think the patchwork man *really* represents in your life, Lena? Let's explore this a little deeper."

I chuckle and Lena pulls the baseball cap off her head and sets it down on the table. Her red hair falls into her face, and she tucks it behind her ears with both hands.

"How did you meet him?" I ask.

Tears gather in Lena's eyes. "My mom was sick. She had cancer. We all thought she was getting better, and then, out of nowhere, it came back."

I blink. "I'm sorry, Lena."

"She passed away two and a half months ago." Her voice catches in her throat. "Afterward, we all kinda fell apart."

I shift on the bench. "That sounds hard. I—I don't know what I'd do if I lost one of my parents. . . ."

Lena wipes a tear away. "Anyway, I took a walk one day. I needed to be alone. I was trying so hard to be strong for my sister, but I couldn't do it anymore. I sat down on a rock and sobbed into my hands, wishing my mom was still alive. All of a sudden—"

"Bones appeared?"

"Yeah. Totally freaked me out. He said I looked troubled and offered to listen to my story." Lena shudders, and color creeps into her cheeks. "I know I shouldn't have talked to him—he was a stranger. But I wasn't thinking. I told him about my mom dying and how hard it was."

"Then he gave you the skeleton flute."

"Skeleton flute?"

I shrug. "It's what I call it . . . because it's made of bone."

"Creepy," she says, shuddering. "Anyway, he told me that if I played it, it would give me my greatest desire. He told me to take it home and think about it, and then he disappeared. It was so silly of me to think . . . to think that weird flute could bring my mom back."

Anger burns in my chest like fire. Bones took advantage of Lena's grief. "It wasn't silly. I believed him too. He tricked you. He tricked both of us."

She shakes her head. "I should've known better. Talking to him was my first mistake. Playing the flute was my second. Anyway, when I woke up the next morning and went downstairs . . ."

I lean forward, my hands gripping the edge of the bench. Lena swallows hard, and a shiver tears through her.

". . . my mom was waiting for me."

My mouth drops open. "No way."

"She was right there in the kitchen, making breakfast like she hadn't been dead for two months. I freaked out. Like, completely freaked."

"Uh, yeah, I would too."

"When I saw my mom, I raced upstairs to my sister's room to tell her, only she wasn't there. None of her things were there either. The room was filled with boxes and old books. It was like she never existed."

Lena's eyes fill with tears. I wanna reach out and comfort her, but it feels weird. I don't know this girl, but I *do* know how she must've felt at that moment when she realized her sister was gone. I felt the same way when I discovered Grayson and Addie were missing.

"So you got your mom back but lost your sister."

Lena sniffles and wipes the back of her arm across her nose. "Lenore. We're twins."

"God, Lena, I'm so sorry."

Her pain washes over me like a wave of heat. This isn't fair. We didn't ask for this. We were tricked into making a choice that was impossible to make without understanding what would happen. I'm tempted to march down the bike trail and call out to Bones, just to give him a piece of my mind.

"That's not all. My mom and dad are different. They're not happy like they used to be. They're so strict. I hate it," Lena says, her lower lip trembling.

"That's awful."

"What about your parents? Are they different?"

I tilt my head. "Yeah, but not in a bad way."

"Lucky."

I remember why I checked the internet in the first place, which led me to find Lena. "Did anyone else answer your post on the message board? Are there others like us?"

Lena shakes her head. "No. I've been trying to find others since I woke up and everything was different. You're the only one who responded to my post."

I shiver, even though the sun's beating down on my back, warming the exposed skin on my neck. It's only been a little over a day for me. I can't imagine weeks of feeling so alone, not knowing what's going on.

"Have you seen Bones since the first time?"

Lena looks up, her dark eyes widening. "No, have you?"

"The day I woke up here, in this twisted version of my life, I went back to the trail to find him."

She sucks in a breath. "You talked to him again?"

I nod. "I told him to put everything back the way it was."

"What'd he say?"

"He said he only offers his services once. Dude seems to think he helped me or something."

Lena lets out a humorless laugh. "Right. If by helping he means destroying. I was too scared to try to find him again."

"Lot of good it did," I mutter.

Lena's quiet for a minute, then her eyes meet mine. "Have the dreams started?"

"The dreams?"

"Yeah." She chews on her lip.

"What kind of dreams?"

Lena shudders. "An awful nightmare place. Dark. Cold. The feeling of being hunted."

"No, I haven't had any dreams."

"You will."

I shift on the bench, hoping she's wrong about that. "Where do you think Lenore is? And Grayson and Addie? How could they just disappear?"

Lena's eyes shift away from mine. "I can't feel her, Sam."

"Feel her?"

"We've always had this . . . connection. It's hard to explain, and maybe it's just in our heads because we're so close, but whenever we're apart, there's like an invisible thread connecting us." She takes a shaky breath. "But now . . . now it's just gone. The thread, Lenore, everything."

I pound my fist on the table. "Argh! What did this creep do to us?"

"I have an idea, but haven't been able to prove anything yet." Lena glances at her phone and then stands abruptly. "I have to go. My parents are expecting me home soon, and they get really mad if I don't follow the rules."

Even though we just met, I feel connected to Lena in a way I can't explain. Maybe it's because she's easy to talk to. Or maybe it's because her being here means I'm not alone anymore. Either way, I don't want her to go.

"Can we meet up again?"

She fits the baseball cap back onto her head, tucking her hair under it again, and nods. "How about the library, tomorrow morning?"

"Why the library?"

"Research," Lena says. "Give me your phone."

I pull my cell phone from my pocket and Lena takes it. She puts her name under my contacts, along with her phone number. "Meet me at ten o'clock. Text if anything comes up."

"I will. Oh, and Lena?"

"Yeah?"

"We're gonna figure this out."

Hope flashes in her eyes, and she gives a little wave before walking off across the park. I watch her until she disappears under the arches, hoping I can make good on my promise.

Chapter 13

WHEN I GET HOME FROM MEETING Lena, my mind's all over the place. She knows what I'm going through: the shock and pain of waking up to find everything in your life has changed. Of finding that someone you love has been written out of history, like a page ripped out of a book. She's just as desperate to figure out what's going on as I am.

Tomorrow can't come soon enough.

"Sammy? Is that you?" Mom calls when I walk through the door. "Dad and I are in the kitchen!"

The sounds of dinner being prepared float down the hallway. I think back to the evening before everything changed—the epic day that was ruined by the announcement of their separation. And here they are, making dinner. Together. A lump forms in my throat.

"What's that?" I ask from the doorway. "Smells good."

"Meat loaf," Dad says. He's peeling and chopping potatoes at the table, while Mom stirs the glaze sauce in a pot. "Sit down and help me with these."

I grab the peeler from the table and pick up a potato. Music drifts through the air. Mom hums along with it, swishing her backside as she stirs the sauce. Dad hops up and grabs her by the hand, pulling her into the center of the kitchen. She throws her head back and laughs, and they spin around, dancing in time with the music.

I close my eyes, potato in hand, and take a deep breath. Am I doing the right thing? Why am I trying to fix things, when Mom and Dad are so happy now? If I manage to get things turned right side up, we'll all be unhappy again. That's not what I want. The whole reason I played the flute in the first place was because I didn't want things to change.

"You're a little rusty on your two-step," Dad laughs, sitting back at the table. "Hey, you okay, Sammy?"

A tear slips from one eye and slides down my cheek. I wipe it off on the back of my arm and start peeling the potato again. "Yeah, it must be the onions you cut for the meat loaf."

"Funny, they've never bothered you before." He shrugs. "How was school today, champ?"

"It was fine."

Dad narrows his eyes. "You sure you're okay?"

"Yeah, I'm fine. Everything's fine."

If he only knew the truth. Nothing's fine at all. Things are as far away from fine as they can be. Guilt slams into me, filling my head with fuzz. For a moment there I got caught up. I was starting to wonder if it wouldn't be better to give up trying to figure out what Bones did to us. That maybe I could learn to live with things the way they are, because they're not so bad.

I shake my head. No. I have to figure out what's going on. For Grayson and Addie. I don't know where they are, but I know they don't deserve this. They should be here to see Mom and Dad dancing around the kitchen. Only . . . if things go back to the way they were before I played the flute, Mom and Dad *won't* be dancing around the kitchen. Dad will be moving out, and everyone will be miserable again.

After dinner, Mom and Dad go into the living room to watch a show together, while I go upstairs to read. It isn't easy focusing on my comic with my mind spinning the way it is. And there's something else. Something I've wished for hundreds of times, but which now has me on the verge of tears.

The silence.

It's been a whole day, but I can't get used to how quiet the house is. I keep expecting my door to burst open and Grayson to come in, talking to me about some ridiculous thing he built in Minecraft. My ears twitch at the thought. I almost can't remember the sound of his voice.

And Addie. I miss the clean smell of her hair and even her sticky little fingers patting my cheeks. My breath hitches in my chest. I sniffle and drop my head into my hands. A tear splashes onto my comic. Then another.

I flip my comic closed, cross the room, and flop down on my bed. The silence presses in on me until my chest feels like it's gonna cave in. The feeling of helplessness is so heavy, I'm sure I'm gonna stop breathing.

I just want my brother and sister back.

My eyes flutter, then open. I frown. I don't remember closing them in the first place. Weird. Goose bumps dance across my skin, and the hairs on my arms stand on end. Something's wrong. The last thing I remember, I was in my bedroom. I was reading, then I lay down on my bed.

Did I fall asleep?

I blink and sit up. I'm definitely *not* in my room anymore. The air sparkles and moves, like sunlight shining through a window into a room filled with dust. Only it's dark instead of sunny. Not so dark I can't see, but dark enough to creep me out. I lift my hand in front of me, like I used to do when I was younger, trying to catch the floating particles. My fingers close around thin air.

What the heck?

Dry, brittle grass crunches beneath me. Above me, a tall tree looms like some kind of creepy watchman. Its bark is inky black and the branches are bare. It reaches upward like a hand, clawing toward the sky. I shudder. Lena's warning about the dreams comes back to me. Is this what she meant?

"Help!"

A voice cuts through the darkness, sending chills racing down my back. I jerk my head in the direction of the voice and struggle to my feet. My shoes sink into dirt, damp and tangled with vines. A sour, earthy smell drifts under my nose, making my nostrils flare. It's like the basement at Grandma's house—mildewy and old.

"Who's there?"

My voice falls flat, sucked away the second the words leave my mouth. A cool breeze kicks up, ruffling leaves and dirt, sending them spiraling into the sparkly air. I shiver and take a step forward. I'm at the edge of a field. In the distance, the sky dances with oranges and yellows, like a fire is burning somewhere. The scent of burning wood moves on the breeze, covering up the other, less pleasant smell of decay.

Dark, angry-looking clouds part above me, revealing a big full moon. I scrunch up my face as it shows itself. There's something wrong with it. Instead of silver, everything the moonlight touches has a sickly orange-yellow tone to it.

Behind me, something scuttles in the dark. I whip around and squint. But the shadows are deeper there, inky black and almost moving, and I can't make anything out. There it is again, the scuttling, scurrying sound, this time to my right. What *is* that? Fear prickles in my chest. This is not cool.

"Help me!"

For one wild moment I convince myself I'm hearing Grayson calling for help. I stumble forward without thinking. "I'm coming! Hold on!"

On the other side of the field there's a short embankment. I charge down it, unsure what will meet me at the bottom. In that brief moment, I picture myself coming down off the grass straight into the jaws of some drooling, snarling monster.

I trip at the bottom and fall to my hands and knees. Broken concrete rises to meet me, and the air rushes out of my lungs. A chaotic, fluttery feeling fills my chest. On the other side of the stretch of concrete, the remains of a building thrust up through the destroyed ground. The front of it is crumbling. Great big chunks of it lie at my feet.

The scuttling noises are all around me now. I can feel eyes boring into my back. The feeling of being hunted threatens to overwhelm me, just like Lena said. Another breeze kicks up, and the smell of decay gets stronger.

"Someone, help, please—"

The pressure in my chest releases and I let out a relieved breath—it's not Grayson. But someone still needs help. My eyes dart wildly, searching for the source of the voice. Something about it is overriding my sense of self-preservation. It claws at my insides, forcing me to move, even though my stomach is clenched tight with terror.

A beastly scream cuts through the night. It's high-pitched and sharp. I clamp my hands over my ears to stop them from vibrating, and a chill shudders through me. Whatever made the noise is close by. And it's *big*. I don't want anything to do with it, whatever it is.

Don't panic, don't panic. If there's one thing I've learned from watching scary movies and playing video games, it's that panicking will only make you dead quicker.

I glance up at the building. It's cement, like the office buildings that line Main Street in downtown Stapleton. The windows are just bare openings, the glass panes broken. Glass litters the pavement below. There's movement on an upper floor. A dark shape flashes by one opening, then another. Whoever's calling for help is inside the building.

"Hey! Wait!" I yell.

The door looms in front of me like a dark mouth, waiting to swallow me up. Going through it will get me out of the open, away from whatever let out that inhuman scream, but everything I know about horror movies says I shouldn't go in. I should turn around and put as much distance between myself and this creepy building as I can. Nothing good will come from going in there.

But the voice pulls me forward.

It's an urge that starts in the pit of my stomach and stretches out toward my legs, pushing me to keep going. I hesitate a moment longer, then run through the door, feeling like I'm running right into the belly of the beast itself.

The air inside is heavy and warm. When I breathe in, it clings to my lungs, filling them with the smell of dust and mold. Shafts of orange-yellow moonlight shine in through the busted-out windows. I'm in some sort of entryway. To my right, a crumbling stone staircase rises up and out of sight.

Frantic footsteps creak across the floor above me. I move through the entryway, tripping on rocks and debris as I go, and stop at the bottom of the stairs. A wave of dread washes over me. Once I climb those stairs, there'll be no quick escape, no turning back.

I lift a foot and place it on a hunk of rock, testing my weight. It makes a grinding, groaning sound, but holds. All right. I'm doing this. I take another step, bracing myself against a crooked iron railing. Black paint flakes off in my hand.

Stone disintegrates beneath my feet as I climb, chunks of rock showering down behind me. The higher I climb, the more the stairs break and come away. Each step becomes a struggle.

I'm halfway up the pile of rocks when a gasp cuts through the stillness. I look up, and it takes everything I have to hold back the scream trying to force its way out. A figure stands at the top of the stairs, looking down at me. It's fuzzy around the edges, but there's no mistaking him. The boy has light brown skin, dark curly hair, and wide brown eyes.

Like me.

I stumble backward, rock shifting dangerously under my feet. A tingling sensation dances across my skin, crackly like static. My mouth drops open and I rub at my eyes, sure I'm seeing things. I pull my hands away. Nope, still there. The boy at the top of the stairs is gaping back at me, fear etched into his face. Our eyes meet and he screams. It's a sound so full of terror, I feel it inside my own stomach.

The boy at the top of the stairs *is* me. I'm looking into my own face.

Chapter 14

I **WAKE UP IN THE MORNING, FUZZY-**headed and confused. I can't shake the feeling that the dream I had wasn't *just* a dream. If it wasn't for the fact that I'm in my bed, I'd swear I was really transported right into the middle of that nightmare world. The memory follows me—remains of a dark, haunted place, and a pale, frightened face that belonged to me.

The smells follow too, a mixture of mold and smoke clinging to my nose. They grow stronger as I come to, sitting up in bed. Just when they start to fade and I'm almost convinced it *was* just a dream, *BAM!* Those awful smells hit me, and I feel like I'm getting pulled right back in again.

But as I put on a hoodie and a pair of jeans, I remember it's Saturday. I get to see Lena again. Maybe we'll actually get to the bottom of what's happening to us. That hope carries me down the stairs. Physically, I feel better too. My head feels lighter, less murky and confused. Mom's in the living room, reading.

She looks up from her book, folding down a corner of the page. "Good morning, sweetie. You're up early for a Saturday."

I shrug. "Can I have a ride to the library?"

"The library?" Dad asks, poking his head into the room. "On a Saturday?"

"Uh, yeah. I have a big project to work on with a partner."

"All right, sure. Mom and I are going to the farmers' market. We were going to make a morning of it. You'll be missing out on a thrilling time perusing produce."

I laugh a little too hard at the joke. "Maybe next time."

Dad nods. "All right, but eat something first."

"I'm not really hungry," I say, "but I'll bring a snack with me."

"You feeling okay?" Mom asks, tilting her head. "Never known you to turn down food."

"I'm good," I say, grabbing my backpack.

Dad pulls a stack of reusable shopping bags from the hallway closet. "What's the project about?"

I freeze, one arm shoved through the strap of my bag. "Uh, it's a group project on voting rights."

Dad raises his eyebrows. *Please don't ask more questions. Please don't ask more questions.*

"I used to love group projects when I was your age," he says.

Dad loved group projects? Since when? Only slackers like group projects, and the Dad I know isn't a slacker. This is just further proof that this bizarre life I'm living is nothing like the one I used to know.

Dad shifts the car into park outside the Stapleton Public Library. The three-story building is made of concrete and glass. Thunder rolls in the distance, and the angry black sky reflects off the windows, making the building look like it's encased in clouds. I scan the entrance, looking for Lena.

"We'll swing back by in a few hours to get you once we're done," Dad says. He looks back over the shiny leather seats and smiles.

I give him a thumbs-up. "Great, thanks. Have fun at the farmers' market."

Fat drops of rain are just starting to fall, splashing onto the ground like little wet grenades. Hopefully that doesn't mean Mom and Dad's trip to the market will get rained out. I don't want my visit with Lena to get cut short. Luckily, the vegetable stands are mostly set up inside buildings. I hop out of the car and race across the parking lot so I don't get soaked.

Lena's waiting in the lobby, her hair pulled into a messy bun on top of her head. She's wearing jeans and a green T-shirt. The color makes her hair seem even more fiery than when I first saw her in the park.

"Sam," she breathes, a smile lighting up her face. "You came."

I grin. "Of course I came."

"I wasn't sure after the other day. That was a lot."

"Hey, I want my old life back just as much as you do."

Lena shifts from one foot to another. "I'm not exactly excited to go back to life where my mother isn't alive . . ."

My face burns. *Open mouth, insert foot.* That was not the smartest thing I've ever said.

"Oh, right. Sorry."

". . . but I need my sister back."

"Okay, where do we start?"

Lena crosses the lobby and stops by a set of elevator doors. I follow, glancing up at the sign on the wall.

"The reference section is on the third floor," she says.

"What exactly are we looking for?"

"I'm not actually sure, but there are computers up

there. We can search the newspaper archives to see if there's anything about Bones in them . . . or maybe something about missing people." I look at Lena sideways and she shrugs. "I know, it's probably a long shot, but it's worth a try."

We step into the elevator and ride it up to the third floor. I'm not familiar with this area of the library at all. My knowledge stops at the graphic-novel section two floors below, and the kids' section because, well, little siblings.

"This way," Lena says, stepping off the elevator.

We're in a hallway with shiny tile floors and a railing that looks down over the lobby. I glance over the railing and jump back, my stomach fluttering like crazy. Lena shoots me a look.

"Sorry," I mumble. "I'm not good with heights."

Lena smirks. "Really? I couldn't tell."

The reference section is dim and deserted. The fluorescent lights buzz overhead, flickering in places. It's a little creepy, but I don't tell Lena that. At the front of the room, a librarian sits at a desk, her nose buried in a book. She glances up when we enter and watches us move across the room.

Lena stops in front of the computers. The walls surrounding us are lined with shelves containing large books with age-yellowed pages. The entire room smells earthy and old. I scrunch up my nose as Lena sits down in one of the chairs.

She points at the chair next to her. "Sit."

I sink into it, and she opens up a browser, then types in a web address. I crane my neck to see what she's doing. "What's that?"

"Most old newspapers and magazines are in online databases. We can search by keyword. If that doesn't work, we've got the local copies right here on the shelves."

"How do you know all this?"

Lena shrugs. "My dad's a researcher. Give me a key-word."

"Okay, start with 'creepy body-snatching dude.'"

Lena turns and looks at me, her eyebrows jumping. "'Body-snatching'? Is that what you think happened?"

Heat creeps into my face. "It was a thought."

She puts a hand over her mouth and stifles a laugh. "Like, aliens, Sam?"

"Look, how am I supposed to know? It's not like this has ever happened to me before," I say, scowling. "And I wasn't thinking aliens . . . anymore."

The smile vanishes from her face. "You're right. I'm sorry. I didn't mean to laugh."

"What do *you* think it is, then?" I slump back in the chair and cross my arms over my chest.

"This probably doesn't sound any better than body-snatching aliens, but I think we're in some sort of alternate universe."

"Wait, what?"

"Think about it. Both of us met this Bones guy when we were upset about something and wished for things to be different. We both played the flute, and when we woke up, everything *was* different."

"But an alternate reality? That doesn't happen in real life."

"And body-snatching does?" Lena asks, shooting me a look.

She's got me there. If I was ready to believe aliens were responsible for all of this, then I have to at least consider Lena's theory could be true. An alternate reality. Like the multiverse in the movies Derek and I like to watch. Or used to, anyway.

"Okay," I say. "Search 'bone flute' and see if that brings anything up."

I lean forward while she types the keywords into the search bar. I clench my jaw, waiting for the results. Pages and pages of articles pop up. There's so much information, I don't know how we're ever gonna sort through it all.

"'The earliest known instrument,'" Lena reads out loud. "This article's all about the history of the bone flute and how they date back to the early ice age."

"That's not super helpful," I say, pulling up the archive site on the computer in front of me. "I don't think Bones is from the ice age. We need something more recent. Keep looking."

I type in the same keyword and search through articles on the next page while Lena scans the first page. In another tab I search for images of instruments made from bone, hoping to find something that looks like the skeleton flute.

I click through pages and pages of images. There are flutes with symbols carved into them, but nothing quite like the ones on Bones's flute. An image of the flute, with its symbols and the snake encircling it, swims in my head.

I clear my search and add "snake" to my keywords. An image pops up on the screen. I lean forward, a fizzy feeling of excitement bubbling up in my stomach.

"Ceremonial flute used by spiritual healers," I read. Lena turns and looks at my screen.

Her hand flies to her mouth. "That's it!"

"It's not exact. See how the snake is wider?" I trace my finger down the screen. "It's not the same flute, but it's similar."

"I could kiss you right now, Sam!"

That escalated fast. My cheeks burn and I shift backward in my seat. "Uh . . ."

Lena rolls her eyes. "I'm not really gonna kiss you—calm down. I just knew two heads would be better than one."

She clears her search results and types "spiritual healer" and "Stapleton" into the search bar. A number of articles jump onto the screen. Lena mutters to herself as she scans them, then lets out a squeal. The librarian looks up from her desk and shoots us a grumpy look. She sets her book down and stands, peering across the reference section at us.

My eyes widen. "Shh! You're gonna get us kicked out of here."

The librarian moves from behind the desk and drifts along the shelves, straightening up books but clearly keeping an eye on us.

Lena shrugs. "Sorry."

"What'd you find?" I ask in a quiet voice.

"You're not gonna believe this."

"What?"

"There's an article here from . . ." She scans the top of the page. "From an old issue of *National Geographic*. It's a series on witch trials in the eighteen hundreds."

I frown. "Witch trials in Stapleton?"

"Apparently," Lena says, her eyes widening. "The author did some digging into Stapleton's history and found some really dark stuff."

"What's it say?"

I'm on the edge of my seat now, gripping the table in front of me so hard, my knuckles are white. Lena clears her throat and reads the article out loud.

"'Stapleton's Children Healed by Traveler Calling Himself a Spiritual Healer. The following information was taken from records discovered, along with a number of items dating back to the eighteen hundreds, in an unknown chamber that was unearthed when renovations were made to the Stapleton Town Hall.

"'In September 1820, a mysterious sickness fell over the children of Stapleton. A traveler passing through proposed a ceremony to heal the town's children of their ailment. The townspeople were afraid of the man, who called himself a spiritual healer, but they accepted his help for the sake of their children.'"

I cover my mouth. "I have a really bad feeling about this."

"'On the evening of September fifteenth, the traveler gathered the town's children in a clearing and performed a healing ceremony, in which he played music on a flute made of bone. It is said that the traveler invoked the spirits, asking for healing and for the town's children to be free of that which plagued them. When the ceremony was completed, the town's children appeared to be completely healed. Despite the apparent miracle, the townspeople flew into a rage, accusing the traveler of witchcraft.'"

An icy feeling flows down my spine like water. "So he was *actually* trying to help."

"'In the grips of terror, they dragged the traveler off to a cave. The traveler pleaded for his life, but the townspeople refused to give him a trial, and they sealed him inside the cave behind a large boulder, leaving him to die.'"

Lena sits back in her chair and takes a shuddery breath. If the words weren't right there on the screen, I wouldn't believe it.

"Does it say what the healer's name was?"

Lena scans the page. "Beaumont Jones."

I chew on my bottom lip, tossing the name around in my head. Beaumont Jones. B. Jones. *Bones.*

I swallow hard. "I think we found our guy."

Chapter 15

I REACH AROUND LENA AND CLICK PRINT at the top of the article. At the front of the room, the printer hums to life. When Lena suggested meeting at the library, I was sure we were gonna leave disappointed. I never expected to find anything that could help us.

This whole thing is turning out to be a lot weirder than I thought. Healers, witchcraft, murderous townspeople. It's like a bad movie plot that's somehow turned into real life. *Our* life.

Lena stares straight ahead, her eyes unfocused. Now that we know *who* Bones is, the question is *how*? How is he here two hundred years after being trapped in a cave and left for dead? There's gotta be more to the story. I stand and move toward the librarian's desk.

Lena snaps out of her daze. "What're you doing?"

"Come on."

Halfway across the room, the pages of the article start sliding out of the printer. I step up to the desk and clear my throat.

The librarian looks up at me. "Ten cents a page for printing."

I reach into my pocket and dig out a quarter, thrusting it at her. She turns and pulls the pages from the printer, glancing down at the article. Her lips move silently, and the papers tremble in her hand.

I clear my throat again. "Can I have those?"

She passes the papers to me, but something in her eyes has changed. "Here you are."

"Thank you. Ma'am, this article mentions some items that were found when Town Hall was renovated. If we wanted to see those items—"

"What would you want to see those old items for?" Her voice is sharp and pinched.

"Uh—"

"We're doing a school project," Lena cuts in. "And it would be really great to get some pictures of things from the time period."

Man, she's good.

The librarian presses her lips into a line, then points to a doorway at the opposite end of the room. A sign above the door reads LOCAL ARTIFACTS AND ARCHIVES. Well, that couldn't have been more obvious.

"Thank you!" we say in unison.

"Don't touch anything!" the librarian calls after us.

The Artifacts and Archives room is dusty and warm. There are no windows, and the light flickers to life when we step through the door. Rows of shelves stand in the center of the room, piled high with old books, boxes full of items, and glass cases full of artifacts arranged according to date.

I walk down a couple of rows, reading off dates as I go. Along the far wall there's a long glass display case. Inside are medicine vials, combs made from bone, clay pitchers, and other items dating back to the late 1800s and early 1900s.

"Lena, over here."

A plaque on the wall beside the case describes the renovation of Stapleton Town Hall in June 2005. It outlines the uncovering of an unknown chamber containing archives and other items. Some of those items were sent to the Stapleton Historical Society, while others were sent here to go on display.

We slide along the front of the glass case, not

knowing what we're looking for. Something, anything, related to the dark past of our town. At the far end are a number of dusty books with a sign in front of them written in faded, feathery ink that says TOWN HISTORY. We might find something in there if we can—

I stop dead in my tracks. Lena sees the book at the same time I do. It's smaller than the history books, bound in worn leather, and the image of a flute is burned into the front cover.

"No way," Lena whispers. "We *need* to see what's inside that book."

"I don't know if we should. . . ."

I want to see inside the book just as much as Lena does, but the librarian told us not to touch anything. If we get caught, she might call the police. Or worse—our parents.

"Come on, Sam, it's a clue. It has to be."

I glance over my shoulder, then reach out and grasp the edge of the glass door.

"Wait!" Lena hisses. She points up toward the corner, where a security camera is fixed directly on the glass case. I freeze. A soft whirring sound comes from the camera a moment later, as it sweeps across the rest of the room. "Now, quick!"

My legs are shaking from the exhilaration of doing something I shouldn't be doing, but also from the possibility that we might've found a major clue. It can't be a coincidence that there's a flute on the front of this book—a book recovered along with other items from a time when we know Bones may have been here in Stapleton.

The hinges on the door let out a high-pitched squeak as I pull it open. My breath catches in my throat. I ease it open just a few inches. Lena's standing close, her breath hot on my neck.

"Quicker," she whispers.

My hand is trembling and beads of sweat break out on my forehead. This is it. The second I put my hand on this book, there's no turning back. It's the start of my life of crime. But I don't have a choice.

"What are you doing?"

My stomach flip-flops at the sound of the librarian's voice. Every nerve ending in my body jumps and grows cold, like someone dumped a bucket of ice water over my head. It cascades down my body, chilling me from head to foot.

I withdraw my hand from the case and turn. The librarian is in the doorway of the archive room, her hands planted on her hips. My heart skips a beat at the angry look on her face. Maybe if I confess, they'll take it easy on me. Give me community service or something. I'm too young to go to jail.

"I—"

"We weren't going to touch it," Lena says quickly. "We were just opening the case to get a better look."

"Follow me." The librarian presses her lips together and marches out of the room. "And close that case."

I push the door to the case shut and it snaps closed with a click. For just a second I consider making a run for it. But where would I go? Security would be waiting at the front doors before I even made it to the elevator.

"Jeez, Sam. You'd make an awful criminal," Lena mutters as we follow the librarian.

"No kidding," I say, wiping sweat from my forehead with the back of my hand. "Oddly enough, you'd make a really good one."

Lena flashes a smile. "You have no idea."

The librarian continues past her desk, all the way to the other end of the room, where the door to an office stands open. She ushers us inside and motions to a pair of chairs sitting in front of a desk. When we're seated, she closes the door behind her.

My heart's thundering in my ears. Which is kind of a relief, because for a minute there I swear it stopped beating completely. The librarian sits down behind her desk and folds her long slender fingers in front of her. Her dark hair is pulled back into a ponytail, and her blue eyes narrow at us from across the desk.

"Who are you?" She leans forward. "And why were you trying to take that journal?"

I blink. "Journal?"

"The journal in the case."

"We didn't know it was a journal, ma'am. Like I said, we just wanted to get a better look," Lena says. "For our project."

"Do I look unintelligent to you?"

Unhappy and definitely a little scary, yes, but not unintelligent.

I shake my head. "No, ma'am."

"Then please stop lying to me."

My mouth opens, and the words come out before I can stop them. "My name is Sam."

Lena's eyes widen. I'm no good at lying. I probably should've warned her about that before we made plans to steal an ancient artifact. Over the last few days I've had to bend the truth so much—having the librarian's intense blue eyes staring me down is more than I can take. I crack like an egg under pressure.

Lena sighs in defeat. "I'm Lena."

Recognition flits across the librarian's face. "I've seen you here before."

"Yeah, I come here sometimes to do research," Lena says.

"Well, Sam, Lena, I'll ask you again. Why were you trying to take that journal from the archive room?"

"We didn't know it was a journal. That part wasn't a lie," I add quickly. "We just wanted to see what was in it."

"Why? And why did you print that article about the Stapleton witch trials?"

I swallow hard and look at Lena. I'm starting to panic. I don't know how to get out of this without spilling everything. Maybe it's best if I just leave the talking to her.

Lena takes a deep breath. "Our school project. We're researching—"

"That's not the truth," the librarian says sharply. "*Why* did you print the article about the witch trials?"

We're at a standstill—Lena and me staring across the desk at the librarian, and her staring back at us—all of us determined not to back down. The silence in the room is so thick with tension, you could cut it with a knife.

"We're trying to find information about a man," Lena finally says. "That article was a clue."

The librarian sits back in her chair and lets out a deep breath. She looks down at her desk, and when she looks back up at us, her eyes are misty.

"You kids don't belong here, do you?"

Chapter 16

MY MOUTH FLOPS OPEN AND CLOSED, trying to form words that won't come. I glance at Lena, and her face has gone pale, her freckles standing out dark against her ashen skin. The librarian's eyes never leave our faces.

I can almost hear the wheels in Lena's brain spinning, trying to think of a way out of this, remembering the last time she told an adult about Bones and got sent to therapy.

"No," Lena says finally. "I guess we don't."

"But how did you know that?" I ask, relieved we're not lying anymore.

"The article was my first clue. The interest in the journal was the second. The two of you also seemed to be hiding something," the librarian says. "It was a guess."

"Pretty good guess," Lena says, raising her eyebrows.

I frown, still confused. No big surprise there. It feels like I spend most of my time confused these days. "Why did those things make you think we weren't from here?"

"That journal the two of you were looking at is almost a hundred years old. When it was sent here from the historical society, I noticed it tucked in with the rest of the items. It's how I discovered I wasn't the only one."

I tilt my head. "What do you mean?"

She takes a deep breath. "My name is Helen Hargrave, and when I wasn't much older than the two of you, I met a stranger who gave me an item that changed my life."

If my eyes grow any bigger, they'll pop right out of my head. I stick a finger in my ear and twist, sure I heard her wrong. A look of relief washes over Helen's face, reminding me of the day I met Lena in the park. The day we both realized we weren't alone anymore.

Lena leans forward in her seat. "The flute?"

The librarian nods. *Holy crap.* If what the librarian says is true, then she's just like us.

Lena's eyes widen. "Ms. Hargrave—"

"Please, call me Helen."

"Helen," Lena continues, "are you saying you know Bones?"

Helen lets out a deep breath, and her cheeks flush pink. "I haven't heard, or even thought of, that name in so long."

"I wish I'd never heard it in the first place," I mutter.

"So," Lena says, "that means you're not from here either?"

Helen shakes her head. "No."

"Then maybe you can tell me if my theory is correct," Lena says.

Helen's eyes light up. "Go on, tell me about it."

"I think Bones sent us to an alternate reality."

Helen nods. "I've had a long time to think about it, and it's the only thing that makes sense."

"How'd you figure it out?" I ask.

"Think about it," Helen says. "We're living a life that's *like* the one we knew, only it's different. Not just the people, but the *place*, too. Haven't you noticed anything different about Stapleton?"

I nod. "At school there used to be a fountain in the courtyard. But now there's a sculpture of an eagle."

"And the other day I took a walk to the place Lenore and I used to hang out—a little bookstore around the corner—only there was a weird coffee shop there instead," Lena says.

"This place—this Stapleton—is the same, but different," Helen says. "I never believed in stories about alternate universes before. I do now."

"You were right," I say to Lena. She makes a face. "I mean, I never doubted you, of course."

She rolls her eyes. "Mm-hmm."

I pull in a deep breath and hold it, letting the pressure build in my chest before releasing it. Okay. Having it confirmed is good, right? Now that we know what happened to us, we can try to fix it. The only question is, How? I press a hand to my forehead and close my eyes.

"Are you okay?" Helen asks.

"It's just, I can't believe this. What are the chances of us finding you, when we just came here to look for clues?"

"I gave up hope of finding others a long time ago," Helen says. "But I guess somewhere in the back of my mind, I was always on the lookout. I took this job thinking it was the logical place for people to look for more information if they were like me. After years of finding no one, I just kind of let it go. And now here you both are."

"How did you get here? Did Bones trick you like he did Lena and me?"

Helen waves her hand. "That's a long, complicated story, but probably not all that different from your own."

The greasy feeling of dread works its way into my stomach. If Helen is still here in the wrong reality, it means she never figured out how to get back home. And if that's the case, then what does that mean for me and Lena?

I swallow. "How long have you been here?"

"Ten years." Helen's eyes are fixed on the desk, and she scratches absently at a spot on her cheek. "I was sixteen when I met Bones."

"You never tried to get back to your own reality?" Lena asks. The idea is shocking. How could she not? But maybe she *did* try to figure out how to get back. Maybe she couldn't.

"Oh, I did, at first. But then . . ."

She trails off. There's gotta be more to her story. I can tell it's painful for her to think about. And we're just a couple of kids she doesn't know.

"What changed your mind?" Lena asks.

"In the reality I left behind, I was a bit of an outsider. But here, things were good. And then I met Julie—the woman who would become my wife—and going back just didn't matter anymore," Helen says, a smile tugging at her lips.

"What about your family?" An image of Grayson and Addie playing on the beach dances in front of me.

They're the whole reason I want to get back home, but it seems like Helen didn't have the same motivation.

"I tried to get back to them, but eventually I thought, what's the point? Why go back to a life where I don't fit in, when I could stay here and be with Julie?" she says.

Lena nods. "If things weren't so weird with my parents, I might want to stay too."

"Why?" Helen asks.

"My mother died two months before I met Bones. The morning after I played the flute, I woke up here and she was alive again."

"That must've been really shocking," Helen says.

Lena nods. "It was."

"If you don't mind my asking," Helen says, raising her eyebrows. "If you lost your mother in your reality, and she's alive in this one . . ."

"Why do I want to go back?"

"Yes."

Lena shifts in her seat and looks down at her hands. I know she's thinking about the version of her parents she's stuck with in this reality and how different they are from her real parents.

"I can't tell you how many times I wished to have **her** back," she says quietly. "It was all I thought about. I would've traded just about *anything* to see her again, to give her one more hug. Anything except my sister, Lenore."

Helen's mouth drops open. "Is Lenore . . ."

"She doesn't exist in this reality."

"They're twins," I add.

"That first morning, it was like a dream come true, seeing my mom there. But . . . she's different." Lena shakes her head. "She's not my real mom. Neither is my dad. They're angry all the time, and they have all these rules I have to follow. It's awful."

"Ah," Helen breathes. "I can understand why you'd want to go back. What about you?"

She looks at me, and I almost don't wanna say it. Knowing how bad Lena has it makes me feel guilty that things are kinda okay for me here. Emphasis on the kinda.

I sigh. "Before I met Bones, my parents announced they were splitting up, probably divorcing. But in this reality they're happy. They go on dates and trips together; they dance in the kitchen. It hasn't been so bad. . . ."

Helen tilts her head. "So what's missing from this reality?"

"My little brother and sister."

Helen nods, and the three of us stare at one another

in silence. My mind is spinning, thinking about every-thing we all lost—and gained—since meeting Bones. I might have a nice new cell phone, parents who go on dates, and clean clothes that are folded and put away, but I don't think I could make the same decision Helen made. Staying in this reality isn't even a choice for me. Grayson and Addie matter too much.

"Did you tell Julie about all of this?" Lena asks when the silence finally becomes uncomfortable.

"No," Helen says. "I don't think I could bear it if she didn't believe me."

I frown. "Why were you still looking for others if you decided to stay?"

"Because I knew they had to be out there. Just because I was happy to stay here didn't mean they would be too. I wanted to help if I could."

"What about the journal?" I ask. "You said you looked through it and it proved you weren't the only one. Is it connected?"

Helen nods. "I'm pretty impressed the two of you found it. There are journal entries from a man named George, dating back as far as 1935. He talks about how, when he was a boy, his father fell gravely ill. On the way home from school one day, he ran into a traveler who gave him a flute and promised it would give him his greatest desire, which of course was for his father to recover. When he woke up the next day, everything in his life was different."

"That's what Bones told us," I say. "I mean, about our greatest desire."

"The rest of the journal entries span years, and they're all about him trying to figure out what happened." Helen pauses. "He never did."

"What did you say the man's name was?" Lena asks.

"George Ashcroft Jr."

Lena gasps, and her eyes slide out of focus. The color drains from her face, and she wraps her arms around herself, shivering even though it's warm in Helen's office.

"Lena?" I say cautiously.

Something's wrong. I snap my fingers in front of her face, and she shakes her head, coming out of her daze.

Lena swallows hard and turns to me, her eyes wide. "You're not gonna believe this, but George Ashcroft Sr. was my great-great-grandfather."

Chapter 17

"**WAIT, WHAT?**" I ASK, BLINKING. "So you're saying that *this* journal belonged to your—"

"Great-great-uncle," Lena finishes.

Whoa. The odds of finding a hundred-year-old journal connected to this whole mess were slim enough. But finding one that belonged to Lena's ancestor?

I frown. "Are you sure?"

"The name was passed down in my family," Lena says quietly. "I'm positive."

I shake my head. "Okay, that's weird. Not gonna lie."

"There's something I haven't told you about my family."

There's a lot she hasn't told me, since we've only met

twice, but now is probably not the best time to point that out. "What?"

"My great-great-uncle disappeared shortly after his brother, my great-grandfather, was born," Lena says.

I frown again. "Wait, wouldn't that make him your great-uncle then?"

Lena shakes her head. "It's confusing. My dad had to explain it to me. That's not important right now."

I shrug. "If you say so."

"The story of my great-great-uncle's disappearance was passed down through my family, just like the name, as a way of honoring him."

"You're serious?"

I wait for her to break into a smile and tease me for being so gullible. But no. She's dead serious. Lena's great-great-uncle met Bones and made a wish for his father to be healed, then ended up here. Was it a coincidence that Lena's ancestor ended up here, and then almost a hundred years later, Lena did too? Or did Bones know exactly what he was doing?

"That's unbelievable," Helen says. "There has to be a connection."

"I was thinking the same thing," I say. "Did George Ashcroft Jr. write anything in the journal that might help us figure out how to get back to our reality?"

Helen shakes her head. "Not that I remember, but it's been a long time since I've read it. I can check again if you think it will help."

"Yes, please. Anything you find, no matter how small, could be the key to getting us home." My phone buzzes in my pocket. I pull it out and read the text message flashing across the screen. "Shoot. I have to go. My parents are done at the market. They're outside waiting for me."

I stand, frustrated that we don't have longer to talk to Helen. If two heads are better than one, three might help us figure out exactly how to get back to our reality.

"I probably should go too," Lena says.

"You'll come back soon?" Helen asks, opening her office door.

I nod. "Definitely."

"In the meantime, I'll read through the journal again and see if I can find any useful information."

"Great—thanks, Helen." Lena takes a step, then hesitates. "Would it . . . be weird to give you my number? You know, just in case there's something *really* important in there and you need to get ahold of us?"

"Good thinking," I say, as Helen hands Lena a piece of paper. "I'll give you mine, too."

I tap on the settings in my phone, feeling silly that

I don't even know my own phone number, and scribble it down for Helen. Lena and I say goodbye, then cross back through the reference section and ride the elevator down to the lobby. Outside, I turn to Lena, who still kinda looks like she saw a ghost back there in Helen's office. Maybe she's thinking the same thing I am: Helen and George Ashcroft Jr. never made it back to their own realities.

"Helen could've missed something when she looked through the journal before."

"Hopefully," Lena says. "I don't know what else to do if she can't help us."

"I'll text you," I say, spotting Dad's car. "Don't lose hope, okay? Not yet."

Lena's eyes cloud with tears. "I'll try."

"We'll meet up again soon."

She nods, and I jog off across the parking lot. The back seat is packed full of bags overflowing with fresh fruits and vegetables. I squeeze in beside them and wave at Lena through the window as we pull out of the lot.

Dad glances in the rearview mirror. "Did you get everything you needed at the library?"

"Not quite."

I stare out the window the whole way home, my mind buzzing. I have a sinking feeling that the next time we meet with Helen, she won't have any new information for us. She already read through the journal before, and it didn't help her figure out how to get home. Of course, she also gave up and decided to stay here, in the wrong reality.

Back at home, I help Mom and Dad bring in the groceries. When everything's put away, Dad turns to me, his eyebrows slanted down. "Hey, Sammy?"

"Yeah, Dad?"

"I got a call from Coach Steve while we were out. He was calling to check on you. Said you weren't feeling good at practice on Thursday. Everything okay?"

My stomach flutters. "Yeah, I'm fine."

"Are you sure?" Mom asks. "You've been acting a little strange this week. We're worried, Sammy."

"Worried? About what?"

Dad nods in agreement. "About you. Does this have anything to do with us going to Hawaii without you?"

I raise my eyebrows. "No, I'm happy you guys are going on vacation together."

"Then what's going on?" Mom asks.

"Nothing's going on, I swear."

Dad frowns. "Who were you with at the library?"

"A friend. I told you, we're doing a project together."

Mom raises her eyebrows. "Not Alex?"

"No, not Alex."

"Then who?" Dad asks.

I sigh. "Her name's Lena."

"Ohhh," Mom croons, her eyes lighting up.

Oh, God. *Don't go there.* "No, Mom. It's not like that. We're just friends."

"It's all starting to make sense," Dad says, winking at Mom.

I roll my eyes. Fine. Let them think what they want, as long as they leave me alone. All the sneaking around and lying is getting hard to keep up with anyway. If I let them think I have a girlfriend, maybe they won't ask so many questions.

"You know, your dad and I met in school too," Mom says in a dreamy voice.

"I know, I know. You've told me all about it. I've got homework. Can I go to my room?"

"Of course. We just wanted to make sure you were okay," Dad says. "I hope you know you can come to us with anything, Sammy. We're here for you."

"I know, Dad, thanks."

I bolt out of the room and sprint up the stairs. Phew, that was close. Hopefully, the girlfriend story will keep them happy, at least for a little while.

In my room I pull out my schoolwork and sit at my

desk. Normally, I wouldn't be caught dead doing school-work on a Saturday—Dad was right. But with every-thing going on, I'm starting to fall behind. I'm not the best student in the world, but this isn't like me. It's just been too hard to focus.

As I read, the words dance across my history book, refusing to settle down. I shove it away from me and sigh. My phone buzzes in my pocket. It's a video call from Alex. I hit accept and hold the phone up in front of my face.

"Hey, Sammy."

"Hey, what's up?"

"What're you doing?"

"Nothing, just homework."

Alex clears his throat. "Are you mad at me, Sammy?"

"What?"

His eyes shimmer with tears. "Did I do something wrong?"

"No, why?"

"Well, you've been acting kinda weird. You haven't come over to kick the soccer ball around in days, and you ditched me that day you went to the park. I thought maybe you were mad at me."

This is so awkward. I can't tell him I'm not the Sammy he knows. He'll think I'm losing it and will probably tell my parents. That's the last thing I need right now. My mind jumps to the moment I realized Derek didn't know who I was, and how terrible that felt. Alex is probably feeling something similar.

I sigh. "I'm not mad at you, Alex."

"Are you sure?"

"Everything's fine, I promise."

He narrows his eyes. "It's like you're a completely different person."

A stab of guilt twists in my stomach. "I know I haven't been the best friend lately, but I'll make it up to you."

"How?"

"I don't know, but I will. I just need some time."

"Okay."

"I've gotta finish my homework. See you in school on Monday, okay?"

Alex nods and I end the call. A bitter laugh surges up in my throat. First Mom and Dad, and now Alex. They think I'm acting like a different person, but they don't know the half of it. I guess from their perspective, though, I *am* acting strange, since I'm not the real Sammy—

Oh my God.

I sit back in my chair and exhale so hard, papers blow across my desk and flutter to the floor. I can't believe it took me so long to think of this. It was there the entire time, the question staring me right in the face, waiting for me to figure it out.

If I'm here, where's the real Sammy?

Chapter 18

MY HEAD IS SPINNING. THE QUESTIONS batter me, one after another, slamming into my skull and leaving me breathless. A dull ache radiates behind my eyes.

When I left my reality and my real parents behind and came to this new reality where everyone knew me—or a version of me, at least—what happened to the me who was here? What happened to the Sammy who was Alex's best friend? The one who was an only child and had no idea that Grayson and Addie even existed?

Oh. My. God.

When I played the skeleton flute and came here, did Sammy take my place? Is he living my life, navigating a strange world with a brother and sister he doesn't know and a best friend who's a stranger to him? Or did he go somewhere else? Lena's great-great-uncle just disappeared, and no one ever heard from him again. That has to mean something.

The wide-eyed face of the boy in my dream swims in front of me—the boy with my face. A chill rips through me and I shiver, wrapping my arms around myself. What if the boy in my dream wasn't me, but Sammy? What if we *didn't* switch places? He could be trapped inside that awful, dark place with no idea how he got there.

I snatch my phone off my desk and type out a text message.

LENA, WE NEED TO TALK. CALL ME ASAP.

I drop the phone and sit back in my chair. One of my legs shakes up and down while I wait for her reply, rattling the things on my desk. *Come on, Lena. Call me.*

Maybe the dreams we're having aren't dreams at all. What if they're some sort of window into a *third* reality? That's how this alternate-reality, multiverse thing works, isn't it? In movies and comics, you start with one reality and then some event—some unknown thing—happens to make the timeline split in two, branching out into different realities. And if it can split into two, why not three?

I need to find out if Lena is seeing herself in her dreams, too. My phone buzzes. *Finally!* I grab it and accept the call before it can ring a second time. "Lena?"

"What's up?"

"How'd you know about the dreams?"

"What? Sam, what're you talking about?"

"Yesterday you told me the dreams were coming. How'd you know?"

Lena pauses. "It was just a feeling, like the dreams I was having were a part of this."

"Tell me about them."

"My dreams?"

"Yes!" I'm trying to be patient, but my head is still spinning from the realization that Sammy could be in the nightmare world.

"Why's this important right now?"

"Lena, please. It's important—trust me."

"Okay, okay. It just freaks me out to think about them." She sighs. "In the dreams I wake up in a field, lying on my back in the grass. It's dark, and I can hear sounds all around me. Creepy sounds, like things moving through the dark, and something big screeching and flapping in the sky. There's these crumbling concrete buildings—"

I let out a hiss. "I'm dreaming about the same place!"

"You are?"

"Yeah, the *exact* same place."

"But how?"

"I'll explain in a minute. Tell me more."

"There's a town, all dark and overgrown. Every time I wake up there, I feel like I'm being hunted."

"Have you seen anyone else in the dream?"

Lena gasps. "Yes, Sam, how—"

"Is it yourself?"

"Yes! Are you seeing yourself, too?" Lena asks.

"I did once, yes."

"At first . . . don't laugh, but at first I thought it was Lenore, since we're identical."

I'd never laugh at her about something this serious, especially when it's something to do with her sister.

"How did you figure out it wasn't her?"

Lena pauses. "There was just something about the way she moved. I knew it wasn't her."

"Have you talked to her? I mean, to yourself?"

"No. I've tried to get close, and every time I do, she gets spooked and runs off. There was a weird feeling when we were close, though, like sparks racing across my skin."

"I felt that too," I say. "Is she all fuzzy-looking?"

"Yeah, it's really weird."

I pause, trying to decide if I should tell her my theory. "Lena, I think I know what the dreams mean."

"What?" She pauses and I can almost hear the laughter in her voice. "Is this like the alien thing, because if it is—"

"No. At least I don't think it is."

"I was kidding. Sorry. Tell me what you think they mean."

"See, now I don't know if I want to."

"Sam!" Lena laughs. "Tell me. Please."

"Okay. What if . . . this is gonna sound a little out there . . ."

"Just spit it out, dude."

"What do you think happened to the Sam and Lena from this reality?"

"I just figured we swapped places. I mean, I wasn't sure, but I thought it was a possibility."

"Okay," I say. "But what if we didn't?"

Lena makes a sound of confusion. "Huh?"

"See, I thought the same thing at first, but the more I think about the fact that your great-great-uncle just disappeared and wasn't replaced with a different version of himself—"

"Ohhh."

"Do you see where I'm going with this?"

Lena gasps. "The dream world?"

"Exactly. What if it's not *just* a dream world? What if it's a third reality, and we're not seeing ourselves—we're seeing the other Sam and Lena?"

"But how?"

"Maybe it's some sort of cry for help, like we're connected to them in some way. If it's true, they're trapped there just like we're trapped here."

"Oh God, Sam. That would be awful," Lena says.

"More than awful."

"Why do you think the other Lena runs from me when I get close?"

I sigh. "Maybe they don't know what's going on any more than we do. . . . Maybe they're scared."

Lena makes a weird choking noise. "This is all our fault for playing that flute. What do we do?"

"We need to talk to them. We need to find out if they're really in the nightmare world."

"That's going to be hard if they run away whenever they see us."

I sigh. "I know, but we have to try."

"If I dream tonight, I'll see if I can get Lena to talk to me. Gosh, that's weird to say."

"I'll do the same with Sammy."

"Okay. I have to go."

"Good luck, Lena."

"You too, Sam."

I set the phone down and let out a breath, relieved Lena didn't think my theory was ridiculous. I change into my pajamas, hop into bed, and slide under the covers. I want to get to sleep and, hopefully, back to the dream world as soon as possible. If I'm right about this—and I think I am—then I need to talk to Sammy. Tonight.

Chapter 19

BRANCHES STRETCH LIKE HANDS above me, bare and clawlike, reaching for the sky. I'm beside the tree again. The ink-black bark is bumpy and thick, kinda like the scab that formed on my knee the last time I wiped out trying to land a jump on my bike.

A shiver rips through me. I was prepared for the darkness and the swirling dust-particle air, but it's still a shock to go from my nice comfy bed in the cool, silvery moonlight to this world where everything is tinted orange. The shadows move like living creatures, darting here and there, never still.

I pull myself off the ground and move down the embankment. The concrete building with its crumbling walls and empty, staring windows is directly in front of me. Something flaps in the dark sky, and a shadow blots out the strange moonlight. I jump and look up, sure I'll find some snarling creature swooping down on me.

There's nothing there, but I can feel eyes on me. Watching. Waiting for an opportunity. I bolt through the doorway, panic rising in my chest, and stop beside the crumbling stairs. Outside, a terrible screech rips through the darkness, but inside, it's eerily quiet. At the moment I'm not sure if that's a good thing or a bad thing. Guess I'm about to find out.

"Hello?"

My voice bounces off the bare cement walls and fades. No one answers. How am I ever gonna find Sammy? He could be anywhere. This is the last place I saw him, but it doesn't mean I'll see him here again. The building seems deserted.

I lift a foot and place it on the first broken step. Somewhere, deeper in the building but on the same floor, a door creaks open.

I freeze. "Hello?"

The door slams, and I push off the step and run blindly in the direction of the sound. My heart is thundering in my ears. That annoying voice in my head returns, frantic this time, asking me if it's such a smart idea to be running after the sound. *What if it's not Sammy? What if it's someone or something else?*

Like I haven't thought about *that* already.

I round a corner into a dark room full of broken furniture and cobwebs. There's a doorway across from me. I charge through it and find myself inside another entryway. Dingy curtains gently sway back and forth over a window set into a door. This must be the door I heard slam shut.

I grab the knob and pull it open. Here, a sidewalk leads down to a street, where two fuzzy figures are running away from the building.

"Wait!" I yell, running through the door. "I just wanna talk!"

The figures, who I think are Sammy and the other Lena, don't stop. They turn off the street, onto another, and disappear behind a house. I have to go after them. I close the door behind me and run down the sidewalk.

The road, flanked on both sides with crumbling buildings, is cracked and choked with weeds. I dodge chunks of broken concrete and fallen branches, my feet slamming against the pavement. My lungs scream in protest, and sweat streams down my forehead.

At the intersection, I turn right. The figures are on a road lined with tall brick houses. The fronts of them are black with mold and crawling with vines, and they sit back from the road on large overgrown lawns. I shiver. It's like time has completely stopped in this place.

I skid to a stop, gulping air in great, heaving gasps. My lungs are on fire. Not just from the running, but from this nasty, rotten air I'm breathing in. The figures come into focus. It *is* Sammy and Lena. They're frozen on the doorstep of one of the houses, watching me approach. I press a hand to my chest, my heart beating frantically under my palm. Then I walk forward slowly, so I don't freak them out and make them run again. I don't think I'd survive another sprint down the road.

Sammy squints through the darkness at me, his eyes growing wide. He says something to Lena, and her shock mirrors his. I stop at the end of the walkway and reach out a hand. Sammy takes a staggering step backward. He mashes his palms into his eyes and wipes at them furiously, then pulls them away, his mouth hanging open.

"No," he gasps. "Not me, you're not me. . . ."

Lena reaches out from behind him and grabs a handful of his shirt, pulling him away from me. My stomach lurches. They're so scared. I need to help them understand what they're seeing. I have to assure them they don't need to be afraid, but I don't know how. I'd completely freak too.

Come on, do something, say something!

I take a deep breath. "I—"

A loud shriek cuts through the air, drowning out my words. Heavy wings flap above us. The whoosh and pull of air being drawn upward and then forced back down ruffles the hair on my head. Inside the house, a chorus of slightly quieter shrieking fills the air.

Lena's face goes pale as a sheet. She backs away from the door, her head jerking up. Whatever's up there, it sounds huge. And angry. Another shriek splits the night, this one so loud the windows on the house shake in their frames.

"We have to get out of here!" Lena yells. "She's protecting her nest!"

My mouth goes dry. "What do you mean, nest?"

Lena jumps off the porch without answering and bolts across the street, Sammy right behind her. I groan. More running. I've barely recovered from the first time. I stumble after them, panic exploding inside me. I can't lose them. Now that I've made contact, I need to stay with them.

As my feet pound across the cracked pavement, I make the mistake of looking behind me. A dark shape dips out of the sky and swoops low over the street. Blood-red eyes flash through the darkness. A mouth full of razor-sharp teeth emits a sound that fills my veins with ice.

It looks like a bat, but that's where the similarities end. This is nothing like the cute little bats that swoop around the backyard at dusk catching mosquitoes. *This one's* the size of the small two-seater airplanes Dad and I sometimes watch take off from the airstrip outside town. It's covered in thick, dark, matted fur and has wings the size of boat sails.

I freeze in the middle of the street, my mouth hanging wide. The voice in my head is screaming at me now. *Wake up, get out of this nightmare! Go back to your room where it's safe!* I fight against it with everything I have. I can't wake up yet. Not without talking to Sammy and Lena. I have to find out if they're really here or if they're dreaming, too.

They duck in between the houses across the street. Another shriek breaks me free of the trance holding me in place, and I run after them, bushes slapping me in the face as I try to keep up. I can hear their frenzied breathing and the sound of their bodies pushing through the thick overgrowth. I think back to not so long ago when Dad moving out was the most not-okay thing to ever happen to me. Correction: *this* is the most not-okay thing that's ever happened to me.

With a grunt, I pull free of the branches just in time to see Sammy and Lena disappear into a small wooden shed behind one of the houses. I wade through the knee-high grass, the sound of wing beats following me, and yank open the door.

They're huddled against the far end, and they recoil when I open the door. I scramble to close it behind me and sink onto the floor, leaning my back against the wall. Not that it'll do much good. If that thing wanted to get in here, I'm pretty sure these thin wooden walls couldn't stop it.

"What was that?" I pant. "I've never seen anything like it in my life. It was huge!"

Lena and Sammy stare at me but don't answer my question. Lena's eyes are narrowed. She's clutching a garden spade in one hand. Sammy is beside her, his eyes wide and confused.

Oh right. They probably want to know how there are two of us.

"Look, I know this is weird—"

Lena stiffens and points up. "Shh!"

The screeching is right above us. The bat creature's wings flap furiously like it's searching for something. Hopefully the thing it's searching for isn't its next meal. If the cute little bats at home eat mosquitoes, it only makes sense that *human* might be on the menu for this ginormous thing.

When the wing beats fade, the tenseness leaves Lena's body. She raises her eyebrows, like she's waiting for me to continue.

I open my mouth. "I—"

"Who are you?" Sammy sputters.

"I'm you. I mean, I'm Sam."

Lena's brown eyes narrow. "Why do you look like that?"

I look down at myself. "Like what?"

"All strange and fuzzy . . ."

"And how are you me?" Sammy adds.

I lift a hand and gaze at it. It's not fuzzy, not like they are. I must look to them the way they look to me. "I'll try to explain—just, please, don't be scared."

Lena sets her jaw. "How do we know you aren't another one of the ether's monsters?"

"The ether?"

"This place," she says impatiently. "There are monsters everywhere. How do we know you're not one of them?"

"I'm not a monster any more than you two are. I'm also not really here."

Sammy scrunches up his nose. "What do you mean you're not here?"

"I'm dreaming. I thought you were too. Like we were connecting in our dreams somehow."

"I wish this was a dream," Lena says.

My shoulders slump. "So you're actually here?"

"What do you mean?" she asks, like I just asked if the sky is blue. "Of course we're actually here."

"That must be why I look strange to you, because I'm not really here and you are."

She sets down the spade. "Okay, explain."

I let out a long sigh and start from the beginning. I tell them about Bones and his skeleton flute, and how he tricked us into making a wish on it. I explain that the other Lena and I realized that the two of them might be stuck here, so I came to find them.

"Wait a minute," Lena says. "I think I've seen the other Lena. I thought she was a monster because she was all fuzzy, like you. I didn't realize she was me."

Sammy gasps. "The other night, on the stairs."

I nod. "I didn't know then that what I was seeing was you and not me."

"This is confusing," he says, his mouth twisting into a frown.

He's not wrong. It's totally bizarre sitting here talking to myself, watching myself move and react without a mirror in front of me. Though Sammy's very clearly me, there are small differences someone else might not notice. My dark hair is slightly longer than Sammy's, his curly ringlets sitting closer to his head. As he crouches in the corner of the shed, the muscles stand out in his legs—the muscles of someone who plays on a soccer team instead of spending most of his time playing video games.

He tilts his head. "Isn't this bad luck? Like crossing the streams or something?"

"Let me see if I understand what you're saying," Lena says, ignoring him. "We're here because some guy with a flute gave you a wish, which sent you to take *our* places in *our* reality?"

"Yeah, that's what we think, anyway."

"But why?"

I frown. "I was hoping you might know the answer to that."

"How would we know?" Lena asks, frustration rising in her voice.

"I don't know," I mumble.

She shakes her head. "I woke up one day and I was here. Same with Sammy."

"Have you tried finding Bones again?" Sammy asks. "Maybe he can tell you."

"Yeah, no dice. I mean, I found him, but he didn't explain anything, and he wouldn't fix things."

"Maybe you didn't try hard enough," Lena snaps.

Sammy looks at her sideways and places his hand on her arm. "Lena, I'm sure—"

"No!" she growls. "He and the other Lena are living our lives. They're not stuck in this awful place like we are. He can just wake up, safe and sound, and not have to worry about getting eaten every day!"

My face burns and I look down at my feet. I probably deserve that. No, I *definitely* deserve that. We made the decision to play the flute, which set all of this into motion. I've spent the last few days feeling sorry for myself—missing my brother and sister, worrying about playing soccer, and having to eat leftovers in front of the TV. But at least I'm not here in this nightmare.

It's all our fault. And that means it's our job to make it right.

Chapter 20

LENA STANDS AND CROSSES THE SHED, her eyes traveling up and down my body. I squirm under her gaze, guilt still tugging at my insides. She reaches out a finger and pokes me in the arm, hard.

I flinch. "Ow. What was that for?"

"If you're dreaming, how are you solid? How can I touch you?" she asks.

I think back to the very real feeling of bushes slapping me in the face as I ran after Sammy and Lena. "I don't know."

"This doesn't make any sense," Lena says, pressing her hands into her temples. "How is this possible?"

"I don't know that, either," I say. "What I do know is

that the man responsible for this knew this would happen. I just don't know why he's doing it. It's like he's pulling the strings, and we're all his puppets."

Lena turns and pushes open the shed door just enough to stick her head out. She tilts it left and right, then opens the door all the way. "I think it's safe. We were going out scavenging when we heard you."

"I'm sorry, I didn't mean to scare you."

She lifts an eyebrow. "Since you're here, you can help us look for food and water."

Lena steps out into the knee-high grass, and Sammy and I follow behind. Another stab of guilt twists in my stomach. They're stuck here fighting for their lives and scavenging for food. All because of me.

"You mentioned monsters," I say warily, as Lena leads us back to the street. "Are there more of them? I mean, other than that freaky bat thing."

Lena shudders. "You have no idea."

"Lena's been here longer than me, so she's seen a lot more," Sammy says. "She doesn't like to talk about it."

I frown. "But where did they come from?"

Sammy shrugs. "No clue."

"Where are we going?"

Lena holds a finger up to her lips. "We shouldn't talk. We don't want to draw the monsters to us."

I nod. "Nope. Definitely do not want to draw them to us."

Lena moves over the broken street, dodging fallen branches, piles of twisted metal, and crawling masses of vines and thick roots like she's taken this path before and has it memorized. How many times has she had to risk her life to venture out in search of food?

In the middle of the street, Lena turns and points at each of the houses across from us, as if counting them.

I frown. "What're you doing?"

She shoots me a dirty look. I lift my eyebrows. I'm really not great with keeping quiet. It's a character flaw.

"Counting," she says quietly. "Last time we were here, we checked the first four houses on the left side of the street. They all look pretty much the same, so I count to keep track."

She hurries toward the fifth house and turns up the walk. I stay close, walking beside Sammy, my heart hammering in my chest. Now that I'm close to him, the air feels charged with static electricity. Sammy notices it too. He rubs a hand along his arm, where the static is causing the hairs to stand on end.

At the door, Lena places one hand on the knob and the other flat against the wooden frame. She twists the knob and eases it open a couple of inches. A breeze rushes in, and a chorus of squeals fills the air. Lena's face goes pale and she yanks the door closed, then glances up at the sky.

"Another nest." She backs down the walk, and we move on to the next house. At the front door, Lena opens it an inch, then wrinkles her nose. "We should be okay in here. But don't touch the pods."

"The pods?" Sammy asks.

I was wondering the same thing, dude.

"Yeah, you haven't come across these yet," Lena says, swinging the door open wide.

"The ether—the place that keeps on giving," Sammy mutters.

Lena steps into the house and motions for us to follow. I edge into the entryway behind Sammy, and shut the door behind us.

As soon as I do, an awful smell washes over me. My stomach heaves. Like a cross between rotten cabbage and dirty gym socks, the stench fills the air inside the house, triggering my gag reflex. I clamp a hand over my mouth.

Beside me, Sammy's clutching his stomach. "What's that smell?"

"The pods," Lena says. "You get used to it after a while. I think it's some sorta defense mechanism."

She reaches into her backpack and pulls out an old metal flashlight with a handle on the side. She cranks it for a minute to get it to turn on, and a yellow beam cuts through the dark. I turn to follow it, and my eyes fall on a sight so terrifying that I almost pass out. The edges of my vision darken, and I fling out a hand, pressing it against the wall to steady myself.

The bottom floor of the house is coated from wall to wall in thick, slimy goo. Sitting on top of the slime, three-foot-tall orbs fill the living room. *The pods.* They're light green and laced with red veins. Each orb has one thick red vein running away from it, connecting it to the orb next to it.

We step around them, moving toward the kitchen. My feet stick to the ground as I walk, every step making a wet squelching noise. Lena said we'd be okay in here, but there's *nothing* okay about this.

I scrunch up my nose. "What are those things?"

"They're like eggs, I think. For the frogmen."

Lena shines her flashlight onto one of the pods. Inside, something wriggles and squirms beneath the beam of light. The pod pulses, its veins bulging thicker and then shrinking back down.

"So this is where they come from," Sammy says.

"Frogmen?" I ask, raising an eyebrow.

Lena shakes her head. "I'll explain later; we have to keep moving. Do *not* touch them."

"You don't have to tell me twice," I say, shivering.

I stay as far away from the pods as I can manage, but in the middle of the room I step into a particularly slippery patch of slime and my feet go right out from under me. I topple toward a pod and Lena freezes, her hands flying up to cover her mouth. Sammy lets out a grunt and lunges forward, grabbing hold of my T-shirt and stopping me before I fall onto the pod.

I let out a breath. "Thanks, dude."

"You're welcome," he says, his eyes wide.

Lena frowns at me. "Try to be more careful."

"Noted."

When we finally make it across the minefield to the kitchen, I let out a sigh. No pods here.

"Check the cupboards for cans. Grab anything that's in good shape," Lena says, moving to the other end of the room.

Sammy slips his backpack off while I fling open cupboard doors. There are cans on the shelves, the labels faded and peeling. There's no telling what's inside them, but most of them seem to be in okay shape. They look like they've been here a really long time.

Once Lena and Sammy fill their bags, we hurry

back out through the front door into the night. I never thought I'd be so relieved to see the orange-red glow of the moon. Sammy must be thinking the same thing. He exhales loudly and bends over, his hands resting on the tops of his thighs.

"You okay?" Lena asks.

"A little heads-up next time we're about to encounter something like that would be nice," he chokes out.

Her face softens. "Sorry."

This Lena might not be *my* biggest fan, but there's something there between her and Sammy. She's much gentler with him than she is with me. I mean, we just met, and she *does* blame me for her being stuck here, but there's something else. I can't help but wonder what they went through together since they showed up in this awful place.

We move down the overgrown walk and turn toward the next house. Movement at the end of the street catches my eye. I stop dead in my tracks. "Lena, there's something there."

Lena stops and turns, her eyes growing wide. The object that caught my attention moves fully into view. Relief floods through me.

"Is it another monster?" Sammy asks. I almost laugh at how high his voice rises. This is a kid who's the *captain* of his soccer team. He's used to performing under pressure, only it seems monsters are his limit.

I smile. "No. It's another Lena."

She spots us in front of the house and moves toward us, her hand waving through the air. I run to meet her, and Sammy and Lena follow.

"Sam," she pants. "You found them."

The two Lenas stop walking and stare at each other. They're almost completely identical, except that my Lena's hair is longer. I can feel their confusion, how disorienting it is to be standing face-to-face with another version of themselves.

"Lena," I say, "meet Lena."

"This is gonna get confusing," Other Lena says.

"Maybe we should call one of you something different," Sammy suggests.

My Lena closes her eyes and takes a deep breath.

"Are you okay?" I ask.

"Yes, it's just . . ."

"You're thinking of Lenore."

She nods. "Yeah."

"Lenore?" Other Lena tilts her head. "Who's Lenore?"

"In my reality, I have a twin sister. Her name is Lenore."

"Oh," Other Lena says. "I don't know if it would be

weird, but that's my middle name. You could call me that instead."

Something flickers in Lena's eyes. She looks down at her shoes and bites her lower lip. I don't think she could handle calling someone by her twin's name, especially not knowing if she'll ever see her again.

"What about Lee?" I say quickly.

Other Lena nods. "That's what my sister used to call me—"

Lena's head whips up. "Your sister? But I don't have a sister in your reality."

Lee presses her lips together and starts walking. Lena shoots me a look, and I shrug. At the corner, Lee turns left, back toward the building where I first saw Sammy. I watch her, thinking of the look in her eyes just now when she mentioned her sister. It was haunted and sad. There's something she's not telling us.

Chapter 21

LEE PAUSES IN THE ENTRYWAY OF THE building and tilts her head, listening. It's quiet, the silence so heavy it feels solid. When it's clear no monsters are lurking in the shadows, she moves toward a back staircase. No one says anything as we follow her. The tension of something unspoken hangs between us, though.

At the top of the stairs she turns right into a narrow hallway and moves to the end of it. A heavy wooden door is on the left, and Lee pushes it open, motioning for us to go ahead of her. We step through, into a stairwell, and she closes the door behind her, then pulls some sort of barricade in front of it.

Lena and I follow her and Sammy up the stairs into

a small, windowless attic with slanted ceilings. A ledge runs along one wall, where rusty canned goods and glass jars full of water are arranged neatly. I look around, sadness twisting in my stomach. Guilt slams into me again, thinking about them hiding out in this small room, trying not to get eaten by bat creatures and frogmen.

"You guys live here?" Lena asks.

Lee nods. "Home sweet home."

There's a hint of bitterness in her words. Sammy sits down cross-legged in the middle of the room and Lee sits beside him. Lena and I hesitate, then join them. Lee takes a long drink from a jar of water, then passes it to me. I accept it, only just now realizing that my mouth feels like I swallowed a bunch of sand. Cool water rushes down my throat, calming the burning. Then the taste hits me— metallic and earthy. I make a face, then feel bad.

"You okay, Sam?" Lee asks.

I clear my throat. "Uh, yeah. Water just tastes a little weird."

"It's from a well pump," she says. "I found it behind the building. When I woke up here, one of the first things I did was look for water."

"Smart," I say, passing the jar to Sammy.

On the wall behind him, someone has drawn hatch marks with a nubby length of charcoal. Six neat groups of five hatch marks and a couple of single marks stand out black against the dingy white walls.

Lena notices them too and frowns. "What are those?"

"The number of days we've been here. There's more for Lena than me since she got here first," Sammy says.

"But there's over thirty marks there. It hasn't been that long," Lena says. "It's been just a little over two weeks since I woke up in the wrong life."

Lee shrugs. "Time moves weird here; it isn't the same as it is at home. I figured that out when Sammy showed up and I asked him the date. It'd been fourteen days since I played the flute instead of seven."

I frown. "How can you even tell when a day's passed? It's dark every time I'm here, and that weird moon is in the sky."

"We count days by the position of the moon, but it's kind of just a guess," she says.

I shiver. "What is this place anyway?"

"It's like a strange, twisted version of our reality," Sammy says. "You probably couldn't tell, but the road behind this building is the main road that runs through Stapleton."

"The only way I figured that out was because of the statue in the center of town. It's the same figure of the founder, just crumbling and crawling with vines," Lee says.

"Lee," Lena says slowly. "What did you mean when you said your sister used to call you Lee?"

Lee shifts and looks down at her hands, which are clasped together in her lap. She clears her throat and when she looks up again, her eyes are misted over. "I had a sister once."

Lena frowns. "Your parents haven't mentioned her."

"No, they wouldn't. We lost her when I was ten. She was nine."

"What happened?" Lena asks, leaning forward.

"There was an accident." Lee pauses. "Lacey—that was her name—and I were walking home from school. A car came out of nowhere. We both got hit, but Lacey didn't make it."

As she talks, she runs her finger across a thick scar on her right arm. A tear slips from her eye and trails down her dirt-smeared cheek. Pain blossoms in my chest. How awful.

Lena puts her hand on Lee's knee. "I'm so sorry."

"Mom and Dad were different after we lost Lacey. Everything changed. They became so cold and unhappy, so strict." Lee pauses, then continues in an almost-whisper. "Sometimes it feels like they blame me for making it when Lacey didn't."

"I don't think that's it at all," Lena says, her face

twisting. She sits up on her knees and grabs Lee's hands. I've seen that look on her face before. It's a look that says she's figured something out the rest of us haven't.

Lee looks at Lena through her tears. "You don't?"

Lena shakes her head. "No, and now that I know what happened, it makes so much sense. They don't blame you, Lee. They're terrified something will happen to you."

Lee is quiet. She bites down on her lip and sniffles. Lena pulls her close and wraps her arms around her.

"I know what it's like to lose someone," she says into Lee's shoulder. "I lost my mom a couple months ago."

"I'm sorry, Lena."

"I'm sorry about your sister, but I'm almost positive your mom and dad are being so strict because they don't want to lose you, too," Lena says.

Lee pulls back and sniffles. "I never thought of that."

"They sent me to a therapist when I told them about Bones. Her name is Dr. Wells. She's really nice, and if—*when* we get you back home, I think you should ask your parents to come with you. I think she can help all of you."

Lee nods. "Okay."

It's impossible not to be ridiculously proud of Lena right now. Not only did she figure out the mystery of why her parents are so awful—so different—from her real parents, but she gave Lee something she's probably not had in a really long time: hope. If I get nothing else out of this whole awful situation, at least I get to be Lena's friend.

"Well," I say, nudging Sammy, "I wish I'd had a breakthrough like Lena, but all I managed to do was mess up soccer practice. You can thank me later."

"Oh no!" he gasps. "I totally forgot about the game against Cedarville."

"It hasn't happened yet—don't worry."

"I take it you're not a soccer player?"

I shrug. "Only if you count in video games."

Sammy groans. "If we ever get back home, I'm gonna have a nice mess to clean up."

My face burns, thinking about Alex. "A couple of messes, actually."

"What do you mean?"

I'm almost embarrassed to tell him. He and Lee are already upset with us for getting them stuck in this nightmare world. Now I have to tell him I'm screwing up his real life too? I press my eyes shut. He deserves to know.

"Alex knows there's something going on with his best friend. I didn't exactly do a great job of convincing him I was you," I say.

He lets out a breath. "I think I can fix things. What about Mom and Dad?"

"Clueless. Too busy planning trips to Hawaii and going on date nights."

"Another trip?" Sammy rolls his eyes. "Guess I'll be spending some quality time with Grandma. That is, if I ever get out of this place."

"At least they're happy." I look down at the floor and pull at a loose thread on my pants. "At least they're together."

"Your parents aren't?" Lee asks.

I shake my head. "That's why I took the flute from Bones in the first place."

"Who is this Bones guy, anyway?" Sammy balls his hands into fists. "He sounds like a jerk."

Lena nods. "He is."

I sigh. "All I wanted was for my parents to stay together."

"No one can blame you for that," Lee says gently. "I'm sorry I was so angry back there when you first told us."

I shrug. "It's okay."

"If someone offered to give me my greatest desire, I'd wish to have my sister back and I wouldn't think twice about it. He tricked you. It's not your fault," she says.

"Yeah, but still . . ."

Sammy gasps, his eyes widening. "Lena, what's happening to you?"

"What do you mean?" Lena looks down at herself, and her eyes widen.

"You're fading," Lee says. "You too, Sam."

I glance down and my mouth drops open. I *am* fading. My body is see-through and growing lighter by the second. "We must be waking up."

"No," Lee says, almost desperately. "You can't leave us, not yet."

"I don't think we have a choice," Lena says.

"We'll come back soon," I say. "We're gonna fix this, I promise."

Lee's eyes are pleading. "You have to get us out of here!"

"We will," I say, nodding. "I swear I won't stop until I figure out how to get you home."

"Is there anything we can do to help?" Sammy asks.

"Yeah," I say. "Stay alive."

Chapter 22

ON MONDAY, I CHECK MY PHONE during lunch. There's a group text to me and Lena from a number I don't recognize.

It's Helen. Meet me after school if you can. Have some info.

Lena's waiting for me in the library's lobby cafe after school, dressed in a pair of overalls that are dotted with different colors of paint. She's sipping on a mug of hot chocolate, her hair hanging loose around her shoulders.

"I got you one too," she says.

I sit in the metal chair across from her. "Thanks."

There's a smudge of paint on her nose. She sees me eyeing it, and wipes the back of her hand across it. "Paint, from art class."

I smile and take a sip of the cocoa. "What school do you go to, anyway?"

"I'm in seventh grade at Stapleton Academy," she says. "It's a STEAM school."

I tilt my head. "STEAM school?"

"Science, technology, engineering, art, and mathematics. It's across town."

"Is that where you live?" I ask, realizing I have no idea.

Lena shakes her head. "I live about a block from Stapleton Town Park, but Mom and Dad wanted me to have an 'enriching school career.' Surprisingly, that's the same here as it is back home."

I chuckle. "Sounds fun. Not."

She rolls her eyes. "It's not so bad."

"So, are we gonna talk about the other night?"

"That was pretty wild," she says, pushing a lock of hair off her forehead.

I nod. "Yeah, it was."

"I feel so terrible, Sam."

Tears blur my vision. "They're stuck in that awful little room, while I get to sleep in my bed—in *Sammy's* bed every night. . . ."

Lena sets down her mug. "Hey, we *both* played the flute."

"We have to fix this," I say, nodding. "We've gotta figure out how to get them out of there."

Lena pushes back from the table and stands. "Then let's go find Helen."

We step into the elevator and Lena mashes the number three to take us back up to the reference section. When the elevator lurches to a stop, we step out onto the tile floor and hurry across the room.

Helen leans forward and waves when she sees us. She's checking books out for an older woman, so we wait off to the side. I twist my fingers in front of me, fighting the urge to tell the woman to check out somewhere else so we can be alone with Helen.

After scanning the books, she hands the stack to the woman and waves us toward her office. Lena and I settle into the chairs in front of her desk. Helen closes the door behind her. Her dark hair is pulled up into a messy bun, and she's wearing a flowery blue dress.

"I'm so glad you two could meet me."

I lean forward in my chair. "Did you get a chance to look through the journal?"

Helen nods. "I did."

"And?" I ask. "Did you find anything?"

"I think so." She pulls a notebook from a bag beside her desk. She flips it open and scans the page, which is filled with feathery handwriting. "George Ashcroft Jr. talked about the stranger being a healer—"

"The article we found about the witch trials said Bones called himself a healer," I say. "And the picture of the flute we found said it was a ceremonial flute used by spiritual healers. What exactly is a spiritual healer, anyway?"

"Don't you pay attention in social studies, Sam?" Lena asks, a smile tugging at the corners of her mouth. "We learned all about that in, like, fifth grade."

I shrug. "We can't all go to fancy STEAM schools."

"I actually found some articles on the topic," Helen says. "Spiritual healers use the spiritual world to help them heal the sick and provide guidance to others. Musical instruments are vital to this process. They're used in healing ceremonies, even today. The music helps the healer transcend this plane of existence."

I tilt my head. "What does that mean?"

Helen glances at her notebook. "According to what I read, music reveals the doorway to the non-ordinary reality."

"'Non-ordinary reality'?" Lena asks, frowning.

"Different worlds. Spiritual healers travel between them to help trapped spirits move on. They also commune with them to gain knowledge," Helen says.

I wrinkle my nose. "Bones isn't trying to help anyone."

"Well, no," Lena says. "But remember the article we found? He tried to cure the town's children when they all got sick, and instead of thanking him, the townspeople locked him in a cave and left him to die. Maybe he *was* trying to help—maybe that changed him."

"The dude is ruining people's lives," I say, scowling. "What happened to him was terrible, but it's no excuse for what he's doing."

Helen's eyes grow dark and she flips to another page in her notebook. "There's something else, something that might explain why he's hurting people. I need to dig into it a little more, but what I found has me concerned."

I raise my eyebrows. "What?"

"I found an article about something called a soul eater in connection with spiritual healers."

"'Soul eater'? What's *that*?" I ask, my voice cracking.

"Healers who have given themselves over to darkness. They work with evil spirits, consuming the souls of others. It makes them stronger, more powerful, and as close to immortal as a person can get," Helen says.

The light above us flickers, and I jump, a chill shivering through me. *Immortal.* That explains how Bones tricked George Ashcroft Jr. into playing the flute almost a hundred years before he tricked us.

I swallow hard. "Does immortal mean he can't be killed?"

Helen shakes her head. "Not necessarily."

I press a hand to my forehead. "So if Bones *is* a soul eater, maybe he didn't start out that way."

"That's exactly what I was thinking," Lena says. "If he tried to help the townspeople, he couldn't have been bad. What happened after, when he was trapped in the cave, must've turned him into one. What if this isn't his fault?"

"Are you kidding me?" I ask, anger burning in my face. "Bones is *choosing* to trick people into playing his flute. It's a choice, Lena."

Lena's eyes shift to the floor. "It was just a thought."

My tongue feels like lead in my mouth. If Bones really *is* a soul eater, we're dealing with something far darker than I thought. I shake out my arms and legs. I need to get a grip. I need to *think*.

"So the real question is, why's he doing it?" I ask. "Why George Ashcroft Jr.? Why us? What does he get by sending the others to the ether?"

Helen freezes. "What did you say? The others? What others?"

Lena and I glance at each other.

"Helen, do you ever have dreams?" Lena asks.

Helen nods. "Nightmares, mostly. Ever since I woke up here. I even tried hypnotherapy to make them stop, but it didn't work."

"In your dreams," I say, "have you ever seen yourself?"

Helen frowns. "I—yes. How did you know that?"

I tell her about the ether and how Lena and I found Sammy and Lee there in our dreams, about how we realized we weren't seeing ourselves, but our *other* selves, the ones whose places we took when we woke up in this reality. Helen's eyes fill with tears.

She pulls a tissue from her desk drawer and blows into it. "I spent all this time thinking I'd been given a gift of sorts. If I'd had any idea the dream wasn't *just* a dream . . ."

"How could you have known?" Lena asks.

"I never would have stopped trying to find a way home. I've just been living her life while she's been stuck in that awful place all these years."

She sucks in a shuddering breath and releases it, a small sob shaking her shoulders. I don't know what to say. Lena and I figured out pretty quickly that Sammy and Lee were our other selves because we had each other to talk to. Helen's been alone for ten years. No one could blame her for not realizing.

"Are you still seeing her in your dreams?" I ask.

Helen nods. "I am."

"That means there's hope. If she's still there, we can save her. Sammy and Lee, too."

"But that would mean . . ." Lena trails off.

"I would have to go back to my reality. The one where Julie isn't my wife," Helen says quietly. "I don't have a choice, though, do I? This isn't my life. I *stole* it from someone else, and I don't have the right to keep it. She's trapped there because of me."

Lena blinks. "You didn't steal it, Helen. You didn't know."

I sit forward in my seat, thinking about someone else who was trapped once. The person responsible for all of this. "Do you think the cave they trapped Bones in still exists?"

Lena chuckles. "It's a cave, Sam. I don't think they just disappear."

"You know what I mean. If we can find it, maybe we'll find a clue or something. Are there any books about caves that might help?"

Helen wipes her nose one last time, then turns to the computer on her desk. "That's a good idea. I think I remember checking in a book about local geology just the other day."

She chews on her lip as she types, her eyes scanning

the computer screen. She stands abruptly and leaves the room, then returns a few minutes later with a book in her hand.

"Did you find it?" Lena asks.

Helen sits down and opens the book, flipping through the pages. "Aha! Here it is. There's a section in this book about caves in the Northeast. There *is* a cave system in Stapleton. Just outside town."

I grin. Librarians truly are superheroes. "What's it say?"

"'More than ten thousand caves lie across the Northeast, and dozens more wait to be discovered, according to the Northeast Cave Society, a nonprofit organization that catalogs and maps them. The Stapleton County Cave System, located along the northernmost point of the town of Stapleton, is a small system, but still vital to the region's ecosystem.

"'You'll find a series of entrances to this largely unexplored system along Route Twenty-Seven, which runs parallel to Lake Ingershall. There may be as many as a dozen entrances located along the sandy shores, although they're likely to be inaccessible due to rock instability and tunnel collapses. Those that can be accessed have been visited by local residents for over a century. The proof is written on the stone walls and ceilings in the form of blackened signatures and dates, scrawled in candle smoke by visitors during the eighteen and nineteen hundreds.'"

"That's it." The memory of a man watching me from the shadows dances around the edges of my mind. "Lake Ingershall is where I first saw Bones. That's gotta be where the cave is."

"Oh my God," Lena breathes.

My body fills with static, like the feeling I got when I stood too close to Sammy in the ether. I know what we need to do. That cave might hold some clue about why Bones is stealing people from their lives and sending them to another reality.

Maybe it'll help us figure out how to save Sammy and Lee and get back home, too.

Helen steps out to return the book to its shelf. When she closes the door behind her and it's just the two of us in the office, I turn to look at Lena. "We have to go there. Now."

Lena looks alarmed. "I'm sorry, what?"

I push back in my chair. "It has to mean something that the cave system is in the same place where I saw Bones for the first time, even if I didn't know then that it was him. We have to go there and see if we can find a clue."

"Okay, I get it, but why *right* now?"

I nod. "We can't waste any more time. Sammy and Lee are trapped in the ether because of us. They're in danger. We have to save them."

The image of the giant bat creature and the sound of its angry cries splitting the night comes back to me. I feel the wind from its wings on my skin as if I'm back there in the ether, reliving it all over again. Going to the cave is the best lead we have. It's also better than sitting around looking through books. It's *doing* something.

"Even if we find a clue, how are we gonna save them, Sam?"

An uneasy feeling wiggles through me. I'm almost afraid to say what I'm thinking out loud. Either Lena will think I've lost it, or she'll agree with my plan, and then we'll have no choice but to go through with it. But if we're gonna save Sammy and Lee, we have to be ready to do whatever it takes.

I clear my throat. "Do you remember what Helen said about healers and music?"

Lena scrunches up her face. "She said . . . music helps healers transcend this plane of existence."

I nod. "Yeah, but not just *any* music."

"Huh? Sam, you're not making any sense—"

"The skeleton flute!" I'm pacing back and forth in

front of the desk now, my eyes darting wildly. "It's how Bones travels between worlds. It's how he sent *us* to the wrong reality. That means the flute will help us get to Sammy and Lee."

The thought of coming face-to-face with Bones again makes my lunch churn inside my stomach. But we don't have a choice.

Lena's face goes pale. "We have to take it from him, don't we?"

I nod. "But first we have to go to the cave."

Chapter 23

"**SO HOW DO WE GET THERE?**" **LENA** asks.

"The bus," I say. "There's buses running past Lake Ingershall all the time."

She glances at her phone and her face crumples. "I don't think I can go with you," she says. "My parents would be furious if they found out. Besides, we have no idea what time the buses run or when the return bus will come by. It could be hours."

I frown. She's right, but there's gotta be a way we can both go. We need to do this together. "How long do we have?"

Lena looks grim. "Dinner's at six. I told my parents I'd be home by then. If I'm late . . ."

I let out a breath. She's right. It's already four thirty. We can't take the chance. I don't want Lena to get in trouble. This is so frustrating. She should be with me for this. Besides, I really don't wanna do it alone.

The door to Helen's office opens and she pokes her head in. "I'll be just a minute more—I have to check someone out."

A smile spreads across my face. "I think I know how to get us there quicker."

When Helen returns, Lena and I put on our best pleading puppy-dog faces. Helen glances from Lena to me, then back again. "What's up?"

"We need a ride," I say.

"A ride?" Helen asks. "Where to?"

"Lake Ingershall. Can you help us?"

She closes her eyes. "You're going to look for the cave, aren't you?"

I nod. "We have to, Helen. We might find a clue there that can help us get home."

Helen glances at her watch. "I'm still on the clock for another hour."

Another hour and it'll be too late for Lena to get back in time for dinner. We need to get out there now. Every minute we waste is at least twice as long for Sammy and Lee. I don't wanna leave them there any longer than we have to.

"Please, Helen. Is there any way we can go now? This is really important."

Helen hesitates, then nods. "Meet me out front in five minutes."

My body buzzes as we take the elevator down to the first floor. Outside, I take a shuddery breath. We're really doing this. This could be the worst idea I've ever had, or it could be the key to helping us get back to our reality. Only time will tell which one it is.

"I'm glad I don't have to do this by myself," I say, glancing at Lena.

Heat creeps into my cheeks, but I don't care. If I've learned anything from all this, it's that I should tell people how I feel instead of keeping it inside. Not just Lena, but everyone. Mom, Dad, Grayson, Derek.

I think back to the way I tried to be strong for Grayson instead of letting him see that I was upset too. And how I wanted to explain to Mom and Dad how much their separation would hurt me, but couldn't. Maybe if I'd talked to them instead of trusting some sketchy dude in the park, I wouldn't be in this mess. Feelings are complicated, but so is getting transported to another reality and trying to find your way home.

Lena smiles. "I'm glad I don't have to miss the adventure."

"I don't just mean going to the lake. I mean all of this. If I hadn't found you, I don't know what I would've done. I mean, without you, I'd still think everyone I love was body-snatched."

She snickers, then reaches out and squeezes my hand. "I feel the same. We're gonna figure this out, Sam. Together."

"Hey, you two! Get in!" Helen calls from the window of a dark blue SUV.

Lena pulls open the back door and climbs into the back seat. I jump in after her. "Thanks, Helen."

Helen glances at me in the rearview mirror. "It's the least I can do."

She pulls out of the parking lot into traffic on the main road, and I wonder if she really feels she has to help or if helping us isn't actually about us at all. Maybe she just feels bad about trapping the other Helen in the nightmare world for all these years. Either way, her willingness releases the knot of anxiety that twisted itself inside my chest when I thought I'd have to go to the cave alone.

Ten minutes later, Helen slows the car and turns off Route 27 onto the road to Lake Ingershall. A thrill of excitement explodes in my chest. I need to reel it in. We have no idea if we'll find anything to help us, but

I can't help the spark of hope growing inside me. This could be it.

Helen glances in the rearview mirror. "We're here."

I nudge Lena. "Here goes nothing."

If she's as excited as I am, she's better at hiding it. I'm starting to think she's superhuman, the way she's always so calm.

The road to Lake Ingershall is long, and it twists off into the woods and out of sight. A vision of Addie's soft brown curls bobbing up and down as she half ran, half waddled from our beach blanket to the edge of the water just a week ago flashes in my mind.

Pain blossoms in my chest, fluttery and frantic. I press my hand against it, gripping my shirt between my fingers. The vision is so strong, I can almost hear them. The sound of Addie's laughter as she chased Grayson down the beach, his fake cries as he tried to escape her. Even the sound of the water lapping against the rusty old ladder that led up to the high dive. I squeeze my eyes shut to push the image of my brother and sister out of my head.

Lena looks at me sideways. "Sam, are you okay?"

"I'm fine," I say through clenched teeth.

"It's okay if you're nervous," she says softly. Her eyebrows are slanted down over her dark eyes. "I mean, if you changed your mind—"

"No, that's not it. It's just . . . my family used to come here all the time."

Lena nods. "This place brings back memories for me, too. Lenore and I used to come here."

We might've swum right past each other and never even known it. I was always so focused on trying to work up the nerve to jump, I might not have noticed if she'd plopped right down next to me on the beach.

"You two were really close, weren't you?"

Lena nods. "We shared a womb. There's nothing closer than that."

"It must be really hard, being without her."

"It's like a really important piece of me is missing," Lena says. "She was the strong one. I feel so lost without her."

I nudge her with my shoulder. "I think you do okay on your own."

"I just miss her so much, Sam," she says, tears shimmering in her eyes.

"We'll get you back to her," I whisper. "I promise."

A small brown booth comes into view, and Helen slows down. During the summer, an attendant collects entrance fees and hands out parking passes from a window on the side. This time of year there's no one inside. A sign on the shuttered window reads BEACH OPEN DUSK TILL DAWN.

Helen turns left, down the last stretch of road that will bring us out by the lake. The green water sparkles through the trees, which are starting to turn different shades of yellow and orange. This is Mom's favorite time of year to visit the lake. She loves driving down the road and looking at the leaves starting to change colors while it's still warm enough to enjoy them. Another stab of pain slashes at my insides.

The lake doesn't feel the same without my family here with me. I swallow a lump that's formed in my throat as Helen pulls into the parking lot and finds an empty space. We get out of the car and wait while she swaps out her slip-ons for a pair of hiking boots she keeps in the trunk. When she's done, she and Lena both turn and look at me.

"Where do we start?" Helen asks.

My ears grow hot. I'm not used to anyone, especially not an adult, looking at me to call the shots. Like the moment at soccer practice when the coach said I was team captain, I'm frozen in place. I think back to the local geology book that led us here in the first place.

"The book said the entrance is along Route Twenty-Seven, which would be on the other side of the lake. We should start there."

I lead the way onto the soft sand of the beach and

stop, looking out over the still, green water. I was just here a week ago, swimming in this water and trying to work up the nerve to jump off the high dive. Well, not here exactly. There are little differences from the Lake Ingershall at home, but it's still very much the same place. I wonder if Sammy has made the jump. The captain of the soccer team wouldn't be too scared, I'm sure of it.

"Sam?" Lena asks.

I take a deep breath. "Sorry, let's go."

We walk along the edge of the beach on the paved path until we reach the other side, where the bathhouse sits dark and deserted. My eyes linger on the tall bushes near the concession stand where, just a week ago in another reality, a strange man watched me from the shadows.

At the end of the paved path, a dirt trail picks up, circling the entire lake. Woods stretch out to the left of it, all the way back to the road. If we're gonna find any hidden entrances, they'll be off this trail. There are thorny-looking bushes, big sharp rocks, and some pretty gnarly plants with spikes on them lining the walkway. I suddenly wish I was wearing long pants instead of shorts. We step onto the path, scanning the woods as we walk.

"How exactly are we supposed to find the cave?" Lena asks.

"Keep your eyes on the rocks," Helen says. "The entrances would be on the left, probably hidden behind bushes and trees."

A large rock formation, covered in moss and vines, juts out of the ground about twenty feet from the trail. In some places it rises fifteen feet into the air, and in others it's no more than a couple of feet high. But it's continuous, which means we're probably in the right place.

Somewhere, under all this rock and overgrowth, the cave where the Stapleton townspeople imprisoned Bones and left him for dead waits to be discovered. I shudder at the thought.

Lena swats at a bug, squishing it on her arm. "Gross."

"Hold on," Helen says, pointing. "What's that?"

There's a spot where the undergrowth has been stomped down into a makeshift path heading toward the rock formation. We step off the trail and follow it. My nerves are lit up like a Christmas tree. Could this be it?

Lena ducks under a low-hanging branch, and Helen and I follow close behind. We emerge in front of a tall section of rock that curves around us in a half circle. There's an overhang providing protection from the rain, and a small fire pit in the center of the space. The back wall is covered in spray-painted graffiti, and trash litters the ground.

Lena moves a crushed soda can aside with the toe of her shoe. "Ugh, why are people so gross?"

"This must be a popular hangout spot," Helen says, wrinkling her nose.

I turn back toward the main path, shaking my head. "I don't think this is what we're looking for."

"Obviously," Lena says.

A few minutes later, after stepping off the path a number of times to investigate places along the rock formation, I stop. Maybe we got it wrong. Maybe this isn't the place they brought Bones. Maybe we're out here wandering around the woods for nothing.

Lena glances at her phone. "Maybe we should head back."

I know she's worried about getting home in time for dinner, about what'll happen if she breaks her parents' rules. I'm worried too, but I'm not ready to give up.

"No!" My words echo, bouncing off the trees. A pair of birds roosting above us startles, squawking as they take off, their wings flapping loudly.

"Sam—"

"I have a feeling we're going to find answers here. We just need to find the cave."

She shoots Helen a look. "What if it's not here? What if we were wrong?"

I throw my head back. "Ten more minutes. Please?"

"Okay, okay," she says, holding her hands up in surrender.

"Thank you."

Her eyes have a faraway look to them, like she thinks this is pointless. Frustration bubbles up inside me. I wish I could explain what's pushing me to keep going, but the truth is, I don't know. Maybe it's just being here, *knowing* that this is where it all started. It has to be the key to getting us back home.

I take two steps down the trail when I see it. I would've missed it if it wasn't for the huge black crow sitting on top of the rock formation. Through the trees, behind the edges of a crumbling boulder, there's an ink-black opening in the rocks.

My breath catches in my throat. "Lena."

She turns and follows my gaze, her eyes growing wide. "Sam."

This is it. We found the cave.

Chapter 24

KNEE-HIGH FERNS SLAP AT MY LEGS AS I step off the trail. Unlike before, there's no beaten-down grass here, no trash littering the ground or graffiti on the rock face. It doesn't look like anyone has walked this section in a really long time. It's like it's been forgotten.

A large rock rests against the opening in the rock face. The top of it is cracked and crumbling, creating a small window that reveals black space beyond. That's what I saw from the trail. This has to be it.

I walk toward it, holding my breath. Lena reaches out and squeezes my hand. Standing on my tiptoes, I try to see through the opening, but it's too dark. We need to get this big rock out of the way. I place my hands on the side of it, the rough stone pressing into my skin, and brace my feet against the forest floor. Grunting, I push against it. Dust rains down from the top of the moss-covered rock, but it doesn't budge.

Lena steps up beside me. "Here, let me help."

"I'll help too," Helen says.

Shoulder to shoulder, we push against the boulder, trying to get it to roll away, or at least shift enough for us to get in. More dust falls onto our heads and shoulders. The muscles in my arms burn, and sweat breaks out on my forehead. But the rock doesn't move.

"It's been here too long," I say, shaking my head. "It's too big. There's no way to move it."

The dark opening looms in front of me, taunting me. Frustrated tears press at my eyes, and I swipe them away, embarrassed.

Lena puts her hand on my arm. "It's okay, Sam—"

I let out a growl. "There's gotta be a way to get in there!"

Lena presses a hand to her mouth, her eyes darting back and forth. She turns suddenly and disappears around a corner of the rock formation. I shoot Helen a look and she shrugs. When Lena returns, she has a long stick the thickness of my wrist in her hand.

I frown. "What's that for?"

Helen's eyes light up. "You're brilliant!"

"Thanks," Lena says, grinning.

"Is someone gonna tell me what's going on?" I ask, feeling totally clueless.

"It's a lever," Lena says. "To help lift the rock out of the way. We just need a fulcrum now."

"A what?"

Lena sighs. "Something to shove under the lever."

"Is that gonna work?"

"It's basic physics," Lena says, leaning the stick up against the boulder. I scrunch up my face. We're in seventh grade. How am I supposed to know anything about physics? She sees the look on my face and smiles. "STEAM school, remember? Help me find a rock."

We start searching the ground, but I honestly have no clue what kind of rock I'm looking for. A few feet away from where we are, I spot one a little bigger than a basketball, hidden beneath the ferns. "Is that big enough?"

"Yes! That's perfect."

Together we roll the rock through the ferns and up beside the cave. Lena takes the end of the stick and wedges it under the bottom edge of the boulder, then rests it on the smaller rock. Shaking her head, she pushes the smaller rock out farther toward the middle of the stick until it looks like a seesaw.

I don't see how that little stick is gonna move such a large object, but Lena seems to know what she's doing, and Helen doesn't stop her. Might as well go along with it. It's not like I have a better plan.

"If we all push down on this end of the stick, it should move the boulder," Lena says. "Strong, steady pressure when I say go."

I take a deep breath. "Okay . . ."

Helen, Lena, and I grab the end of the stick and brace our feet wide in the dirt. As I wait for Lena to give the signal, doubt creeps in, but I push it out of my head. This has to work.

"One, two, three, go!" Lena cries.

The muscles in my arms quiver as we push down. Helen lets out a grunt and squeezes her eyes shut. The rock starts to shift, but not enough. A wild cry of built-up frustration rips from my mouth. I don't think a grown man could get this thing out of the way, even with a lever and a whatever Lena called it.

"Come on!" Lena yells.

It's no use. We release the lever. Disappointment washes over me until my stomach is burning. I step back and look closer at the boulder. It's about five feet high and semi-flat on the side facing us. It's not exactly natural—it looks like it was made specifically to fit the cave opening, and the edges along the outside are rounded.

"Someone rolled this thing into place. There *has* to be a way to roll it out of the way," I say, walking around to the left side of it. Sticks, rocks, and other debris are piled up around the base of the boulder. I bend down and start pushing the stuff out of the way. "Help me clear out this side."

Lena's eyes light up, and she rushes over, grabbing at the sticks and rocks and hefting them away. Once we clear the ground around the outside edge, she grabs a flat rock and begins scraping the dirt we just cleared, moving it down and away from the boulder.

I frown. "What're you doing?"

"Trying," she grunts, "to make a bit of an incline."

"Gravity. We can use it to our advantage," Helen says, moving along the front side of the boulder. She pulls away vines and ferns from the bottom edge. When the ground around the boulder is clear, she uses a stick to scrape off any moss covering the part of the boulder closest to the rock formation, removing anything that might keep it in place.

Lena drops her rock and smiles. "I think this'll help. Let's give it another try."

I'm almost afraid to. I won't be able to stand the

disappointment a second time if we can't get the rock to budge. But we cleared it off the best we could, and all that's left to do is try.

We move to the end of the lever and grab ahold of it. Lena's eyes meet mine. "One, two, three, go!"

The sound of rock scraping against rock is music to my ears. The gap at the top of the boulder begins to widen, and the rock shifts slowly, steadily, to the left.

"Keep going!" Helen cries.

My arms are shaking. My legs are too. But I keep pushing and the rock keeps moving. Once we get it over the divot in the ground that it's been resting in for who knows how long, the incline helps the boulder move as we push down on the lever. The dark opening to the cave slowly comes into view. My breath gets faster. We're actually doing it, we're—

A crack splits the air.

"Look out!" Lena cries.

The lever snaps, sending us, and half of the stick, flying backward. I hit the dirt with a thud. Lena and Helen land beside me, and the stick flips over our heads, missing us all by just a few inches. That was close. Searching for clues with a concussion might be a little challenging.

I let out a rush of air and look myself over. My legs and shorts are streaked with dirt. "Oof."

"Are you guys okay?" Helen asks, scrambling to her feet.

"I think so," Lena breathes. "That was not supposed to happen."

I get to my feet and reach out a hand to help Lena up. She brushes the dirt from her backside, and we turn toward the cave.

"Well, the good news is, it looks like we can squeeze through. You wouldn't happen to have a flashlight in your bag, would you?" I ask Lena.

She smiles. "No, but we've got phones."

"You're brilliant."

Lena's cheeks blush. "That's the second time I've heard that today. If you're not careful, I might start believing it."

"You should," I laugh.

She opens her bag, rummages around in it, and pulls out her phone. She grins, then taps the flashlight button.

Grabbing my phone from my pocket, I take a deep breath and do the same. "Here goes nothing."

It's a tight fit, but I manage to slip my right arm and leg through the opening and pull the rest of my body through and into the cave. If the rock was sharp, even just the tiniest bit, it would've been impossible. I would've been gutted like a fish.

I move off to the side to give Lena room to get through. She squeezes in with a grunt. Behind her, Helen attempts to join us. She sucks in her stomach and reaches an arm through. Then a leg. The opening isn't wide enough for an adult. It was barely wide enough for us.

"It's no use," she says, backing out. "I can't fit."

I poke my head through the opening. "We'll be quick. Promise."

"Be careful!"

Lena and I turn away from the opening. My hand trembles as I hold my phone out in front of me, the yellow beam flashing back and forth on the walls like some weird dance party. The cave is small—no more than twenty feet deep and maybe ten feet wide—and the air is heavy. If this wasn't such an important moment, I'd crack a joke about it. But this is no time for jokes.

As I take another step forward, my ears fill with pressure, like they're stuffed full of cotton balls. I can hear Lena breathing beside me, but the sound is muffled, like we're underwater. Every sound gets sucked deeper into the darkness, like the cave is trying to swallow it up.

I lift my phone up and shine it onto the back wall. When the beam sweeps across the dark stone, something white catches my eye. I scream.

Chapter 25

THE YELLOW BEAM FLASHES ACROSS the tilted, smiling face of a skeleton. Dark, empty eye holes surrounded by bleach-white bone stare at us—stare *through* us. Slumped to the side against the back wall of the cave, the skeleton is still dressed in the clothing it died in. Time has faded it, but there's no mistaking the multicolored patchwork suit jacket.

No way. No freaking way.

"Sam! Lena!" Helen calls from outside. "I heard a scream!"

"We're okay!" I yell back, taking a step toward the skeleton.

"Bones," Lena whispers.

I shake my head. "But how's he *here*, and also out *there* tricking people?"

Lena frowns. "How's he not dust after all this time?"

A gold tooth, still attached to the skull, glints in the beam of light. I edge forward, my legs shaking. I've never seen a dead person before—unless you count the fake skeleton hanging at the back of Mr. Cheney's science classroom. Derek says it's real, but it looks like plastic to me.

One of the skeleton's hands sits in its lap, and the other is outstretched, the bony fingers reaching toward a dark puddle in the center of the cave. It glistens as my light sweeps over it.

"Water? What the—"

The surface of the puddle is as smooth as glass, and it's dark, almost black. I shine my phone at the ceiling, checking for a hole where rainwater could've gotten in. I'm almost relieved not to find one. If we did all that heaving and shoving for nothing, and could've just climbed in through the top of the cave—

Lena frowns. "Sam, I don't think that's water."

When the light moves across the puddle, it sinks down into the dark substance and disappears. A shiver runs down my back, making the hair on my arms lift away from the skin. I crouch down beside the black, tarry-looking substance and peer into it.

"You're right." I make a face. "It's definitely not water."

"Be careful," Lena says. "I don't like the look of that."

I pass my phone to Lena and lean in close, studying the puddle, trying to make sense of it. Up close, there's a slight movement I didn't notice before. It swirls slowly, silently, in an almost rhythmic way. Almost like it's alive.

My vision goes fuzzy and my head swims. I feel like I'm spiraling down a black hole. The substance is mesmerizing, but not in a good way. Something's not right. My brain starts to scream at me: *Back away! Back away!* But instead, almost like I'm being pushed by an invisible force, I reach for the puddle.

"Sam, no!"

Lena drops both phones, sending them into a spin on the cave floor. The lights flash and darken across the walls. She closes the distance between us to try to stop me, but she's too late. I press my palm into the dark substance, surprised to find it warm beneath my skin.

My stomach drops, yanked violently from where it should be, like the moment at the top of a roller coaster when you've just come over the peak of a hill and you start to plummet down the tracks on the other side.

Oh no. What have I done?

My head is spinning, picking up speed, and the cave blurs into flashes of light and dark. Lena screams. Her hands clamp down on my shoulders. She tries to pull me away, but it's useless. I'm cemented in place, my hand resting on the swirling puddle and my mind spiraling down, down, away from the cave.

And away from Lena.

I squeeze my eyes shut against the spinning waves of nausea washing over me. Icy fingers prod my brain, like something evil is pushing images into my head, cramming them in there against my will. They come one after the other, fighting to be seen. Emotions overwhelm me, but they're not mine. They're *his*. Somehow they're his, and I panic. I don't wanna feel this. I don't want these visions.

But they come anyway.

The images splash across my mind like a movie: Bones being dragged through the streets, his arms and legs bound tight with rope that digs into his skin and rubs it raw. A crowd of men and women chanting and jeering at him, their children peeking out from between their legs.

A pair of men toss him into the back of a wagon. His eyes are wide with fear. Confusion. Anger. *No! I helped you! I saved your children! You should be grateful!*

The wagon takes off, followed by a caravan of angry townspeople. Bones's pleas for mercy are ignored. Inside my head they catapult against my brain, a high-pitched sound blasting my eardrums.

Witch! the townspeople chant over and over. *Heathen!*

They cut him free and push Bones into this very cave, bruised and bloodied, then seal him in behind a boulder. He screams and pounds on it until his fists are raw, but there's no way out. He's trapped.

My heart thuds against my rib cage. The rage coursing through Bones washes over me. I feel it in every inch of my body. His thoughts are in my head, his anger taking over. I shudder, trying to push it out, trying to clear my head and gain control of myself.

But the visions keep coming.

It's like the dark substance has the events of the past imprinted into it, and it's passing them along to me because I put my hand into the puddle. I remember a movie I watched about a man who was driven mad when he found an old pocket watch that was haunted by a dark spirit. It made him see things and do things he didn't want to do, just like what's happening to me.

Oh God, make it stop.

Bones gives up trying to escape, collapsing on the ground in defeat. He turns his flute—the one he used to heal the town's children—over and over in his hands, looking down at it helplessly. The power inside it is meant to heal. Not to get him out of a tomb. And if he doesn't do something, that's exactly what the cave will become—*his* tomb.

And so he digs down deep inside himself, calling to the healer within, calling to his spirit guide to help him.

Oh, spirit guide, release me from this cave. My intentions were pure in saving those children. I've done nothing wrong. Oh, spirit guide, come to me, save me, I beg of you.

No one comes.

As time passes, Bones grows weak. And desperate. He decides to try something else—something he was told by his elders never to do. He knows that once he makes the decision, there's no turning back. But he doesn't have a choice. He calls to the dark spirits, to the restless souls wandering the earth. He feeds them his anger and his betrayal, pleading with them to help.

And *they* answer.

A dark spot appears on the floor of the cave. It grows, bubbling up through the rock, thick as tar and black as night, pooling on the ground in front of him. The rotten smell of sulfur fills the air. It's the very same puddle that has sent me tumbling into these awful visions—an echo of Bones's past that I was never supposed to see.

He hesitates at the sight of the dark substance, then plunges his hands into it, giving himself over to the darkness. His eyes roll back in his head, and the darkness—the corruption of a thousand souls—fills him up like an empty vessel.

I struggle to free myself, afraid it will happen to me, too. Acid burns in my throat, sharp enough to make my eyes water. *It's okay, it's okay. Just breathe. What happened to Bones isn't happening to me.* The words tumble through my head as I try to convince myself that I'm safe, that I'm still *me*.

But these visions . . .

When Bones comes to, an image of himself appears in the inky surface of the puddle. But it's not himself he's seeing, not exactly. The dark spirits have thinned the veil between worlds, revealing a window between realities. The vision in the puddle is a different self, one from another place. He looks like Bones, sounds like him too, but he is not Bones. He's Beaumont Jones—a version of Bones from another reality—the person he might've been if he hadn't been trapped inside the cave and forced to make a deal with evil spirits.

And he's the answer to Bones's prayers.

Using his new, dark powers, Bones speaks to the other version of himself in his dreams. *Deep in a forest,* beside a lake, you will find a cave, and within that cave a puddle. All you need to do is put your hands into it and you will release me from my prison. Please. Save me, Beaumont.

When Beaumont finds the cave, he doesn't hesitate to try to help. He's a good man—like Bones was before he was consumed by burning rage. My stomach drops. *Don't do it!* Whatever Bones has planned for him can't be good. But, of course, I'm just an observer. Nothing I say will make a difference.

As Beaumont presses his hands into the puddle, they sink into the thick substance. He immediately tries to pull himself free, but it's too late.

"This is wrong," he whispers, a tear rolling down his cheek. Bones grabs him from the other side.

Beaumont gasps. *No! What are you doing? I came to help you!*

And help you will....

Bones tugs, and he feels something fracture and break off. It's a piece of Beaumont's soul, pulled away, separated from his body and leaving nothing but emptiness behind. Beaumont is released from the puddle, and he claps his hands over his ears. The air fills with the screams of countless tortured souls.

Then, with a whoosh, Bones rushes in, his soul crowding in beside what's left of Beaumont's, stomping it down until it lives in only the smallest corner of his mind. Freed from his prison on the other side, Bones is there to stay.

And to get revenge.

I look on, horrified, as the skeleton flute appears in Bones's hand—just like when it came back to him after I played it. His words crowd into my head:

It served its purpose, so it returned to me.

But the flute he used to heal the town's children has changed. It's dark and different. Bones throws his head back and laughs. The cool bone warms, tingling against his skin, vibrating with the fragment of soul that's trapped inside it. The fragment of Beaumont's soul. My stomach clenches, and my mouth fills with a metallic taste.

Bones—controlling Beaumont's body—takes charge. Beaumont, his soul fractured, is left helpless, weak. Like me, he can only watch as Bones dives deeper into the dark practice that allowed him to break free of his prison. He speaks to the dark spirits and they make him promises—power, control, *immortality*—in exchange for his devotion. Everything Bones has ever been taught by his elders is forgotten in this moment.

Not long ago, he was faced with death. Now, not only does he have a chance at living the life that was stolen from him, but it comes with the promise of living forever.

Over time, the world that belonged to Beaumont becomes corrupt. The evil inside Bones seeps out like a sickness, poisoning everything it touches. Grass shrivels up, animals die, and buildings crumble. The sun stops rising, even the moon is affected—turning a sickly orange instead of silvery white. And the people who live there begin to change. This corruption feeds Bones—and in turn the dark spirits.

It starts with violence and hatred, one person against another. There's fighting in the streets; wars break out. Every ounce of their humanity is erased. Then they change, evolving into wicked creatures unlike anything known to humankind. They swarm across the land in hordes, twisted versions of what they once were.

Bones's cackling vibrates in my ears. *Rise, my children, rise! For you are borne of me, you are borne of chaos, and chaos you will bring down on the heads of all who have wronged me!*

With each soul he corrupts, Bones gets stronger, more powerful. Powerful enough to seek revenge on the people of Stapleton for what they did to him. His need for revenge turns into a fire, consuming him and threatening to destroy everything in its path.

A chill shivers through me. *Revenge*. This is all about revenge.

They were ungrateful, selfish. They'll pay for what they've done to me.

Beaumont tries to stop what's happening, but he's too weak. He's forced to watch Bones destroy his home and everything in it, completely helpless. His fractured soul is no match for the evil one living inside him.

Please, let me go. I can fix this—it's not too late—

Bones laughs at Beaumont's pleas, a sound that makes the air crackle. *Fix it? What makes you think I want you to fix it? No, my friend. You will stay right where you are for all of eternity. There's nothing you can do to stop me.*

A scream cuts through the visions in my head.

Lena.

The sound of her voice stops the spinning just long enough for me to regain control, to yank my hand free of the dark substance. I gasp and fall back onto the cave floor. My chest heaves in and out, my mouth gulping in the musty cave air. Lena kneels beside me, her cheeks wet with tears.

"Sam, are you okay?" she gasps. "Your eyes were black. What just happened?"

Shivers rock through me, and I wrap my arms around myself, trying to stop the chattering of my teeth.

Ghosts of the visions swim around my head. The skin on my palm where I touched the dark puddle is bright red and blazing hot.

Outside the cave, Helen calls to us, her voice high-pitched and frantic. She's grunting and pushing at the boulder, trying to move it aside so she can get to us.

I open my mouth, but the words won't come out. How could I explain it, anyway? The dark substance on the cave floor showed me something terrible, but it also showed me the truth, something I knew all along: Bones is evil. And, more importantly, it showed me that he's holding Beaumont hostage in his own body.

Chapter 26

OUTSIDE THE CAVE, HELEN'S STILL screaming our names. Lena hurries to the opening and speaks through it, reassuring her that we're okay. "Okay" might be a stretch; I'm not even close to okay. But Helen stops yelling, and Lena returns to my side.

When my heart stops thrashing against my rib cage, I tell her about the visions. As I talk, the fear Beaumont felt when Bones rushed into his body ripples through me again.

"Oh my God," she whispers.

"I could feel their pain, Lena, both of them. What Bones did was horrible, but what the townspeople of Stapleton did to him was too. He felt like he didn't have a choice."

I shudder, remembering the avalanche of emotions that assaulted me when the images claimed the space in my head, plunging me into Bones's story. Back in the library, it almost seemed like Lena was defending Bones because of what the townspeople did to him. I was angry then, but I understand it a little more now.

Lena sucks in a breath. "But still, how could he do that to Beaumont?"

I think about Sammy trapped in the ether. No matter how desperate I was, I could never do to him what Bones did to Beaumont. My wish led to Sammy getting trapped in the nightmare world, but it was an accident. I didn't know Sammy even existed. I would never do something like that on purpose.

I shake my head. "I don't know."

"We've gotta help Beaumont," Lena says. "We have to set him free."

I nod. "Maybe if we free him, it'll help us free Sammy and Lee, too."

"Maybe," Lena says. "The question is, How?"

I chew on my bottom lip, going back through the visions, searching for something that might tell me what we need to do to fix everything. Nothing. I got nothing. I drop my head in my hands, frustration building in my chest and tightening, like a balloon filling with air, ready to pop.

I struggle to my feet, my legs still shaking. Lena helps me up, making sure to keep her distance from the dark substance. I cross to the skeleton and crouch in front of it, staring into its smiling face. "How do we fix this?"

"Sam—"

"Tell us how to make it right!"

I reach out and grab the skeleton by the shoulders and shake it, hard. With a crack, the skull tips off the neck and clatters to the floor. It lands smile side up. The image of Bones holding up the skeleton flute flashes in front of me.

"The flute," I say. "The visions showed me where the missing piece of Beaumont's soul went. It's trapped inside the flute."

"Huh," Lena says, scrunching up her face. "I feel like that should've been obvious."

I want to laugh, but my mind is spinning. "I think the flute is the key to fighting Bones."

Lena frowns. "If what you told me is true, then this is *serious*, Sam. Dark magic, evil spirits. Do you really think two kids can go up against a *soul eater* and win?"

"It's not just the two of us," I say. "We have Helen and Sammy and Lee. And we have Beaumont."

Lena frowns. "True . . . but what can Beaumont do if he's being controlled by Bones?"

"We have to figure out how to make Beaumont whole again. If we return the missing piece of his soul, maybe he can fight back," I say. "In my visions, the dark spirits opened up a window between worlds. That's what this dark substance is. That's how Bones got to Beaumont."

"Okay, so what?"

"So what if . . . we go to the ether."

Lena's eyes bug out of her head. "Go to the ether? Like, for real?"

I nod. "Yeah."

"Sam, that sounds like a terrible idea."

Ouch. I guess I can't blame her for that. But going to the ether makes the most sense. The corruption of that world is feeding Bones, like some twisted all-you-can-eat buffet. It's what's keeping him strong. It's also Beaumont's original reality. Maybe being there will help him fight back.

I'm guessing at all of this, which might be dangerous with everything that's at stake, but it's the best plan I can come up with. I press my hands to my forehead, frustration building in my chest. Everything's just so messed up. It's like trying to put together a puzzle where most of the pieces are missing and others have warped edges and blurred images.

Nothing makes any sense. Except this.

"Hear me out," I say. "If we can lure Bones to the ether and help Beaumont fight for control, maybe he can send Bones back through the window."

"Ooh, good one," Lena says. "He's just a skeleton here—his soul would have nowhere to go."

"Right," I say, nodding. "If Beaumont boots him out, maybe he'll just disappear."

"You realize you're talking about using ourselves as bait," Lena says, raising an eyebrow.

I shrug. "I didn't think about it like that but . . . yeah, I guess that's exactly what I'm talking about. If we take the skeleton flute, I'm sure Bones will come after us to try and get it back."

"Why don't we just steal it and wish for things to go back to the way they were?" Lena asks.

The thought hadn't occurred to me. It's not a bad idea, but . . .

"Do you *really* want to risk that? Look what happened the first time," I say. "We have no idea if it would work the way we want it to. No, we have to go there."

Lena shudders. "Yeah, you're right."

I know my plan sounds impossible, but we don't have a choice. Now that I know what Sammy and Lee are dealing with in the ether and what Bones did to Beaumont, nothing matters to me except getting them free. "In my visions Beaumont said he could fix things if Bones just let him free," I say. "I think that means he can put things right—get us all back where we belong."

Lena swallows, then nods. "Okay."

I grin. "Okay?"

"Yes, but only because I don't have a better plan," Lena says. "So if it fails, it's all on you."

"Gee, thanks."

She nudges my shoulder with her fist. "I'm kidding. We're in this together."

I turn and look at the now-headless skeleton one more time, then squeeze through the opening and out into the sunlight.

Helen rushes us when we emerge. She grabs us both and pulls us into her arms. "Oh, thank goodness. I was so worried—what happened in there?"

I force a smile. "We're okay, Helen."

She presses her hand to her chest. "I heard Lena screaming your name."

"I think I figured out how to get the others free," I say, turning toward the trail.

Helen follows behind. "How?"

"We have to go to the ether."

Her mouth drops open. "You . . . what?"

I nod. "We think it's the only way."

As we walk back to Helen's car, I tell her about the visions in the cave.

"So wait," she says, stopping short. "Help me understand. Bones used dark magic to create some kind of portal between worlds. Then he reached through into Beaumont's reality, trapped a piece of his soul in the flute, then took over his body?"

I nod. "That about sums it up."

"And whatever evil he tapped into to help him do that turned all the people in Beaumont's reality into those monsters you told me about?"

"Mm-hmm."

Helen shudders. "And you want to go there?!"

Okay, so it's a terrible idea. Hearing her say it out loud like that makes my plan seem reckless. Maybe it is. The problem is that my heart and my head are telling me two different things. Going to the ether is risky. It's dangerous, and it might not solve our problem. But it also might be the only way to save Sammy and Lee. So we have to try. They don't deserve to be stuck there.

"There's something that's bugging me about this whole thing," Lena says. "If Bones ended up in Beaumont's body in *his* reality, then how was he in *our* reality? How did he get there to trick us into playing the flute?"

I shrug. "It's gotta be the flute. In my visions I saw

it change. It became dark and evil—just like Bones. If it could send us to another reality, he must be able to use it to travel between realities himself."

Lena frowns. "But why? If he's really trying to get revenge on the descendants of the people who trapped him in the cave, why'd he need us?"

"That's a good question," I say. "The one piece of the puzzle I can't figure out."

When we reach the car, Helen hesitates with her hand on the door handle. "You know I'd go with you two and try to help if it wasn't for—"

I nod. "Julie. I understand, Helen."

To be completely honest, we could use Helen in the ether. Like Lena said in the cave, we're just kids. But what we need to do could possibly get us killed or trapped in the ether forever. I can't blame Helen for being afraid. Or maybe it's that she's afraid we will succeed. If we do, we'll all go back to our own realities, and she'll lose Julie forever. Either way, I can't be mad at her.

Back on the road into town, I stare out through the window, watching the world blur by. I can't stop thinking about Helen wanting to stay here in this reality instead of going back to where she belongs. Maybe if I'd been here for ten years, I'd feel the same. But I don't. I need to get back to my family, my *real* family. Even if Mom and

Dad are separating, it's better than this. Isn't it?

Lena leans over and bumps me with her shoulder. "Whatcha thinking about?"

"I know the right thing to do is to get everyone back where they belong," I say. "But if we manage to do that, I'll still be in the situation that got me here in the first place. My parents are separating. How is that better than being here, where they're together?"

Lena looks at me sideways. "What about your brother and sister? Don't you want them back?"

"Of course I do," I say without hesitating. "But I also want my parents to stay together."

Helen looks at us in the rearview mirror. "I'm sorry about your parents, Sam. I know that has to be hard."

I swallow. "I feel like this—all of this—is my fault."

"Adults have problems just like kids do," Helen says. "No one's perfect. You have to give your parents the chance to figure it out. You can't fix them or blame yourself for it. You're just a kid."

"But why do Sammy's parents get to be happy?" Tears sting my eyes. "How come they can make it work, but mine can't? Is it because Sammy's an only child? Did having three kids tear my parents apart somehow?"

Helen looks up at me again. "We don't know how these alternate realities work exactly. Why did I have a miserable life in my reality, but I'm happy here? It's not for us—for you—to figure out. You have to leave it to your parents, Sam, as hard as it is. And I don't think it has anything to do with there being three of you."

I suck in a shaky breath. "How do you know?"

Helen's eyes return to the road. "I *don't* know. Not for sure. But when adults have relationship troubles, it usually has to do with *them* and not the kids. I can guarantee you that your parents love you—*all* of you—even if they're struggling themselves."

"I just want things to be the way they were."

"I can understand that," Lena says quietly. "I'd give anything to be able to go back and fix things so my mom was still alive. No one wants things to change, but they do."

Heat creeps into my cheeks. Here I am worrying about my parents separating. At least both of them are still alive.

"People have a way of surprising us, usually in the best ways," Helen says. "Maybe your parents will work it out, and maybe they won't. Be patient with them, Sam. And with yourself."

From the very beginning, all I've wanted is to keep my parents together. But not for them, not entirely. I want it for myself. And for Grayson and Addie. Because

I don't want things to change. I don't wanna be just one more kid with split-up parents. But is that selfish of me? Don't my parents deserve to be happy—even if it means separating?

Helen said I should be patient with myself. Maybe she's right. My feelings are all jumbled up inside me, and I don't know how to sort through them. What I do know is that when I played the skeleton flute, I stole Sammy's life from him to make mine better. If I don't fix things, that makes me no better than Bones. No matter what my life looks like when I get back to my reality, I know I can't stay here.

"So," Lena says, "how do we get to the ether?"

"You two are determined to do this?" Helen asks.

"We need to get the flute," I say, ignoring the question. "That's what started all this, and that's how we'll get there."

"Are you sure?" Lena asks.

"No."

She blows out a breath. "Great. Okay, let's say it will take us to the ether. How do we get it from Bones?"

"I think I have an idea," I say. "He tricked us—now it's his turn. We have to go back to Stapleton Park and get him to show himself. When he does, I'll distract him, and you can sneak up behind him and grab the flute."

Lena tilts her head. "Oh, that easy, huh? Just like that?"

I shrug. "It's worth a try."

"Okay, then," Lena says. "I guess that's the plan."

I laugh. "The worst plan ever."

"True."

I sigh. "I know it's not solid, but it's all we've got. We have to do this, Lena. For Addie and Grayson, for Lenore and Beaumont. For us—both versions."

Chapter 27

HELEN DROPS LENA OFF FIRST—DOWN the street from her house so her parents don't get suspicious—right before six o'clock. When I get home, the house is silent. I expect Mom and Dad to rush out and ask where I went after school, to demand to know who dropped me off, to tell me to get upstairs and get my homework done or I'll be grounded. Everything my real parents would do if I was dropped off by a stranger well past dinnertime.

Instead, there's a note stuck to the fridge:

> Sammy—
> Mom and I are out shopping for Hawaii.
> Dinner's in the fridge.

Love you, champ

—Dad

Okay, then. I guess I should be happy they're not here to ask questions. It would make everything I've been doing for the past few days—trying to figure out how to get back home—completely impossible. I should be happy, but I'm not. The silence and emptiness press in on me, squeezing my chest tight.

Grayson should be here, bugging me to help him with one of his models. Addie should be shoving her stuffed animals in my face or building big block towers just to push them over and watch them crash to the floor. Mom should be making dinner while Dad grades papers at the dining room table. The house shouldn't be this empty.

Sammy didn't seem surprised when I told him his parents were going to Hawaii. I kinda feel bad for the kid. No brothers and sisters, parents constantly taking trips and leaving him out of things. If I'm lonely after just a few days, I can only imagine how Sammy feels living this life all the time. Maybe that's why he plays soccer—to feel like he's a part of something.

A sharp ache blooms in my chest. There've been moments when I've gotten caught up in living his life. It's been amazing having my parents in love again—

going on date nights, dancing in the kitchen, cooking together. But there's also so much about it that makes me want to run screaming.

I slide into a chair at the kitchen table and drop my head into my hands. A tear splashes onto the tabletop, then another. I miss my mom and dad. I miss my brother and sister, and Derek.

I wanna go home.

After inhaling a slice of cold pizza, I rush up to my room and change into my pajamas. I slide into bed, exhaustion weighing on me like a ton of bricks. It's been such a long day already, and my work isn't done. I need to prepare Sammy and Lee for what's coming. We're about to wage war, and they need to be ready for it.

As I'm drifting off, I remember George Ashcroft's journal. I shudder, imagining how it must have felt not having any idea why everything in your life was suddenly different. At least I have Lena and Helen. He was all alone.

"I can't get you home to your family, George," I whisper, "but I'll stop the man who took you from them and make sure this doesn't happen to anyone else."

My eyes flutter shut and fly open again almost immediately. I scramble off the ground and gaze up at the dark, swirling sky beyond the skeletal tree. In the distance, dark shapes move through the sky, dipping and sailing, then shooting upward. The sound of wing beats drifts on the air.

I move away from the tree and the field as quickly as I can. I don't wanna hang around and wait for the monsters to notice me here in the open like a sitting duck. Nope, nope, and more nope.

I barrel down the embankment, Sammy and Lee's building rising in front of me. I dart through the door and plunge into darkness. When my eyes adjust, I move away from the Staircase of Doom, heading straight for the much safer back staircase.

I climb the stairs two at a time, anxious to get to Sammy and Lee and tell them what we have planned. I'm halfway up when an earsplitting scream stops me in my tracks. I freeze, my foot raised in the air. The scream echoes through the building, a horrible, inhuman sound that's guttural—like a croaking frog—and high-pitched at the same time.

My blood turns cold; the icy fingers of terror scrape down my spine. I'm not alone.

The smell of dirty swamp water floods my nose. My eyes fill with tears and I clamp a hand over my face. It's heavy and earthy, tangy like sweaty socks that haven't been washed in weeks. I glance down the staircase, squinting through the darkness. Another scream shakes the building, followed by a squelching sound, like the sound your feet make when you walk through thick mud. My stomach flip-flops, and saliva floods my mouth. I swallow, trying not to hurl.

Move, Sam, move!

But my legs won't listen. I stand there, my eyes growing wider, as the creature comes into view. It's impossibly tall, with pale, shiny skin. It's unclothed, but there are no humanlike features. It's a blank canvas of smooth, sickly gray skin. It walks hunched over, its long arms swinging in front of it as it shuffles toward the bottom step. I bite down on my tongue, fighting back a scream.

This is it. This is how I die.

The creature turns its elongated head to look up at me. The sides of its neck puff in and out as it breathes, the skin blowing up like a balloon and then shrinking back down again. A scattering of different-sized eyes covers the creature's face, stretching from just above a pair of puffy pink lips and up over the top of its head.

The frogman. One of the ether's monsters that Sammy and Lee told me about. It grins with needle-sharp teeth, and each of its eyes blinks in turn, like a wave, revealing pale orange irises and slit-like pupils. A long, slimy tongue rolls out of its mouth, and thick, yellow saliva oozes down its chin. The tongue draws back, like a snake ready to strike.

That's enough to get me moving. This is *not* cool. Not cool at all. I stumble up the stairs, tripping over each step, but before I can make it to the top, the frogman leaps forward and closes a webbed hand around one of my ankles.

"Gah! Let go! Let me go!"

It pulls down on my ankle with inhuman strength, yanking me right off my feet. I slam onto the stairs, my elbows banging against the concrete. Stars blossom in front of my eyes. *This is a dream! How is this happening?* Dream or not, the frogman has a hold of me, and he's pulling me closer to that slimy tongue and those needle-sharp teeth.

The vision from the cave comes back to me—images of Bones corrupting the people from this world and turning them into monsters. This was a person once. It didn't choose to be a monster. Its life was stolen from it, just like Beaumont's.

Well, person or not, I'm not about to lie here and let it eat me.

"Let! Go!"

I kick at the creature with my free foot, my toes sinking into its gross spongy skin with each blow. It rears back and lets loose another screech that vibrates my eardrums. Kicking it made it angry. Angry is bad. I try to scramble away again, but it pulls down on my ankle even harder. I slide down a step, then another, closer to the monster's deadly teeth.

I'm inches away from it and can see thick drool glistening on its tongue when the smell of cigar smoke drifts under my nose. I know that smell, but . . . how?

A breeze kicks up inside the stairwell, rustling the hair on my head and stirring the swamp-water smell around until my eyes are watering. The frogman yanks me free of the stairs and pulls me down into the entryway. Its slimy hands grip my arms as it wrestles me into a standing position.

The cigar smell is stronger down here, so strong it gags me. Through my streaming eyes, I see a tall figure come into focus. An ice-cold chill races through me as a familiar voice comes out of the darkness.

"Hello, son."

Bones steps forward from the shadows, a grin stretching across his face. His dark eyes are black in the orange moonlight coming through the dirt-caked windows. I shiver. Where'd he come from? My mouth drops open, and for a moment I stop fighting to get free of the frogman's grip.

"What are you doing here?"

Bones nods at the frogman. "I see you've met my friend."

"Your friend?" I grunt, trying to pull myself free. "More like your servant."

Bones makes a tsk-tsk sound.

"Call it what you will." He turns to the frogman. "Release him."

The frogman lets go of my arms and sinks down onto its haunches, watching and waiting, its chest heaving in and out.

I stumble forward. "How did you find me in my dreams?"

A smile stretches across Bones's face. "The gateway in the cave. You touched it. I can *feel* you."

A wave of nausea washes over me. Did touching that awful puddle create some kind of connection between us? The thought sends shivers racing through me. I'd rather be connected to the disgusting frogman.

I take a step back, inching toward the stairs. "What do you mean?"

A deep laugh rumbles in Bones's chest. "There's so much you don't understand, maybe some things I still don't understand myself. But now I can sense where you are."

I narrow my eyes. "Why are you here?"

"To deliver a warning," Bones says, his eyes flashing.

"A warning? About what?"

"About helping the others. It's pointless. They're mine. Stop trying to save them." He snarls the words between his teeth, spit flying with each one. I flinch, a chill shivering down my back.

"No way," I say, still inching closer to the stairs.

"Maybe," Bones says, rubbing his chin, "you need an incentive."

"There's nothing you can say—"

"What if I offered to send you back home, like you wanted?" Bones says with a sly smile. "I'll even throw in your wish, absolutely free of charge."

My mouth drops open, and a chill prickles across my skin. "But you said you couldn't."

"There might be a way," Bones says. "*If* you agree to forget about the others."

"What about Lena? Would you send her home too?"

He grins. "I could be persuaded."

Would he—could he—*really* fix everything? Everything he's ever said to me has been a lie. I have no reason to trust him now. He told me there was no way to undo what he did to us. But what if he's telling the truth this time? Everything I've done since I woke up the day after playing the flute has been to get back home to my parents and to Addie and Grayson. What if I could fix it all, right now, by agreeing?

Bones leans forward as I wrestle with his offer, that ridiculous grin still plastered on his face. My heart thuds in my chest. If only Lena was here. I don't want to make this decision on my own. What if I make the wrong one?

An image of Sammy and Lee swims in front of me. Their tired faces and dirty clothes. The fear in their eyes at having to go out into the nightmare world looking for food. My own words come back to me as Bones's carrot dangles in front of me.

I swear I won't stop until I figure out how to get you home.

I can't break my promise. I can't leave Sammy and Lee in the nightmare world. Just like it would've been wrong to choose to stay in Sammy's reality and learn to live with things, this is wrong too. And I know Lena wouldn't want me to leave them, even if it meant never seeing her sister again. How could we live with ourselves if we just went back to our lives and left Sammy and Lee to whatever horrors Bones has in store for them? Especially since it's our fault they're there in the first place.

I ball my hands into fists. "I'll never stop trying to save them."

A shadow passes over Bones's face, the smile disappearing. "Then you'll suffer too."

He nods his head toward me, and the frogman leaps forward, brandishing its needle-sharp teeth. Wind rushes through the entryway, bringing with it the smell of swamp and sweaty gym socks. Bones steps back, fading into the shadows, and a chorus of screams cuts through the darkness. A squelching sound echoes off the walls, then another and another.

More frogmen are coming.

I run toward the staircase, darting back and forth in a zigzag pattern, then sprint up the stairs. I'm almost at the top when a hand closes around my ankle. I let out a scream and pull against it, but the frogman is impossibly strong. I'm too weak from fighting it before.

"Sam!"

My head whips up. Feet pound the floor above me. Lee and Sammy are racing down the hallway. I've never been more relieved to see anyone in my entire life. And I'm totally not exaggerating.

"Sammy, Lee, help! It's got me!"

They skid to a stop. Sammy reaches down and grabs my hands. It's a game of tug-of-war now between him and the frogman. I hope Sammy has more upper-body strength than I do. If he's anything like me, this game will be over pretty quickly. And not in my favor.

The voices of the approaching frogmen get louder, closer, more urgent. Lee peers down the stairs, her eyes widening. "Guys, there's more coming."

She edges in to grab my upper arms, helping to tug me away from the creature. It's not working. The thing is too strong. Pain rips through my shoulders, and my ankle screams in white-hot agony.

"Just go!" I yell. "Get out of here!"

I won't let Sammy and Lee sacrifice themselves to save me. Not after I just seriously considered leaving them behind in this terrible place.

Lee shakes her head. "Not a chance."

She bends forward to adjust her grip, and the old crank flashlight she's holding clatters onto the steps. The beam of light splashes across the frogman's face. The monster rears back and screams, all of its orange eyes widening in shock. I drop to the steps as its hands fly to its face, slapping at it to shield itself from the flashlight beam.

"The light!" I gasp.

I grab the flashlight and twist around, swinging it up so it's shining full-on in the frogman's face. A rage-filled scream rips through the stairwell. The frogman leaps away, down the stairs, and disappears from view.

Still shining the beam down the stairs, I fall onto the top step in a heap. Sammy and Lee come down next to me, panting loudly. The creatures' angry screeching fades.

I suck in a breath. "Thank goodness you heard me screaming."

Lee scrambles to her feet. "Let's get out of here before the rest of them show up."

"Are you okay?" Sammy asks, reaching out to help me up.

I move my arms in a circle. "Yeah, I think so."

In the attic room, after barricading the door, Lee sinks to the floor and pulls in a shaky breath. I drop down beside her, my arms and legs still trembling from the encounter with the frogman. I press my fingers into the tender flesh of my ankle and hiss through my teeth.

Lee looks at me with concern. "Are you sure you're okay?"

I nod. "Nothing's broken."

My gaze drifts past her to the hatch marks on the wall. Another four have been added since the last time I was here. For me it's only been two days, but they look like they've suffered for much longer than that. Sammy's clothes are smudged with dirt and Lee's T-shirt is ripped at the shoulder. They look worn down and weak.

"No offense, but you two look awful," I say.

Lee frowns. "Gee, thanks."

"The longer we're here, the weaker we feel," Sammy says. "Like this place is sucking the life out of us."

A chill shudders through me. *Soul eaters consume the souls of others to make themselves immortal.* I don't know if that's what's happening to them, but one thing is clear: I have to get them out of here.

"So what'd you find out?" Lee asks, leaning forward.

I tell them about our trip to Lake Ingershall and what happened to me in the cave when I touched Bones's gateway. They listen in silence, their eyes getting wider and wider as I talk.

"Holy crap," Sammy says. "I can't believe this."

"It gets worse," I say, remembering Bones's warning. "He knows we're trying to save you."

"H-how?" he asks, his face going pale.

"Something happened when I touched the dark substance. I'm connected to him somehow. He *knew* I was here and used the frogman to get to me."

"Oh God," Lee says, running a hand through her hair. "We're never getting home, are we?"

For a second I'm afraid she knows about Bones's offer, and that I was seconds away from agreeing to it. The look on her face is enough to tell me I made the right choice.

"Lena and I have a plan."

"What is it?" she asks.

I grin. "We're coming to the ether—for real."

Sammy's eyes light up. "How?"

"We're gonna steal the skeleton flute and use it to lure Bones here, where we can all fight him together."

Lee pulls in a sharp breath, pressing a hand against her cheek. "Do you think that's going to work now that he knows you're trying to save us?"

"I hope so. It's our best shot. But I need you two to gather some supplies—water, food, weapons if you have any. You need to be ready. I think I know how to get us all back where we belong, but it's gonna be dangerous."

Lee sets her mouth in a firm line. "Every day here is dangerous, Sam. Whatever you have planned, we'll be ready."

Chapter 28

THE NEXT MORNING, I TRUDGE DOWN the sidewalk toward Stapleton Town Park. I told Mom and Dad I was walking to school— getting in some extra exercise for the upcoming game against Cedarville—then came here instead. It's the second time in a little over a week that I've skipped school. Too bad this time it's not to lounge at the beach and eat hot dogs with Grayson.

My breath billows out in front of me, leaving foggy trails in the air. I tighten the straps on my backpack, which is heavy with supplies. After the frogman's reaction to the beam of light in my dream, I gathered every single flashlight I could find and shoved them into my bag before leaving the house.

It's been a week since I played the skeleton flute. A week too long. It's time to get my life back. I cross the parking lot to where Lena's perched on a bench beside the basketball court. She texted me this morning freaking out about getting caught skipping school, so I'm more than relieved to see her. Her hair is pulled back, hidden beneath a baseball cap. Just like the first time we met.

"You made it," I say.

"Barely," Lena says, rolling her eyes. "Mom likes to watch me like a hawk when I walk to the bus stop."

"So, how'd you get away?"

"I walked to the end of the street, then ducked behind a tree right as the bus came into view," Lena says, sliding off the bench.

I nod. "Impressive."

"So, we're really gonna do this, huh?"

She's probably hoping I'll say no, and—not gonna lie—part of me wants to. But then I think back to the morning before everything changed, the moment I stared up at the high-dive and chickened out. There's no chickening out this time. Sammy and Lee are counting on us.

"We have to, Lena. There's no other choice."

"I know." Her voice wavers. "I'm just seriously freaking out here."

"Me too."

"What if it doesn't work? What if Bones doesn't even show up?" The words tumble out of her mouth.

I place a hand on her shoulder. "They *need* us, Lena."

"We could die, Sam."

I scrunch up my face, trying to decide if I should tell her about Bones's offer. I don't want her to be disappointed in me. But she has the right to know.

"He came to me last night."

Lena's eyes widen. "What do you mean?"

"In my dreams. Remember I told you that I went to Sammy and Lee to tell them to be ready? Well, he showed up. With a warning." I look down at the dew-covered grass, afraid to meet Lena's eyes.

"What was it?"

"He told me to stop trying to help the others, that it was pointless."

Lena smirks. "And I bet you told him to shove it—"

"There's something else."

"What, Sam?"

"He offered to fix everything for us, as long as we agreed to leave the others alone."

Lena's hand flies to her mouth. "Oh my God."

I swallow hard, avoiding her gaze. "I told him I'd never stop trying to save them. I'm sorry, Lena. I know it wasn't fair of me to make that decision without you, but I just couldn't leave them there. I—"

"Sam!" Lena shouts over my rambling apology. "Sam, it's okay. I'm not mad."

I meet her eyes. "You're not?"

"No," she says, shaking her head. "I'd like to think I would've done the same. I'm kinda glad it was you and not me, though."

"Wow," I say. "Thanks a lot."

"You know what I mean," she says.

"Do I, though?"

Lena laughs. "We can't leave Sammy and Lee in the ether. We can't just go back to our lives and pretend they don't exist."

I let out a breath. "You don't know how happy I am to hear you say that."

"You really thought I'd leave them?" she asks, bumping my shoulder with her fist.

I shrug. "No, not really. I can't say I didn't think about it, though."

"I'm sure it was tempting," Lena says. "But I'm glad you said no. That was very brave of you."

I shrug, heat blooming in my cheeks. "I guess."

"It was. I mean it."

I nod. "Okay, are you ready?"

"No." Lena flinches at the look I give her. "Fine, let's do this."

We cross the playground, moving toward the bike trail. The leaves on the trees and bushes are starting to change, the deep greens fading into bright shades of yellow and orange, fiery red. It's like we're walking through a tunnel of flames. I just hope we aren't about to get burned.

"Whatever happens," Lena says, "I'm glad we met. I couldn't have gotten through this without you."

"Why does it sound like you're saying goodbye?"

She glances at me sideways, then steps off the dirt path into the trees. We've reached the bend in the trail. I watch her go with a sinking feeling in the pit of my stomach, and stop at the spot where I've called to Bones twice now. Lena crouches behind a tree and gives me the thumbs-up.

"Bones!"

My words echo and fade into the forest. My palms begin to sweat, and I swipe them across my pants. What if Lena's right? What if he doesn't come this time? I tilt my head and sniff the air, waiting for the smell that I know will come. If Bones is gonna show, so will the scent of cigars. And the fog. I glance frantically at the tree where Lena's hiding. *Come on, come on!*

"Bones! I need to talk to you!"

It's faint at first, the smell drifting through the trees in a lazy way without a breeze to carry it. It slithers along the ground with the fog until it surrounds me. I shiver, waiting for him to appear.

A rasp of hot breath rushes across my ear, licking the side of my face. "Hello again, son."

I spin around. Bones stands on the path, his patchwork jacket and dusty brown shoes a welcome sight. He's here. That means it's go time. Goose bumps dance across my skin.

"H-hello."

"What can I do for you?"

"I need to talk to you."

Bones tilts his head. "Okay, talk away."

"I know what you are," I say through clenched teeth. "If there's some connection between us, like you say, then you know what I saw inside the cave."

Bones narrows his eyes, watching me like a lion watches its prey. He tilts his head to the side, and a humorless smile spreads across his face. "Okay, I'll bite. What exactly is it that you think you know?"

I jab a finger in his direction, heat rising into my face. "I know you don't belong in that body."

"Ahh," Bones says, giving a low whistle. "Maybe you're smarter than you look."

I'm trembling now, but doing my best to stay calm. I can't let him see how shaken I am. I clench my fists, my fingernails digging into my palms. "I know you say you're helping, but you're not. You're just trying to get revenge for something that happened two hundred years ago."

Amusement twinkles in his eyes. "Well, you've got half of it right, at least."

"What the townspeople did to you was wrong, but what you're doing is wrong too," I growl. "Don't you see that?"

"I see nothing now but the satisfaction of destroying the lives of those whose ancestors wronged me," Bones says. "If you saw what happened to me, you should know that."

Rage radiates from him. I take a step backward, away from his flashing eyes, then hesitate. I can't back down.

"You stole Beaumont's body. You should give it back and stop ruining people's lives!"

"*I'm* ruining people's lives?" Bones snarls suddenly. "What about my life? I was robbed of it when all I wanted to do was help. I cured those children, and the towns-people hunted me down like an *animal*."

I let out a breath. "So you're making Sammy and Lee pay for what their ancestors did? How is that fair?"

"Their ancestors threw me in that cave and left me to die," Bones says, his face twisting with rage. "They stole my life from me, and now I'm claiming what I deserve by making their children *pay*. Just like I've been doing for the last two centuries."

A sour taste surges into my mouth. "How many others are there?"

"An entire town came together to condemn a man who did nothing but help," Bones says. "How many descendants is enough to make that right?"

"What about Lena and me? Why are we being punished?"

"Punished?" Bones laughs. "You did this to yourself, son. *You* made a wish."

"You tricked us," I growl. "You lied about *everything*."

"I did no such thing," Bones says, brushing off the front of his patchwork suit. "You wanted your parents together—I gave that to you. You never *asked* if it would be in another reality."

I throw my hands in the air. "How would I know to even ask that?"

"It's all in the details, my boy."

"Why did you need Lena and me to get revenge on Sammy and Lee? Were we just pawns in your sick little game?"

Bones shrugs. "Haven't you heard of the domino effect?"

I shake my head. "No."

"Action and reaction, my boy."

A dull ache throbs at the back of my head. "What does that mean?"

"You have a connection to the others, like two versions of the same soul."

I frown, thinking about Bones and Beaumont trapped together in the same body. *Two souls within one body.* But that's not what he means. When Lena and I first met, she told me about a connection she had with Lenore—like a fine thread attached to each of them. Maybe it's like that.

"The dreams," I whisper. Maybe this connection is the reason Lena, Helen, and I started having dreams about the others when we woke up in the wrong reality.

Movement catches my eye. Behind Bones, Lena is crouched low to the ground. My eyes dart back to his face. "So when we played the skeleton flute and wished for things to be different, we somehow changed things for Sammy and Lee, too?"

"In order to displace the others and send them to the dark realm, I needed you to set it all into motion by playing my flute," Bones says, nodding. "Like one domino falling into another, as you left your reality and came to this one, you pushed the others into my realm."

"And you couldn't push them into the realm yourself because . . ."

Bones makes a sour face. "The worthless soul inside my flute stops me from using it to directly harm the others. It's still connected to the soul inside me, in a way. Every time I tried, he interfered. The only way around it was to get you to push the others out."

I grit my teeth. "Beaumont isn't worthless. He doesn't deserve this."

"He's weak," Bones spits out. "And gullible. If he was worthy of this body, if he was even half the healer he proclaimed himself to be, he never would have helped me in the first place."

I sneer at him. "This isn't really about revenge, is it?"

Bones tilts his head. "What do you mean?"

"This is all because of the evil inside you," I say. "You sold yourself to dark spirits in exchange for power. You became a soul eater. *That's* what this is about."

Bones tips his head back, and laughter shakes through him. "That is an added benefit, I must admit."

Lena is right behind him now, her shaking hand reaching toward the pocket of the patchwork jacket where the skeleton flute is just visible. Her fingers close around it. Bones notices me looking past him and whips around, grabbing hold of her still-reaching hand.

"Nice try."

Chapter 29

LENA CRIES OUT, THE COLOR DRAINING from her face, as Bones clamps a hand around her wrist and drags her around in front of him. She releases the flute and it clatters to the ground. My eyes dart to it and I take a step forward. Bones waggles a finger at me.

"Uh-uh," he says, gold tooth glinting. "Stay back."

There's poison in his voice. His face clouds, and a sneer turns up the corners of his mouth.

I puff out my chest. "Let her go."

"You thought you could trick *me*? Of all people? The *master* of tricksters?"

"*Let her go.*"

"Why should I?"

Lena pulls against Bones's grip, pain twisting her face as he squeezes her arm tighter and tighter. My lower lip trembles. This was my idea. If Lena gets hurt because of it, I'll never be able to forgive myself. A tear slides down her cheek.

"Please," I beg. "If you let her go, we'll leave. We'll stop trying to save the others."

Bones lets out a laugh. "Too late for that, son. You should've taken me up on it when I offered."

"Please," I say, desperate for him to release Lena. "We'll stop."

"What were you going to do with my flute, anyway?" Bones asks, tilting his head. "You don't have the power to make it work."

My face burns. I didn't even consider that it would require some special power to take us to the ether. I thought the flute's magic would be enough. This never would've worked, even if we hadn't been caught. Frustration rises in me. Bones twists Lena's arm and she cries out again.

I take a step forward. "Let her go!"

With a hiss, Bones releases her. Lena stumbles away from him, and I throw my arm out in front of her. She rubs at the spot on her arm, which is angry red and already starting to bruise.

Bones snatches his flute from the ground. "It wouldn't matter if you went there anyway. Two versions of a person can't exist in the same realm together."

"Why not?" I ask, my voice trembling.

Bones rolls his eyes. "I was wrong about you being smarter than you look. Action and reaction, remember? A single realm cannot handle the chaos of two versions of the same person trying to occupy the same space. Eventually the realm will send one version away. But there's nowhere for them to go. The dark realm is the end of the line."

My head spins, trying to make sense of what he's saying. I picture the pendulum toy on the desk in Dad's office, how one orb swings into another, and that one swings into the next, transferring the energy from orb to orb. Eventually they turn and go back the other way, but if the last orb couldn't move, the momentum would stop. The energy would just fizzle out.

A cold feeling comes over me. Bones said he needed *us* to set everything into motion, but he really needed the skeleton flute. The flute was kinda like the hand that sends all the orbs crashing into one another. And now I realize just how important it is for us to get to the ether. Because we sent that first orb into motion when we played the flute, we were knocked into another reality and Sammy and Lee were pushed into the ether. So it just makes sense that if we want everyone back where they belong, we need the flute in the ether to send the orbs back in the other direction. But how do we do that if we can't both exist in the same reality?

I swallow. "What happens if we're both there at the same time?"

"Well . . . ," Bones begins. "Since the others are already there and can't be pushed out, they have . . . dibs, shall we say? If you crossed over, it would only be a matter of time for the two of you."

Fear prickles in my chest. "A matter of time before what?"

He smiles, an evil grin that contorts his face. "Before you're ejected into the emptiness between realms. You would be erased from your reality like you never existed. The people who know and love you would forget you, and the others would be trapped in my dark realm forever."

"How long would we have?" I demand, anger pulsing in my ears.

Bones waggles a finger. "Uh, uh, uh. What fun would it be if I told you?"

"But that's not fair—"

He moves like lightning and stops inches from my

face. "Who said anything about any of this being fair *for you*? Do you know what it's like to be locked inside a cave for *days* without a single drop of water or bite to eat? My organs began to fail, cracks formed in my skin, and my body began to consume itself. Fair. Was any of that fair to me?"

"How long?" I whisper, taking a step back.

"Time moves faster in the dark realm. I'll say no more about it." Bones waves the flute back and forth. "Not that it matters. You can't get there without this."

He throws his head back and lets out a laugh that echoes through the forest. It rolls like thunder, bouncing off the trees, so deep I can feel it in my chest.

Lena's eyes meet mine, and she nods her head ever so slightly. In that moment I know exactly what she's telling me. Going to the ether knowing what we now know is risky, but it's a risk we'll have to take. We have to save Sammy and Lee.

I take a deep breath. "Beaumont! Can you hear me?"

Bones blinks and furrows his bushy eyebrows down over his dark eyes. "What are you—"

"I know you're in there, Beaumont. Help us! We're trying to set you free. Help us!"

Bones staggers backward and presses a hand to his forehead. "Stop it!"

"You have to fight him! We need you, Beaumont, please!"

"Please," Lena cries. "Help us use the flute!"

Bones's face snaps up toward the sky. The muscles on the side of his neck stand out, tight against the skin. When he lowers his head, a faraway look has taken over his eyes. One of them bulges suddenly, and he jerks his neck to the side with a loud crack. The hand holding the flute begins to tremble.

"I'm . . . not . . . strong . . . enough . . . not here," he croaks in a voice that sounds like it hasn't been used in a long time.

Not here. Does he mean in this reality? If so, then that's more proof that my theory about getting us all to his original reality is right. My resolve strengthens.

"You can do this, Beaumont," I say. "Help us get to the ether!"

He thrusts his hand out in front of him, pushing the flute at me. A cry full of rage, full of hatred, bursts from his throat. "Nooo!"

Birds in the surrounding trees take flight, squawking and flapping to get away. I almost wish I could go with them. "Yes! Give us the flute, Beaumont."

The more I say his name, the harder Beaumont fights his way to the surface. He grits his teeth, his arm trembling violently as he tries to keep control.

"Come on, Beaumont, we need you!" Lena says.

The skeleton flute begins to glow, just like it did the night I played it. I take a tentative step forward, afraid that at any second Bones will take control again.

"Can't . . . hold . . . him . . ."

My hand shoots out and snatches the skeleton flute from Beaumont's trembling hand. "Thank you!"

"You must hurry," Beaumont pants. "I can keep the flute from returning to him . . . but only for so long . . . hurry!"

With Lena behind me, holding tight to my arm, I lift it to my mouth and blow. And for one terrible moment, nothing happens. The low note carries through the air and fades.

Tears well up in my eyes. "Lena—"

An invisible force tugs me from behind, just below my belly button. I'm jerked backward, off my feet. I brace myself for the hard ground to rise up and meet me, but it doesn't. Lena's hands grip my arm, and she gasps at the sensation of falling backward.

"It's working!" she breathes in my ear.

Bones's angry cries follow us as the bike trail fades. "I don't need the flute to come after you! Not anymore! You can't stop me, do you hear me? You can't stop me!"

I hit the ground with a thud, pain jolting through the left side of my body. Somewhere beside me, Lena groans. I sit up, reaching for her. "Lena? Are you okay?"

I can't see more than a couple of feet in front of me, but I know where we are immediately. I don't need to see it to know we're at the edge of the field, just beyond Sammy and Lee's building. Dry, brittle grass crunches beneath me. I breathe in a lungful of sour air.

Lena's voice croaks out beside me. "I'm here. Sore, but here."

My hand finds hers. She takes it and squeezes, her skin warm against mine. I struggle to my feet, pain shooting through my left ankle. It throbs in time with the beating of my heart, then fades to a dull ache. I wince. It's bruised a bit, but probably not sprained.

Shadows dance in front of my eyes. The familiar tree with its dark, scabby bark and bare branches thrusts up from the ground beside us. I brace myself against it, the surface rough beneath my palm. I test my weight on my ankle again, relieved that it seems to have mostly faded.

"Oh my God, Sam," Lena says. "It actually worked. We're *in* the ether."

I gaze up at the steel-gray sky, at a deep orange moon peeking out from between black clouds. I spin in a circle. In my dreams, the air in the ether sparkled and moved like it was alive. Now it's heavy and full of shadows. It wraps around me like a wet blanket. Each breath I take is sharp and tangy, like I can *taste* the wrongness of the place.

A jagged arc of lightning splits the sky, highlighting the field in a sickly glow. The ground is crawling with vines, black and snakelike. They glisten in the orange light. Deep, rolling thunder swells on the tail of the lightning, shaking the ground beneath our feet.

I shudder. "This place is even worse in real life."

"Tell me about it," Lena says, pinching her nose. "And it smells awful."

I reach around, checking for my backpack, and let out a sigh of relief. "Beaumont did it—he helped us."

"What now?" Lena asks.

"Now we find Lee and Sammy and make a plan to stop Bones once and for all."

"What if we don't stop him in time?" Lena's eyes are wide. "What if we're erased from reality?"

I shake my head. "I can't think about that right now."

"But, Sam—"

"We just have to keep moving forward. We have to believe that we can stop him before it's too late. What other choice do we have?"

"Okay," Lena says, her voice thick. "Let's do this, then."

I turn to the embankment, my eyes darting to the sky, alert for movement. I don't know what would've happened to me if one of the ether's monsters had gotten me when I was dreaming, but now that we're here for real, I don't have to wonder. We need to get out of the open as soon as possible.

Lena and I hurry down the grass and across the concrete. With every step I'm alert—listening, watching, hoping nothing attacks. We rush through the door to Sammy and Lee's building. Once we're inside, I can breathe a little easier. I stop in the entryway, listening for movement, waiting for my heart to slow. I don't wanna be snuck up on again. And I *definitely* don't wanna run into a frogman—or something worse—in real life.

I point to the left. "This way."

It's an odd feeling, being in a place that's so familiar but that I haven't ever actually set foot in. The air is heavier and less dreamlike. Lena and I head to the back staircase, up and across the upper floor, and to the door to Lee and Sammy's hideout. I hesitate, then knock softly. Footsteps move across the floor, then down the stairs. A whispered voice calls out from the other side of the door.

"Who's there?"

"It's me, Sam. I've got Lena with me. Let us in."

There's a thump and then the sound of something heavy sliding across the floor. The door cracks open an inch, then swings open wide. Lee and Sammy stand at the bottom of the stairs, no longer fuzzy, but perfectly solid.

Lee throws her arms around my neck, warm tears pressing against my cheek. "You came."

"Of course we did," I say, breathless.

We follow Lee and Sammy up to their attic room, and I stop short at the top of the stairs. My eyes drift to the dark hatch marks on the wall. Bones's warning echoes in my ears.

"Sam?" Lena asks. "What's wrong?"

"The hatch marks."

She frowns. "What about them?"

"Time," I mutter. "We have no idea how long we have before we're erased."

Sammy looks stricken. "Erased? What do you mean?"

I turn from the hatch marks. "We have a lot of catching up to do."

Chapter 30

"**D**O YOU THINK HE WAS TELLING THE truth about you getting erased from reality?" Lee asks.

I shake my head. "I don't know."

Sammy's chin quivers. "And you still came. . . ."

"Of course we did," Lena says.

We're sitting in a circle on the floor, Lena and me on one side and Sammy and Lee on the other. It's like sitting in front of a mirror, only the reflections have minds of their own. Super weird.

"If Bones *was* telling the truth, we have to move fast," I say.

It's bad enough I got us into this mess. If we get

erased from reality, what hope will Sammy and Lee have of getting back home?

"So, what's the plan?" Lee asks. "You've got a plan, right?"

I clench my teeth, looking down at my hands. "Kinda?"

"What do you mean kinda?" Sammy asks, frowning.

All eyes are on me. I shift under their gaze, wishing someone else was in charge. I'm no good at leading people. I crack under pressure. Like the time I got volunteered for spokesperson when we had a group project for social studies. I fumbled over my note cards so bad, Derek pushed me out of the way and gave the whole presentation himself.

Sammy raises his eyebrows. "Sam?"

I swallow hard, sweat tingling on my upper lip. "We know there's a cave in this reality, because I saw it in my visions. It's where Bones stole Beaumont's soul and took over his body."

"Okay," Lee says. "So what?"

"So we have to go to the cave. That's where we'll find the gateway that connects this reality to yours."

Sammy's eyes grow wide. "Go to the cave? Are you serious? With all those monsters out there? How far away is that?"

I let out a breath. "It'll take us a while to get there on foot, and it's gonna be dangerous. But maybe if we can lure Bones there, where all of this started, we can help Beaumont send him back through the gateway."

Everyone's silent and I know what they're thinking. It's risky. Probably too risky for a "maybe," but it's all I have. Beaumont helped us get to the ether, and we'll need him again if we're gonna get back home. He showed up for us once when we needed him. He's ready to fight back now, I'm sure of it.

I raise an eyebrow. "If any of you have a better idea, speak now or forever hold your peace."

Lee chews on her lip. Sammy scrunches up his nose. Lena nods. But no one speaks up with a different plan.

"Okay," Lee says. "Say we do this. How do we keep from getting eaten before we get there?"

I grab my backpack and unzip it, reaching in to grab a flashlight. "With these."

"Flashlights?" Sammy narrows his eyes. If his brain works anything like mine does, I know what he's thinking. Heading out into a world filled with monsters, armed with nothing more than a few flashlights, is a suicide mission.

"Don't you remember when the frogman attacked me and the light hit its face? It was painful. I could see it." I'm desperate to make him understand. I need him to believe in this plan. I need him to believe in me. If he doesn't, how am I going to believe?

Lee's face lights up. "No, it makes sense. It's always dark here; the creatures aren't used to the light."

"Okay." Sammy nods. "Then let's do it. Let's go to the cave."

We stand, and I hand out bottles of water, shoving them into backpacks along with some light snacks Lena and I brought with us. No offense to Sammy and Lee, but metallic-tasting well water isn't what I want to drink while I'm fighting for my life. When that's done, I double-check the batteries in the flashlights and distribute them between our bags.

My hands tremble as I work. They're counting on me to get them to the cave safely, but I have no idea if my plan is gonna work or if these flashlights will keep us safe. Just in case, as we line up at the top of the stairs, each of us holds a weapon of some sort in our hands. Lee grasps a sharpened stick, Sammy holds a heavy-looking wrench, Lena has a hammer, and I found an iron pipe wedged in behind an old wooden desk. I shift the pipe from one hand to the other. "Ready?"

Three heads nod in return, though no one speaks.

We descend the stairs together, and at the bottom, Lee moves the barricade from in front of the door.

She takes a deep breath. "Here goes nothing."

We move through the upper floor of the building. Silence presses in, with only the occasional grunt breaking it as someone climbs over a discarded piece of furniture or broken cement beam. The old, forgotten building puts up a good fight, but we make it to the back entrance in one piece.

Lena pushes the door open, and we step out onto the sidewalk. I look up, scanning the sky. We need to stay alert. There are things out here that wanna eat us.

"Sammy, you take the lead, and I'll bring up the rear. If something sneaks up behind us, I'll be the first to know," I say, falling behind the others.

Sammy nods, but he shoots me a look. Leading the group means he'll be the first to get eaten if anything comes at us from the front. Even so, he moves to the leader position without complaining. Team captain to the rescue.

We're close to the center of town, where the crumbling founder's statue is the best landmark for the direction we need to travel. What was once early Stapleton is unrecognizable. Not just because of the crumbling buildings and the overgrowth, but because it became corrupt with the evil seeping from Bones long before the town developed into the one we know.

The road out of town is choked with grass and weeds. The cracked pavement shifts under our feet as we walk. The air is still and heavy, cool but not quite cold. Still, I shiver. We move in silence so we won't draw attention to ourselves, but the tension and fear walks beside us, as solid as a fifth person.

Lena falls in line next to me. "Do you really think this is gonna work?"

"Beaumont fought back against Bones to help us get here, but he said he didn't have much strength there. I think he might be stronger here, in his own reality. And giving him back the missing piece of his soul while he's in control should help."

Ahead, Lee stops suddenly beside Sammy and sucks in a hissing breath. She's frozen in the middle of the road, a finger pressed to her lips. She motions, and I squint through the darkness to see what she's looking at.

A thick, slimy substance stretches across the road. Huge round orbs glisten in the moonlight. A familiar smell drifts on the breeze, filling me with both nausea and dread. The pods shiver and pulse as we get closer. Lee waves us off the road into the knee-high grass.

"What are those?" Lena asks.

"Pods," Sammy moans.

The smell intensifies, wafting up from the group of pods, stinging my eyes. It's earthy and sour and tickles the hairs in my nose. I fight the urge to be sick, pressing a hand against my churning stomach.

Lena's eyes are wide. "What's in them?"

I remember that she wasn't with us when we discovered the pods. "You don't wanna know," I answer.

Lee points. "They stop right up there—"

A disgusting, wet cracking sound cuts through the air.

My stomach drops. Looks like Lena's about to find out what's in the pods after all. The frogman from my dream flashes in my mind—its pale gray skin, needle-sharp teeth, and long, slimy tongue ready to strike.

Sammy shakes his head. "No. Move faster. Go, go, go!"

We stumble through the grass, tripping over roots and tangled vines as we try to put some distance between ourselves and the pods. Another wet sound assaults my ears. I freeze, making the mistake of looking behind me.

My eyes land on one of the pods. It's quivering violently, splitting open right there in the middle of the road. A gooey crack forms along the side, and a gush of foul-smelling liquid spills out onto the ground, pooling around the base of the pod. My eyes well up with tears as the stench snakes into my nostrils like poison.

A small gray arm reaches toward the sky, then another, pushing the wet pieces of the pod to the side. The others make it to the opposite side of the pod field, but I'm frozen in place, watching as more of the pods shudder and crack open. Half a dozen pairs of gray arms emerge from them, reaching up toward the sky, shedding their slimy casings. A symphony of screeches fills the air.

"Sam!" Lee calls. "Come on!"

I sprint through the grass and catch up to the others just as the baby frogmen leap from the pods. They land on the road. *Splat! Splat! Splat!*

Chills shiver through me. The frogmen turn their eye-covered faces toward us. More pods start to shudder. *This is bad. This is really, really bad.* Lee reaches into her backpack, grabs a flashlight, and fumbles with the switch on the side.

She clicks it on and shines it at the frogmen. I hold my breath, praying this will work. The creatures screech and squeeze their eyes shut, rearing away from the beam. They hop blindly off the road and into the trees on the other side, where the light can't reach them. No one speaks. We just turn and run, letting the sound of our feet pounding the pavement drown out the echoes of the newborn frogmen's screeching.

Chapter 31

WHEN WE'RE CERTAIN WE'RE alone on the road, we slow to a walk. Every muscle in my legs is screaming. My T-shirt is soaked with sweat, and it clings to my body like a second skin. The blood rushes through my ears, pounding against my eardrums.

I point to the tall grass on the side of the road. "Let's take a break."

With a sigh, I flop down on my back, my arms and legs splayed out wide. My chest heaves in and out from running so long and so hard. The others join me in the grass, each of them just as sweaty and out of breath as I am. Well, everyone except Sammy, who's used to running drills on the soccer field.

The air is still and quiet, but I can't get the sound of the hatching frogmen out of my head. A chill shudders through me, raising goose bumps along my arms.

Lee sits up and opens her backpack, tucking her flashlight inside before pulling out a bottle of water. My stomach grumbles, and I reach into my own bag and grab a package of pretzels I snagged from the kitchen this morning. I take a handful, then pass the bag to Lena.

She pops a salt-coated pretzel into her mouth. "It's hard to believe those *things* used to be people."

Sammy freezes. "What did you say?"

"The ether's monsters," I say. "They used to be people. When Bones corrupted this world . . . they changed. I saw it in the vision in the cave."

"Oh my God," Lee says, wrapping her arms around herself. "Those poor people."

I think about the darkness descending on this world from the evil Bones let in, changing everything it touched. Then I think about the others. The others who Bones tricked into playing the skeleton flute. They must be here somewhere. Unless they changed into monsters too.

I shiver. "Have you seen anyone else here?"

Lee shakes her head. "No one."

"That can't be right," I say. "We met a woman in your

reality and she helped us. She played the skeleton flute ten years ago, and she's having dreams just like Lena and me."

Sammy shakes his head. "We haven't seen anyone at all. Just monsters."

My stomach tightens. We told Helen there was probably hope since she was still seeing her other self in her dreams. I was so sure that meant she was still here. But if Sammy and Lee haven't seen her . . .

Lena looks at me sideways. "You okay?"

I shake my head. "We have to stop him. We have to make him pay for this."

Lee stands up. "Let's get going, then."

"Lena!" Sammy's eyes are wide. "What's happening to you?"

I follow his gaze and the breath explodes from my lungs. Lena's body is semitransparent, faded a little, like when we were waking up from our dream. Only this isn't a dream. Lena looks down at herself, then back up at us, her mouth puckered in confusion.

"Sam?" she says, panic rising in her voice.

I reach out and press my hand into her arm. It's solid, but a strange fuzzy feeling tingles against my fingertips where they touch her skin. My eyes linger on my own hand. I'm starting to fade too. I close my eyes and take a deep breath. It's too soon. We need more time. We have to finish what we started. What was the point in coming all the way here, just to fail before we even get a chance?

"We're running out of time," I say quietly.

Lena looks up at me, her eyes full of tears. "Sam, no."

Sammy lets out a strangled cry. "We have to do something!"

I plunge my hands into my hair, my eyes darting from side to side. We're fading from existence and there's nothing I can do to stop it. Nothing except getting to the lake and stopping Bones once and for all.

"We're still here," I say firmly, getting to my feet. "It's not too late. Let's keep moving. The faster we get to the lake, the faster we can end this."

By my calculations there are still a couple of miles to the entrance to Lake Ingershall. Up ahead, the shape of a bridge huddles in the darkness. I recognize it from our reality. It's a wooden bridge, with a fast-moving river running below it. On the other side, the road is lined with sheer rock walls on each side.

The river swirls beneath us as we cross the bridge, a fine mist dotting our upper bodies with little beads of water. Halfway across, I come to a stop. There's movement above the rock walls. Dark shapes swoop through the sky, backlit by the orange glow of the moon. At the front of the group, Sammy notices them too. He turns, placing a finger in front of his lips, then points upward. Lee stiffens, the color draining from her face.

I follow her gaze. *Good God.* The walls are crawling with bat creatures. White droppings streak down the rock face, and we can hear their shrieking cries as they dart through the air. There's no way around. We have to continue along the road and hope they don't notice us. We huddle together on the other side of the bridge, bringing our heads in close.

"Bat creatures," Sammy says. "Everywhere. We need to be quiet."

Lee's voice wavers. "This is a bad idea."

"There's no way around them," I say. "Not without having to travel miles out of our way, and by then it'll be too late. We're already starting to fade. Stay close to the cliff face, watch where you step, and let's get through them as fast as possible."

We pull apart and turn. Lena slips her hand into mine. I squeeze it and flash a smile, but inside I'm screaming. My legs tremble as we step around fallen branches and dry leaves, edging along the side of the road close to the cliff face. One wrong step—

"Gah!"

My head whips up from where my eyes were trained

on the ground. Sammy stepped into a hole in the cracked concrete and twisted his ankle. He's fallen forward, onto his hands and knees.

A screech cuts through the air.

The first bat creature launches itself down off the top of the cliff, its wings flapping furiously. It moves through the air with surprising speed. Sammy struggles to his feet, his eyes bulging at the sight of the monster closing in on him. Lee pulls his arm over her shoulder and helps him move.

The other bat creatures are right behind the first, swooping down from the top of the cliffs. *Oh God. This can't be happening.* Black dots swim across my vision.

The scream tears out of me like a battle cry. "Run!"

I throw my arms over my head and take off running. The heavy, panicked breathing of the others, mixed with the screeching of the bat creatures, is the stuff nightmares are made of. Lena cries out, a sound so full of terror that the blood in my veins turns to ice.

A dozen creatures hurtle after us, their frenzied wing beats filling the air. One of them darts at Lena's fading form, its talons reaching for her. It snarls and snaps, and I skid to a stop. *Oh no you don't.* I rip my backpack off and reach for the zipper. My fingers are trembling so much, I can't hold on to it.

Come on, come on!

Lena is sobbing now, zigzagging ahead of me as the creature pursues her. It dips down and swipes at her, grabbing her baseball cap and pulling it from her head. My chest tightens. We should've had the flashlights out the entire time. We should've been ready. If anything happens to her, I'll never forgive myself.

I squeeze my eyes shut and count to three. *One . . . two . . . three.* With a rush of breath, I open them, grab hold of the zipper, and yank it to the side. I plunge my hand inside my backpack and pull out a big metal flashlight. I jam my finger onto the on switch and swing my arm around, directing the bright yellow beam toward the creature above Lena's head.

An earsplitting screech fills the air. The creature rears back, its flapping wings sending waves of sour-smelling air rushing over us. I gag but hold my light steady.

Lee and Sammy pull flashlights from their bags too. Three beams slice through the darkness, directed right at the bat creature's drooling face. It gives one last shriek, then soars up and away from the light.

The others follow, settling back onto the top of the rock walls. They watch us as we rush to Lena's side. She's on the ground, tears streaking her dirt-smudged face.

"You're safe." I wrap my arms around her. "It's okay."

She swallows and looks up at me, then climbs to her feet. "There was *nothing* okay about that."

"Guys," Sammy says, his voice rising. "They're watching us. Let's get out of here."

We keep the flashlights out and run, darting along the rock walls without stopping. When we reach the end, I double over, my hands resting on my thighs, gulping air into my burning lungs. Sweat trickles down the sides of my face.

I search the wide eyes and pale faces of the others and guilt slams into me. I brought them out here, I made them risk their lives, and now everything's going wrong.

"That was close," Lee says. "Too close."

"At least the lights worked," Sammy says.

His vote of confidence is reassuring but doesn't really make me feel better. I can barely look Lena in the eye.

I glance behind us. "From now on, we keep them out and ready. Now, let's get out of here before those *things* get any more ideas—"

A flash of black wings darts down from the sky. Before we can react, a snarling, drooling bat creature sinks its claws into Sammy's shoulders. I fumble with my flashlight, but it's too late. The creature lifts him into the air.

"Sammy!" Lee jabs at the creature with her stick, but it's already out of reach.

Sammy's cries float down to us from above. "Ahh! Help!"

The bat creature sails up to the top of the rock wall. I scramble across the road, looking for a way to get up the wall face, with Lee right beside me. The rock crumbles each time I try to pull myself up, chunks of it coming away in my hands.

Lena circles around off the road. "Over here!"

I step off the concrete and run around to where she stands, knee-deep in grass, pointing upward. Here the rock is jagged, a series of ledges jutting out from the earth like a rough staircase leading all the way to the top of the cliff wall. I look up, butterflies surging into my stomach.

Somewhere above, Sammy screams again. I can almost feel his terror clenching in my own stomach, the staticky feeling of panic that must be surging into his chest. Now I think I understand what Bones meant when he said we were connected. We're not twins like Lena and Lenore, but there's definitely something between us. I felt it the first time I dreamed of the ether, when an invisible force pushed me to answer his cries for help.

Beads of sweat break out on my upper lip. *Come on,*

Sam. You can do this. Sammy needs you. I dig my hands into the dirt and roots, the muscles in my arms screaming, and pull myself onto the first ledge. Lena and Lee struggle to climb up behind me. I reach out a hand to try to help.

Sammy screams again, and agony washes over Lee's pale face. "Just go! Hurry!"

On the second ledge I can hear the bat creature calling to the others. *No way am I letting you turn Sammy into dinner.* Onto the third ledge, I'm more than halfway up. I glance down at Lena and Lee twenty feet below. The ground tilts, and I press a hand to my head. That was a bad idea.

I'm frozen in place, unable to move. Memories of the time I made it out to the end of the high dive and couldn't force myself to go any further wash over me. A group of kids from school laughed as I stood there, legs shaking, frozen like a statue. I had to sit on the board and scoot back to the platform, my face burning with shame.

"You can do it, Sam!" Lena calls from below. "Just don't look down!"

I shake my head, trying to knock loose the memory. I can't let fear stop me. I can't let the shame of failure keep me from getting to Sammy. There are no kids from Stapleton Middle School here to laugh at me now. There's just one kid, and he needs me.

"Sammy!" I yell, pulling myself onto the next ledge. "Hold on, I'm coming!"

The rock scrapes and cuts my bare legs as I climb. Warm blood soaks the tops of my socks. One more ledge to go.

"Get back!" Sammy screams wildly. "Get away from me!"

I come up over the top of the wall at full speed, trip, and fall into a nest the size of a swimming pool. It's made out of dry grass and branches, and the smell wafting from it brings tears to my eyes. Broken eggshells and bones litter the floor. I shudder, trying not to think about what or who the bones belonged to.

On the other side of the nest, Sammy's surrounded. The bat creature looms over him. Thick drool drips from a mouth full of razor-sharp teeth. Smaller baby bat creatures hop around him, excited for their dinner.

"Hey!" I raise my hands over my head, waving them wildly. Knee-deep in bones, I can't run. I wade through the nest, closing in on Sammy and the bat creatures. They turn to look at me. "Your light, Sammy! Turn it on!"

Sammy is still gripping his flashlight in his hands. In his panic, he forgot all about it. He fumbles with it, then switches it on. The light flashes, blinks, and goes out.

"No!" he moans.

The mother bat creature leans in close, her breath sweeping Sammy's curls back off his forehead. I swing my flashlight beam up, pointing it into the bat creature's eyes. She stumbles back, away from Sammy, and lets out a screech of anger. The little monsters are still closing in, but I can't take my beam off the mother.

As I stand there, chest heaving in and out, trying to figure out what to do, two beams of light slice through the dark. Lena and Lee are on the opposite edge of the nest, their flashlights thrust out in front of them. Their lights sweep over the little bat creatures. Panicking, they squawk and run behind their mother's wings to hide.

I struggle over to Sammy, grab his arm, and help him to his feet. With my flashlight held out behind me, we wade back to the other side of the nest. One of the little creatures, feeling bold, darts at us. Lena swings her hammer. The mother lets out an ear-splitting screech as the hammer connects, and the creature falls back against the side of the nest.

"Nice one." I help Sammy over the side, onto the rock ledge. "Now move!"

But I don't have to tell them. They're already climbing down the wall, scrambling over the ledges, eager to get away from the nest. I'm right behind them, and as I slide down the first ledge, my stomach is oddly still. No butterflies surge into it now.

"What're you smiling about?" Lee asks when I join them on the road.

"Nothing," I answer. "I'm just happy we got Sammy back."

Chapter 32

THE DIRT ROAD LEADING TO LAKE
Ingershall is barely visible. Bushes reach
across it from both sides like clawing hands.
The wooden sign is broken in half, the two
pieces hanging from the post. They swing lazily back
and forth in the breeze as we approach. If the lake was
once a popular place for the people of Stapleton, you
wouldn't know it now.

I close my eyes and take a deep breath. "This is it.
This is where we put an end to everything."

"We hope," Sammy says, only half joking.

I give him the side-eye, but I know what he means.
Our plan isn't as much of a plan as it is a bunch of kids
charging into danger, completely unprepared. But we

don't have a choice. It's either face Bones or give up. And I'm not ready to give up.

I turn down the road. "Stay alert. Eyes and ears open, and flashlights *out*. I don't wanna be surprised again."

The others nod, and we make our way down the winding road. Now that we're here, my stomach's all tied up in knots. We walk in silence, except for the sounds of our feet on the gravel road, each of us looking from side to side, alert for danger. Sammy walks beside me, limping slightly from twisting his ankle back at the rock walls. His hands are gripped tight around the wrench.

"Thank you for saving me back there," he says finally. "And for coming for us."

I frown. "Did you think I'd just leave the two of you here?"

"No, it's just . . . no one would blame you if you didn't wanna leave our reality, you know, since our parents are still together there."

"That's the thing. They're not *our* parents. They're yours. I thought it was better there at first. Seeing Mom and Dad so happy, dancing around the kitchen—"

Sammy groans. "Oh man, I hate when they do that."

"Don't. Enjoy it. It's not a bad thing; it's just not *my* life. I'm ready to give it back."

Sammy tilts his head. "Even with your parents splitting up?"

I nod. "Even then. I miss my brother and sister. Besides, we can't both stay there, and you've got a soccer game to play."

The sparkling water of Lake Ingershall looks more brown than green underneath the bright orange moon. Old-fashioned beach chairs and towels litter the sand, abandoned. I freeze, noticing a dark stain on the ground, just up ahead. My eyes linger on it; thoughts of what it might be catapult against my brain.

We walk along the edge of the gently lapping water, around to where, in my reality, the bathhouse would be. Somewhere, beyond where we stand, is the cave where we'll confront Bones. Where we'll free Beaumont and finally get to go home. As long as Bones shows up when we call him.

In my reality the path into the woods is covered in gravel. In the ether it's just a narrow dirt trail, barely visible beneath a tangle of weeds. We step off the sand, onto the trail, and switch on our flashlights.

Sammy shivers. "It's creepy out here. And so *quiet*."

It's not until he says that, and we enter the silent woods, that I notice the lack of night sounds. A light breeze rustles the trees and bushes, but there are no birdcalls or owl hoots. No crickets chirping. The absence of sound makes my skin prickle. Bones's evil wiped out everything that makes the forest feel alive.

"How much farther?" Lee asks after a while.

"Keep going," I say, squinting through the trees. "It took us a while to find it the first time."

The truth is, I don't even know for sure. There aren't any of the landmarks I would've had in the reality we came from. Park benches, trail markers, dog-waste stations— they don't exist here.

"I think I see it," Lena whispers, stopping short. Lee bumps into the back of her, dropping her flashlight. It clatters to the ground, the beam flashing into the trees.

The dark mouth of the cave stands open, tucked in behind high bushes. The entrance in this world isn't blocked by a boulder. At least *one* thing will be easy. There's no need to use levers and fulcrums to get into it. I step off the trail, pushing branches aside as I move. The others are right behind me.

"I don't believe it," I whisper. "We found it."

"What do we do now?" Sammy asks.

My mouth fills with saliva, hot and tangy. The pretzels I ate churn in my gut. "I guess we call him."

"Oh God, oh God, oh God," Lena repeats, wringing her hands in front of her.

I want to tell her to be strong. I want to remind her that this is why we came here, but I can't. I'm panicking too.

We stand in a line facing the cave. Lee points her flashlight at the mouth, her hand trembling. I close my eyes and take a deep breath, then open my mouth and bellow his name as loud as I can.

"Bones! I have something that belongs to you!"

Inside the cave, the shadows shift. Something stirs and moves. A wind picks up and thick fog rolls across the ground, inching toward us. The smell of cigar smoke swirls around us, filling the air.

Bones steps out of the cave and toward the beam of the flashlight, a slow smile spreading across his face. In the shadows, his pitted face looks twisted and deformed. It sends chills racing up and down my spine.

"A party? Just for me? You shouldn't have." His voice is deep and menacing. A muscle twitches in his jaw.

Lena rolls her eyes. "You really don't know how to read the room, do you?"

A fluttery feeling stirs in my stomach. Red-hot, raging anger surges through me. Bones took Addie and Grayson away. He made it so Derek didn't know me. He corrupted this world and the people in it, and ruined the lives of so many others.

My nostrils flare. "We're here to end this."

"Are you, now?" Bones laughs, throwing his head back. "Here I was, thinking you'd come to give me back what you stole."

Sweat trickles down my forehead, running into my eyes. "You're not getting the flute back. Not until you let Beaumont go free."

"And what makes you think that's going to happen?" His eyes flash, and his smile turns into a snarl. He raises his hands above him, and the bushes and trees around us begin to shake. A chorus of inhuman cries rises up, filling the air.

Lena trembles beside me. "Sam . . ."

"Come, my children, come! I've brought you a feast!"

In the bushes to my left, something lets out an angry snarl. I whirl around, directing the beam of my flashlight into the shaking bushes. What I see emerging from them sends my head into a spin.

A new creature, one we haven't seen before, steps out into the open. It slinks at the edges of the light, a pair of luminous yellow eyes flashing at us. It's shaped like a wolf, only much, *much* bigger, and it has thick, greasy gray fur that bristles on its back like spines. Black lips peel back into a vicious snarl, revealing sharp yellow teeth that drip with slobber.

"We're done for," Sammy croaks.

I shake my head. "No, we're not going out like this, not after we came this far."

My heart thunders in my chest as I sweep the flashlight toward the wolf monster. It retreats back toward the bushes, staying just out of reach of the beam.

"What is that?" Lena whimpers.

"One of my pets," Bones says. "Cute, isn't he?"

Lee glares at him. "He's awful. Just like you."

"Aw," Bones says. "Now that's not very nice."

He sticks two fingers into his mouth and lets out a sharp whistle. His creatures surge down the trail and through the woods, swooping between the trees, answering his call like hungry children answering a dinner bell.

"Sam," Lena says. "We're surrounded."

"It's so cold." Sammy wraps his arms around himself. "Why's it cold all of a sudden?"

"It's him," Lee says. "He's doing it."

The previously quiet woods are alive with monsters snarling and snapping, darting back and forth through the shadows. Fog covers the ground, swirling at our feet and blocking out the direct light from our flashlights. If we don't do something, we'll be defenseless against Bones's creatures. The others look at me, hoping I'll tell them what to do. But I'm not even sure I can keep the pretzels I ate earlier inside my stomach, let alone figure out what to do.

I'm no good at this. I'm too weak. Too scared.

Wait, that's wrong.

I've had it all wrong this entire time. I was the one who led Helen and Lena out to the cave. I put my hand into the dark substance and discovered what really happened to Bones. It was me who figured out that Sammy and Lee weren't just dreams, but actually trapped here in this nightmare. And it was my idea to bring everyone here to the ether, to the cave where this all started, to put an end to Bones's destruction.

Maybe I don't *like* being a leader, but I've been one all along. It's time to step up and start acting like it.

I puff out my chest. "Call them off."

Another grin spreads across Bones's face. "Give me back my flute, and I will."

The skeleton flute is hidden safely at the bottom of my backpack, wrapped in a piece of scrap fabric I found in Sammy and Lee's attic. I'll die before I give it back to him and allow him to continue destroying lives.

"You can travel without it," I say. "Why do you need it back?"

"So I can take what's owed me."

"No one owes you a thing." I plant my feet firm

on the ground. "Maybe Sammy's and Lee's ancestors trapped you, but *they're* innocent. They didn't do anything to you."

Bones tilts his head to the side. "That means nothing to me."

"Too bad," I say, shuffling forward a step. I won't let him intimidate me, and I won't back down. "I'm not giving you the flute."

Without warning, Bones flashes forward, his hand shooting out in front of him. His fingers close around my neck, his ragged nails digging into the skin, choking off my breath. My eyes widen, and both the iron pipe and my flashlight fall from my hand. The light blinks, then goes out. Bones lifts me off my feet.

"Let him go!" Lena screams.

Tears stream from my eyes, and I claw at the hand that has hold of my neck, desperately trying to pry his fingers loose. Darkness crowds my vision. The others rush forward, but Bones sweeps his other hand downward, and his creatures move in.

Chapter 33

IT'S LIKE THEY WERE WAITING FOR THE signal. There's not a second of hesitation. Bat creatures swoop down from the trees where they were perched, their deep red eyes flashing. A half dozen wolf monsters leap from the bushes, snapping and snarling. Frogmen slink out from between the trees, their wet gray skin glistening in the moonlight.

Lena screams at the sight of them, a sound so full of fear that I temporarily forget I'm being choked to death. I struggle to get free, kicking my feet and swinging my arms. Bones is too strong. The others move into a circle, standing back to back. They swing their flashlights wildly, trying to keep the creatures away. It's no use.

There are too many of them.

Just when I'm sure Bones is going to choke the life out of me, he opens his hand and drops me into the swarm of creatures, like feeding time at the zoo. I land on my feet and stumble backward, sputtering and coughing. Pain blossoms behind my eyes like fireworks on the Fourth of July.

A cry of triumph bursts from between Bones's smiling teeth, urging his creatures on like some sort of twisted cheerleader. I take one last heaving breath and scramble across the dirt, searching through the fog for my weapon.

A wolf monster springs from the bushes, its jaws wide.

"Come at me, bro!" Sammy cries. He swings his wrench at it, bringing it down on the top of the creature's head. The wolf monster lets out a yelp and shoots off into the bushes.

"You might as well give up!" Bones cries, his arms raised. "They'll never stop coming."

Lena screams as a frogman grabs her from behind. "Sam!"

"No!" My voice comes out in a raspy snarl. "Lena!"

I'm searching blindly now, patting the dirt and leaves in search of my weapon. Panic swells in my chest.

I can't find it. It's not here. Lena shrieks again and my head whips up.

The frogman opens its mouth, and a long, slimy tongue shoots out, wrapping itself around Lena's neck. Her eyes bulge out of her head and she plants a hand against the frogman's chest, slowing the pull toward its needle-sharp teeth. But it's not enough.

"Fight, Lena," I say, breathless. "You can do this!"

"No, Sam," she chokes out. "I'm too scared."

She holds the hammer in one trembling hand, her grip loosening as the frogman's grip on *her* tightens. Thick drool drips down the side of her face now, the frogman's deadly teeth way too close to her neck for my liking. I have to help her.

I'm still on my hands and knees, searching for my weapon. My fading, reaching fingers finally brush something cold and hard. I grab it and pull my pipe up through the fog.

"I'll help you," I say, closing the distance between us. "When I say so, swing the hammer behind you."

She swallows, then nods. "Okay."

"Okay, swing!"

Lena lets out a little scream and swings her arm backward. The frogman jerks in surprise, and its tongue rolls back into its mouth with a slurping sound.

"Now duck!" I yell.

Lena bends her knees and slides through the creature's arms, dropping to the ground. The frogman blinks in surprise, and I step forward, bringing the pipe up hard into its side.

There's a loud squelching sound. The frogman staggers.

Lena scrambles around and shines her flashlight into its eyes, her own wide with fear. The frogman screeches and takes off running, darting behind a tree to escape the bright beam.

"Yes!" I say, pumping my fist in the air. She did it. We did it.

But our victory celebration doesn't last. Lena's trembling now, and her eyes have a faraway look to them. She wraps her arms around herself and slides down to the ground, landing with a thud. Her body rocks back and forth.

"I can't do this," she sobs. "I'm not strong enough, not without Lenore."

Fear flares in my chest. She can't give up. She has to fight.

I shake my head. "You're wrong, Lena. Remember when I froze back there on the ledge and you told me to keep going? You told me I could do it, and you were right."

"No, I c-can't—"

Lee ducks under the reaching arm of another frog-man and steps up beside me. "Yes you can! When Lacey died, I thought I'd never be whole again," she says, breathless. "But I was wrong. You're wrong too. You can do this, Lena. You are *whole*."

I nod. "You're the strongest person I know."

Lena shakes her head. "Sam, I can't—"

"I wouldn't be here if it wasn't for you. None of us would," I say forcefully. "You're smart, you're funny, and you're brave. Now *fight!*"

Lena looks up at me, the spark coming back into her eyes. *There's* the Lena I know. She gets to her feet and lifts the hammer, gripping it tight in her hand. A bat creature swoops down from a nearby tree, and Lena swings at it, the hammer connecting with a solid thwack.

Bones stands in the center of the chaos, a smile stretched across his face. Laughter rumbles in his chest. We fight off his creatures with everything we have, but it's not enough. When one creature goes down, another one is there to take its place.

"Sam!" Lee cries. "Sam, we have to get out of here!"

I shake my head. "No!"

Sammy grabs my arm and pulls as a wolf monster snaps at his heels. "We're all going to die if we don't,

Sam. I know you wanted to fix things. I know you wanted to get us home, but this isn't working."

Tears cloud my vision as I glance at Lena, who's barely visible in the dim light. "There's too much to lose, Sammy! We're almost out of time. We can't give up!"

"Give up? Who said anything about giving up?"

The voice comes from behind us. I spin around and my eyes land on a familiar face. It's smudged with dirt, but there's no mistaking her.

"*Helen?*" Lena and I cry at the same time.

"I saw the commotion from the beach," she says. "Came to investigate. Looks like you kids could use some help."

A laugh bubbles up in my throat. I can't believe my eyes. It's definitely Helen, but not the one we met back in Sammy and Lee's reality. This is the other Helen— the one who's been living in the ether since our Helen got tricked into playing the flute. Her hair is shorter, framing a face that's thinner than our Helen's, and her clothes are tattered. But it's her.

She steps off the trail waving a strange contraption in her hand. It looks like a flashlight, a really *old* flashlight, but it has a round metal disc the size of a dinner plate welded to the top of it. She swings it up in front of her and turns a crank. The filament in the center of the bulb begins to grow brighter.

It takes a few seconds, but once the light bulb has gotten enough power from the crank, the beam bounces off the metal disc and back out, flooding the area with bright white light. Bones's creatures back off, scrambling over one another to escape. Humor twinkles in Helen's blue eyes. I'm so happy I could kiss her . . . if it wouldn't be completely inappropriate and weird, of course.

I take a deep breath. *It's go time, Sam. It's now or never.* I take a step toward Bones, hesitation and fear transforming into determination. My chest heaves in and out. "Beaumont! We're here! It's time to fight back!"

"That won't work this time," Bones snarls. "I've put him back where he belongs. He won't get control again."

He raises his arms to the side and a strong wind kicks up, blowing through the trees and bushes, sending dirt and leaves swirling into the air along with the thick fog. They begin to twist and turn around him, gaining speed, blocking out the light from Helen's flood lamp.

"You don't have the right!" I shout to be heard over the sound of the wind. "This is his life and you've stolen it."

"I took back what was stolen from me."

"Beaumont," Lena pleads. She blinks and disappears for a moment before reappearing in the clearing. "Please! Help us!"

Bones swipes at me, his lips curled over his teeth.

"This is my realm now. He has no power here."

"No," I say, dodging him. "You're wrong."

A bat creature shrieks and swoops down from the trees. My eardrums vibrate and I clamp my hands over my ears, ducking as the creature soars over the top of us. A clawed foot reaches out and scrapes across Lee's outstretched arm. She cries out, and a line of blood shimmers against her pale skin.

This isn't working. Even with the light from Helen's flood lamp, he's too strong. I need to do something. I wrestle my backpack off and reach into it. My heart thrashes in my chest, pounding against my rib cage. My fingers close around the flute. The fabric wrapped around it is warm to the touch.

"Keep holding them back!" I call to the others. They turn their flashlight beams, aiming them through the gaps in the fog. I pull the flute free of the fabric. "Beaumont! You *have* to fight him!"

The ground begins to tremble beneath my feet. A crack splits the earth, and from it foul-smelling green smoke hisses into the air. I stagger backward, thrown off by this unexpected twist. Something's emerging from the crack, something dark, thick, and slimy. It slithers up through the belching green smoke—a tentacle of some kind—reaching from the depths of who knows where. Bones cackles, and more tentacles push through the earth.

"Hurry, Sam!" Lena cries.

The cracks in the ground surround her like spider-webs. A dark tentacle shoots toward her, and she dances around it, swinging at it with her hammer. Helen gasps, and I spin around just as a wolf monster leaps at her from behind. It rams into her, knocking both her and the flood lamp to the ground.

She's still, and everything goes dark.

Sammy darts past the wolf monster, jumps over Helen, and snatches the lamp from the ground. His fingers close around the crank and the lamp blazes to life again. "Go, Sam, go!"

I turn back to Bones, thrusting the flute out in front of me. He's encased in a churning cloud of dust and debris, but a smile spreads across his face. "There it is."

"I have what was stolen from you, Beaumont!" I yell. "Fight him! It's time to take it back!"

Something strong and slimy wraps around my ankle. The skin above my sock burns like acid. I grunt but hold the flute steady, fighting against the tugging tentacle. Something else grabs at me from behind, pulling hard on my upper arm. Hot, swampy breath washes over me. *I. Am. Not. Gonna. Die. Like. This.* Not with that smell singeing my nose hairs.

"A breath mint every once in a while wouldn't kill you." Fueled by a renewed sense of determination, I twist my arm free of the frogman's grip and inch forward, pulling the tentacle along, holding the flute out in front of me. "Take it Beaumont, take control!"

"It's not working," Lee sobs. "Sam, it's not working."

"Break it!" Lena cries, her eyes widening. "You have to break it, Sam."

My entire body goes cold. Break the flute? No. That *can't* be what has to happen. If I break it, how will we get home? And what if she's wrong? What if I break it and we still can't stop Bones? My eyes dart from side to side. I need to think. There has to be another way. If I break the flute, we'll be trapped here forever.

Trapped.

Beaumont's soul is trapped inside the skeleton flute.

Lena's right. I don't have a choice. I have to release it.

I hold the flute high above my head and bring it down hard against my knee. For a second, I worry that I'm too faded for this to work, but then it snaps in two with a loud crack, sending a jolt of pain through my leg. My breath catches in my throat. A glittery silver cloud rises from between the fragments of the skeleton flute. It hovers in the air for a moment, then darts toward Bones and circles his head.

"No!" he wails, waving his hands wildly. "No!"

The cloud surges into his mouth and nose. He's powerless to stop it. A sputtering sound bursts from his lips. One eye bulges from the socket, and his neck turns unnaturally to the side. The muscles pulse and tighten, throbbing beneath the twisted skin. He gasps, reaching a hand toward me.

"Please let this work," I whisper. "Please, please, please . . ."

Bones sinks down on one knee. The air around him stills; leaves rain down around him. The attacking creatures falter and stop, watching their master. I take a step forward, pulling my leg free of the tentacle's grasp.

"You . . . can't . . . do . . . this," Bones sputters.

I smile. "You're right—I can't. But Beaumont can."

"Nooo!" Bones twitches and shudders as he crouches in the dirt, trying to fight the soul inside him that's finally fighting back.

His head snaps up. A bloodcurdling scream pours from his mouth. His face contorts, a flash of something evil—something beyond evil—rising to the surface. I shudder, glimpsing the true darkness inside him. Then he shoots into an upright position, his body stiff, and with one last cry he falls backward, landing hard in the dirt.

Chapter 34

"**S**AM?" LEE'S EYES LIFT TO MEET mine.

I stare at Bones's motionless body, afraid to even breathe. The forest is eerily quiet.

"Is he . . . is he dead?" Sammy asks.

I take a step forward. I need to know if Bones is gone or if he's tricking us again. We came here to stop him, and I need to know if we did that or if we failed. If I failed.

"Be careful," Lena says.

I crouch down in front of him and move in close, holding a trembling hand under Bones's nose. Soft breath tickles the hairs on the back of my hand. His chest rises and falls ever so slightly.

I shake my head. "He's still alive."

A hissing sigh escapes from his parted lips, and a plume of black smoke snakes out of his mouth. I recoil, watching as it drifts into the air, spins around, and then fades away.

"Ugh," Sammy says. "What was *that*?"

"I'm not sure," I say, tilting my head. "Maybe it was the evil leaving him."

Sammy frowns. "Gross."

"Look!" Lena whispers.

I turn in a circle. Bones's creatures are frozen in place, their bodies trembling. They're fading around the edges, their solid forms turning to ink-black smoke that drifts up, disappearing too.

Bones groans.

I jump back and snatch the iron pipe from the ground, holding it like a baseball bat. If this dude comes at me again, I'm ready to swing and hit one right into the outfield. The others grip their weapons tighter too.

He sits up and shakes his head, pressing a hand to his temple. "For two hundred years I've been a prisoner inside my own body."

"Beaumont?" The muscles in my arms relax, and I drop the pipe to my side. "Is it really you?"

If there's one thing I've learned through all of this, it's that you can never be too careful. Things aren't always what they seem. Beaumont groans again, then struggles to his feet. His eyes meet mine. I tilt my head, holding his gaze. There's a softness to his face that wasn't there before. It's him, all right.

"Yes," he says. "It's me."

"What about Bones?" I ask.

Beaumont's eyes are serious. "I can feel him inside me. He's weak now, but he's fighting back. I—I don't know how long I can hold him off."

"The puddle," I say, pointing toward the cave. "Can you send him back through? There's nothing on the other side but a skeleton. He won't have a body to go into."

Beaumont winces. "Yes, yes, of course. That's it."

He takes an unsteady step toward the cave. I follow behind, switching on my flashlight. Inside, the dark substance is just a small splash of black against the pale stone.

"It's shrinking," I gasp.

"The evil that created this cursed thing has been released," Beaumont says, kneeling down in front of it. "I have to hurry."

He presses his hand into the substance and closes his eyes. He murmurs to himself, the muscles in his arm tightening and releasing, then tightening again. I hold my breath, surrounded by the others, watching as Beaumont shudders on the cave floor.

Finally he sucks in a deep breath and yanks his hand free. The dark substance shimmers one last time, then disappears like it was never there.

"I don't know how to thank you all for freeing me." He stands and steps out of the cave. He turns his face upward and draws in a deep breath, then releases it, as if tasting the air for the first time in a long time. His shoulders sag, like the weight of the world has been lifted off them.

"Is Bones gone for good?" Lena asks.

Beaumont nods. "Yes. Finally."

"And so are his creatures," Sammy says. Sweat glistens on his forehead, and there's bright red blood smeared across one cheek.

Helen groans and sits up, pressing a hand to her head. "Is someone going to tell me what just happened and *why* I'm seeing double?"

A laugh bubbles up in my throat and I let it out, sinking to the ground, my shoulders shaking with laughter.

Helen looks at me. "Well?"

"It's a really, *really* long story," I say. "And you probably won't believe me."

"Try me."

The four of us piece together the story of how we all ended up in the ether. When Lena and I get to the part about meeting Helen for the first time, *this* Helen sucks in a sharp breath.

She nods her head at Beaumont. "So I've been stuck in this nightmare all these years because of him?"

I nod. "Well, not him, exactly. It was Bones."

"And the other Helen has been living my life, pretending to be me?"

"She didn't know," Lena says quickly. "She didn't figure out that there was another version of herself trapped here until *we* figured it out and told her."

"She feels awful," I say. "She would've kept trying to find a way back if she knew."

Helen nods and lets out a breath. "I can't fault her for that, I guess."

Lena turns to me. "You were right about us all needing to be here."

She sounds impressed, and to be honest, I kinda am too. The visions showed me where Beaumont's soul was trapped, but I didn't know for sure that getting us all here was the key to freeing him and getting rid of Bones. I only hoped it would be.

"How did you know?" Beaumont asks.

"When Lena and I found the cave, I touched the

dark substance on the ground, and somehow it showed me what he did, how he tricked you," I say, shivering at the memory.

Beaumont's eyes drop to the ground. "I was a fool."

"He lied to you," I say, shaking my head. "It wasn't your fault."

"I could've stopped all of this before it started. I knew what he asked me to do wasn't natural, but I wanted to help him," Beaumont says weakly.

"You couldn't have known what he was going to do to you," Lee says. "Or to us."

Beaumont shakes his head. "No, but I was a healer. I knew that he had done what no healer is supposed to do—he called on the dark spirits. Once he took over, once he stole a piece of my soul, I was too weak to fight him. Even when I saw what he was doing. He destroyed this world."

"Will it heal?" Lee asks.

Beaumont shrugs. "I don't know. It might be too far gone."

"There's no one here besides us, anyway," Sammy says.

"That's not entirely true," Helen says. "There are others."

I frown. "There are? Where? How?"

"In a compound about three miles from here, back toward town."

Lee gasps. "We thought we were alone. We were too scared to go that far with all the monsters around."

"How many of you are there?" Lena asks.

"Quite a few. Our numbers have grown over the years," Helen says. "We've settled in quite nicely."

Relief explodes in my chest. "Descendants of the townspeople of Stapleton. They *weren't* all turned into monsters."

"How did you survive in this place after all this time?" Lee asks. "Sammy and I weren't here that long, and every day we woke up feeling like a year had passed instead of a day."

Helen shrugs. "We felt the effects of this place too. Like your soul was being sucked right out of you—"

"That's because it was," Beaumont says gravely. "That's how Bones stayed alive all this time: stealing people, sending them here, *feeding* off them."

"I think that when we formed our community and resisted the darkness of this place, we counteracted whatever that Bones guy was doing. It helps to have friends," Helen says, winking. "But I think you all know that."

I look down at the broken pieces of the skeleton flute

lying in the dirt. Any hope I had before escapes my body with one explosive breath. My relief at defeating Bones and freeing Beaumont goes with it.

"The flute," I whisper. "We'll never get home now."

I'll never get to hang out playing video games with Derek again; I'll never see Addie and Grayson again, never give Mom and Dad another hug—either version of them.

Beaumont smiles. "I think I can help."

I lift my eyes to meet his, hope flaring inside my chest like the sun breaking through dark clouds. "How?"

He bends down and picks up the splintered remains of the skeleton flute. He fits them together and closes his eyes. I hold my breath. Watching. Waiting. An arc of white light flows from Beaumont's palms and traces along the fracture. When it fades, the flute is whole again.

He looks down at it, turning it around in his hands. "The damage this thing has done . . ."

"It's not your fault, Beaumont," I say. "That was Bones, not you."

"Well, I'm going to make it right, if I can." A sad smile spreads across his face. "And then destroy this thing."

"What'll you do after that?" Lena asks.

"Oh," Beaumont sighs. "I'm not sure. The evil that

Bones tapped into is gone now. The dark magic that kept him alive all this time will fade. Maybe I will too, now that he's gone. Shoot, I'm over two hundred years old. My life is long past due. In the meantime, I'll do as much good as I can. Help the others here get home, if they want. Become the healer I never had a chance to be."

I smile. "I like that idea."

"Now stand around me in a circle and hold hands." He looks at me and Lena. "I'm going to undo your wishes. Once I play the flute, it should send you back to your own realities, before all of this started."

"Just a minute," I say.

I turn to Sammy and reach out a faded, almost see-through hand. He shakes it, a smile pulling at one side of his mouth. It's too bad I won't get the chance to get to know myself a little better. He seems like a cool dude, even if he *is* a jock.

"Thank you," he says. "Thank you for saving us."

"I didn't do it alone."

Sammy nods, then reaches out and takes Lee's hand into his. He pulls her close and they hug.

Lena, so faded now she's nothing more than an outline, catches Lee's eye over Sammy's shoulder. "Stay strong, Lee. It's going to be okay. Remember what I said about your parents."

Lee swallows hard. "Thank you for helping me understand."

Something unspoken passes between them, and Lena gives a weak smile. "Find Sammy in your reality. You'll need each other."

Lee nods. "I will."

Lena turns to me, the two of us like ghosts. "Promise me you'll find me too."

I grin. "A pack of wolf monsters couldn't keep me away."

She throws her arms around me and hugs me tight. "Thank you, Sam. I don't know what I would've done without you."

"Will you be okay, you know, going back without your mom there?"

Her eyes shimmer with tears. "No, not really. But I've got my dad. And Lenore. We have each other, and eventually we'll be okay."

I nod and turn to Helen. "Ready to go home?"

She shakes her head. "I'm not going back."

"What do you mean?"

"I have people I care about back in the compound. I have a family," she says. "Maybe now that the monsters are gone, we can work to rebuild this world."

"Thank you for helping us," Sammy says. "We couldn't have done it without you."

Helen waves her hand dismissively. "You all were doing just fine without me. I've never met such brave kids in my life."

Though I know she's just saying that, because we totally *did* need her help, it's nice of her to say so. I know I'll never forget what she did for us, and the others won't either.

I turn to Sammy. "Will you find Helen in your reality and tell her what happened? Tell her she can stay?"

He nods. "Of course."

The four of us move together in a tight circle, with Beaumont in the center, and join hands. Four kids who came together to defeat evil and put things back the way they're supposed to be. I look across the circle at their faces and can't stop the grin that spreads across mine.

I'm ready to go home.

It's not gonna be easy for any of us. The reality back home is scary, but I'm not as afraid to face my parents' separation anymore. I've gone through a lot of things over the past week I never thought I'd have to—never thought I *could*. As long as I have my brother and sister, as long as I have Derek and now Lena, I can handle whatever's thrown at me next.

I just hope that the others are ready too—they each

have their own challenges to face. It makes me feel better knowing that Sammy and Lee have each other now.

I nod, and Beaumont raises the flute to his lips. A long, low note rings out through the forest, bouncing off the trees and fading into darkness. It carries with it his sadness and desire to fix the damage Bones has done, and the hope that we're all going back home, where we belong.

Chapter 35

SUNLIGHT STREAMS IN THROUGH THE
curtains of my bedroom, splashing across the
far wall. My eyes flutter open, then immediately squeeze shut again. After the orange-tinted shadowy light of the ether, it feels like it's been years since I've seen the sun.

Somewhere across the room, my alarm clock rings out, a rhythmic beeping that's music to my ears. I yawn and sit up, shielding my eyes with my hand. Every inch of my skin is tingling. I scan the room. A pile of clothes sits in front of the closet door. The clock on my desk reads 7:35 a.m.

A smile slowly spreads across my face and quickly turns into a grin. I'm home. Beaumont did it. *We* did it.

Still grinning, I climb out of bed, cross the room, and slap my hand down on the clock to turn off the alarm. In the mirror above my desk, I stop and stare at my reflection, relief expanding in my chest. I'm solid. Perfectly solid.

I snag a T-shirt and pants from the floor and put them on quickly, anxious to see Addie and Grayson. In the hallway, a laugh floats through the air. I race toward Addie's door, my bare feet slapping against the wood floors. I slide to a stop, my hands trembling against the metal knob. *Please, please, please.* I push the door open, squeezing my eyes shut for just a moment, afraid of what I'll find on the other side.

Addie's in her bed, playing quietly with a stuffed animal. She sits up when I open the door and rubs her little fists into her eyes. The breath explodes from me in a rush. I cross the soft, carpeted floor, remembering how the last time I was in this room, it was bare and empty, filled with Dad's office supplies.

"Hey, Addie!"

She looks up at me, her eyebrows slanting down in confusion. I reach out, pluck her from her bed, and scoop her into my arms. She stares into my eyes for a moment, and her little mouth puckers. She looks like she's going to cry. What the heck?

Bones's warning that the people in my life would forget me, that I'd be erased from my reality like I never existed, echoes in my ears. My stomach fills with ice, chilling me from the inside out. What if we were too late? I bend forward and plant a kiss on Addie's nose. She hesitates, then breaks into a smile. Her little arms wrap around my neck, and she hugs me close, her breath warm against my skin.

"Sammy!"

"Yes!" I kiss her again. "Yes, it's me!"

"No more!" She giggles and presses her pudgy little hands against my forehead, trying to fend me off.

I squeeze her one last time and whisper into her ear. "I love you so much, Addie-bug. I'm so happy to see you."

"Mom's gonna kill you for waking her up." Grayson's standing in the doorway, hands on his hips.

I put Addie down and grin. "Grayson!"

A frown turns down the corners of his mouth. "Where've you been?"

"What do you mean? I've been here. Sleeping."

"Oh." He blinks. "Right. I . . . I don't know why I asked that."

I laugh and pull him into a bear hug. "You goof."

"Gah! What're you *doing*?"

"Just showing my little bro some love."

He squirms out of my arms, and his face scrunches up. "What're you so happy about this morning?"

"Everything. You and Addie, this room, this *house*."

"But Dad's moving out. . . ."

Coldness plops down in my stomach, racing through my veins. It surges into my arms and legs until I'm numb all over. Beaumont said he was sending us back to before this all began.

Today's the day Dad's moving out.

Grayson's lower lip trembles. Helen's words come back to me now—kinda like a gift from another place, to not only help me deal with what's coming, but to help Grayson, too. I let the tears pressing at my eyes fall. They slide down my cheeks, leaving little warm trails behind them. I wasn't helping Grayson by hiding my feelings before. Feelings are *meant* to be felt, even the hard ones. And he needs to know he's not alone.

"I'm not gonna lie," I say, wiping my arm across my face. "It's gonna suck. But we've got each other, right?"

"I guess." He tilts his head. "Didn't you say you had a plan to fix things?"

I shake my head. "I was just being silly, that's all. I was upset. I wanted to fix things, but the truth is that there isn't anything we can do. We're just kids. Mom and Dad have to work on this themselves."

Grayson nods miserably. "Okay."

"We'll be okay," I say. "I promise."

"And what if we're not? What if they get divorced?"

The question stings. The frustration of not knowing the answer burrows down inside me, wriggling deeper with every beat of my heart.

I let out a slow breath. "We'll figure it out together."

Downstairs, Mom's at the kitchen table. Her eyes are red, and she sips from a mug with a faraway look on her face. She barely glances at me when I walk into the room.

"Morning, Mom."

She startles. "Oh, Sam. I didn't hear you come down."

I slide into the chair across from her, and she stares at me, her eyebrows slanted down over her eyes. Confusion flits across her face, like she's struggling to remember something. She opens her mouth and closes it, then tilts her head to the side.

I reach for a box of cereal. "Where's Dad?"

She gives a sad smile. "Packing up his car."

I dump the Frosted Flakes into a bowl and shove a spoonful into my mouth, only just realizing how hungry I am. "Mmm, this is so good," I say more to myself than to her.

"Don't you want milk with that?"

"No . . . ?"

"Okay . . . Hey, Sam? I know this is really hard for you. . . ."

My chest tightens. "Yeah."

"It's okay if you're sad, you know. I'm not okay. Dad's not okay. It's okay to not be okay," she says softly.

"I know it is."

The back door slams, and Dad walks in. Mom avoids his gaze, and a flash of my other mom—the one from Sammy's reality—swims in front of me. The loving way she gazed at my other dad, the dreamy look on her face after date night, and the way they both giggled like teenagers when they got home after midnight.

Maybe that's where things started to go wrong.

It's not that Mom and Dad are having trouble because they spend so much time taking care of the three of us. It's that they forgot to take care of each other, too. But like Helen said, it's not our fault. And maybe it's not really their fault either. Maybe it's something I won't understand until I'm older. Maybe I won't ever understand it.

Maybe that's okay.

Mom stands and pours herself another cup of coffee, then sips it slowly, her eyes sliding out of focus. Grayson trudges into the room and plops down in a chair at the table. He watches Dad gathering his boxes, a frown etched into his face. His eyes swim with tears. Poor little dude.

"It's gonna be okay," I whisper.

The words are for me just as much as they are for Grayson. I *have* to believe it's gonna be okay. My friends believed in me when I told them we could defeat Bones. And we did it. I have to stay positive. For myself, and for my family. I almost wish they could've gone through what I did so they'd know how lucky we are to have each other.

I clear my throat. "I know you guys need some time to . . . work on things. I wanna help if I can."

Dad sets down a box on the counter and crosses the room, stopping behind me. He puts his hands on my shoulders. "Thanks, bud."

I shrug. "We're family. That's what family does."

Mom tilts her head to the side. "When did you get so grown-up?"

"Must've happened overnight."

A wild giggle bubbles up in my throat, and I almost choke trying to swallow it down. If only they knew the half of it. But that's a secret I'll take to my grave. They wouldn't believe me even if I tried to explain.

"Love you, bud," Dad says. "Now go get ready for school."

I stand and drop my bowl into the sink, then turn toward the stairs. "Just promise me you'll remember, okay?"

Mom frowns. "Remember what?"

"What it was like before."

She nods, and her eyes dart up to meet Dad's. A spark of hope flares in my chest. Magic or no magic, I can't fix Mom and Dad's marriage. I know that now. I should've realized it before, but I was so caught up in the idea of not wanting things to change. If it wasn't for Helen, I might've never understood that it's not up to me.

Mom sets down her coffee cup. "Dad and I love all of you so much. Whatever happens with us, nothing will change that."

"This is something we have to do right now," Dad says. "But we're not giving up. Not on each other and not on our family."

I nod. I understand. I don't like it, but I understand. When Mom and Dad told us they were separating, it felt like my life was over. I thought nothing would ever be the same again. And maybe it won't. Things might be different, but at least I have both my parents—my *real* parents. And I have Addie and Grayson. Lena lost her mom, and in a way Lee lost *both* her parents because of their grief.

At least we're all *here.*

I shift in my seat. "If you ever need me to watch Grayson and Addie so you can work on things, I will."

Mom raises her eyebrows. "Thanks, Sam."

Dad lifts the box from the kitchen counter. "We might just take you up on that. Now hurry, before you miss the bus."

"One more thing," I say. "I was wondering if we could go to the beach again before it closes this weekend."

"What for?" Mom asks. "We were just there."

I smile. "I've got a date with a high dive."

When the bus pulls away from the school, rumbling down the driveway and leaving me standing in a cloud of exhaust, my stomach clenches. Derek wasn't on the bus this morning, and even though everything seems like it's back to normal, I'm suddenly terrified of walking into school and finding him by the vending machines, one of the cool kids instead of my best friend.

The warning bell rings out for the start of homeroom. I jog up the steps and through the front door, my heart thundering against my rib cage. Sweat quivers on my upper lip, and my breakfast churns in my stomach.

Please, please, please be the Derek I know.

As always, he looks flawless. I break into a grin when

I see him. His short locs, collared shirt, wrinkle-free shorts, and spotless sneakers are just as they should be. For once, I don't feel self-conscious about having pulled my own clothes from a pile on the floor. The only thing I feel is relief.

"You weren't on the bus," I breathe.

"Mom dropped me off—I had an early dentist appointment."

"Thank goodness."

He nudges me with his shoulder. "You okay, dude?"

"It's been a rough night."

His eyes turn serious. "Your dad's moving out today, right?"

I nod. "Yeah."

"I'm sorry." He nudges me again. "I'm here for you, Sam."

My heart squeezes in my chest. Derek has no idea how much his friendship meant when I needed it most. The thought of losing him almost broke me. If I didn't have him, and Grayson and Addie, I might not have fought so hard to find my way back home. This is one of the worst days of my life, but at least I have people— Derek included—who care about me.

I really messed things up when I played the skeleton flute and tried to change things. All I wanted was for our family to stay together. I never stopped to think about the consequences. It was so easy to look at what other people had and wish for my own life to be different. I realize now how wrong I was. The guilt I've been feeling all this time starts to fade. What was once a heavy stone permanently sitting in my stomach lightens. The most important thing about making mistakes is learning from them. It's what Dad always tells me.

Outside homeroom I almost bump into a skinny kid with messy brown hair and thick glasses. He stumbles and drops a book he's holding. I bend down, pick it up, and thrust it at him.

"Hey, sorry, Alex. I didn't see you there."

He takes the book, then tilts his head. "Uh, thanks, Sam."

"How's it going?"

Alex blinks at me and hugs his books close to his chest. "F-fine."

He slips into the classroom and sits across the room, glancing back at Derek and me as we enter behind him.

Derek shoots me a look. "What's up with that?"

"What?"

"Talking to that kid."

"Alex? He's a cool guy. We should invite him over to play video games sometime."

Derek slides into his seat and looks at me like I have two heads. Someday I'll tell him about everything that happened. I know he'll believe me, because that's what best friends do. But I need some time.

And there's something I need to do first.

After school I race down the sidewalk away from home. A couple blocks away, I veer off, the familiar sign calling to me again. Stapleton Town Park. Where it all started.

My feet can't carry me fast enough as I hurry across the grass, my eyes darting from side to side. A girl with long red hair sits on a picnic bench, her back to me. My stomach fills with a million butterflies.

I stop behind her and clear my throat. She turns, and her eyes travel up and down my body, then settle on my face. It takes everything I have not to vault over the top of the bench and throw my arms around Lena.

"Hey," I say.

The girl's eyebrows furrow over her dark brown eyes, and her mouth turns down in a frown. "Do I know you?"

My mouth drops open. "I . . . I . . ."

The words are like a slap to the face. I take a stumbling step backward, blinking back tears. *No, this can't be.* How can I remember her, but she's forgotten me? I promised to find her, and here she is, but she's looking at me like I'm a stranger. After everything we went through together.

The world around me starts to spin. A lump forms in my throat. The faint note of a flute floats across the park. I press a hand to my forehead, pulling in a deep breath. This can't be happening. She *can't* have forgotten.

Cold surges into my stomach. Maybe that's not it at all. This whole time, we thought we came from the same reality. We didn't even think to question it. But what if we *didn't*? What if she's in another world altogether and this is a different Lena?

"I knew you'd come!"

The voice comes from behind me. I whip around, and there she stands, a red baseball cap fitted on her head, just like the first time I met her. Lena grins as I look back and forth between her and the girl on the bench.

"What, how—"

Lena grins. "Sam, meet my sister, Lenore. Lenore, this is Sam, the boy I told you about."

Lenore waves. "Hey, Sam. Thanks for un-erasing my sister from reality."

"It was nothing," I say, shrugging.

Lena lets out a sharp laugh and leaps forward. Her arms crush me in a tight hug. I hug her back, letting out a rush of air.

"So humble for a guy who just saved the world," she says, releasing me.

After thinking I'd lost all the people I knew and loved, after traveling to another reality and risking my life to save Sammy and Lee, after fighting off monsters and an evil soul eater, having Lena here means everything. For one terrible moment, I thought I'd never see her again.

"You have no idea how happy I am to see you."

"A pack of wolf monsters wouldn't have kept me away," Lena says with a smirk. "And now you'll never get rid of me."

I nudge her shoulder with my fist. "Same."

"You okay?" Lena asks, narrowing her eyes.

My mind drifts back to this morning. Dad's old blue beater car packed to the roof with boxes, driving off down the street. Grayson slipping his hand into mine as we watched him go. Mom wiping the tears from Addie's cheeks as she cried for him, not really understanding what was happening.

I nod, swiping my eyes with the back of my hand before Lena can see what a hot mess I am. "I think so."

"I'm here for you," she says. "We're in this together, remember?"

Warmth spreads from my stomach, into my chest. *Together.* Even if my parents aren't.

I smile. "After what we went through in the ether, this should be a piece of cake, right?"

Lena laughs. "Totally."

Today might not be easy. And it'll probably only get harder from here. But I'm not alone, and that's what's most important. Going up against Bones and helping to save Sammy and Lee showed me that I'm so much stronger than I realized. I can do hard things. We all have it inside us. Lena did; Sammy and Lee did. Beaumont, too. Sometimes we just have to dig deep to find the strength. It doesn't always mean that things turn out the way you want them to. It means learning to roll with the punches. And looking at my new friend, I know that whatever new reality life has in store for me, I can handle that, too.

Acknowledgments

There are so many people I want to thank for helping *The Skeleton Flute* become a real, live book. I can't possibly name everyone, but here are a few, and named or not, thank you to everyone who walked with me on this journey. First and foremost, my amazing husband, Hugh, for encouraging me to chase after my dreams when I felt like I was too old and too mediocre to catch them. You were right all along. Your endless support meant everything—from listening to my early drafts, letting me toss ideas around, and helping me solve my impossible plot holes. I wouldn't be here without you. My mother, for passing on your love of reading, encouraging my writing as a child, and supporting me in any direction I chose to go with my life. My best friend, Helen, for believing in me, encouraging me, and being the best cheerleader I could ask for. My good friend, Kristal, for being one of my first beta readers and encouraging me to keep at it (despite those awful first drafts). Katie, for being the first person outside my circle who I trusted with my words, and who made me feel that maybe I wasn't awful at this writing thing. My good friend, Nicole. I couldn't ask for a better person to scream with. You're one in a million, and I'm lucky to call you a friend. Thank you for believing in me. Elinor, for your immense patience with the annoying, needy little girl across the street who was so desperate for attention. Thank you, from the bottom of my heart, for being there for me when I needed it the most. I think you listened to readings of those early stories more than anyone else, and you made me believe in myself a little more each time.

My PitchWars mentors, Sandra and Shannon (Team Stellify), who helped me shape this book into the beginnings of what it is today. Your guidance and support meant everything to me. My amazing, talented Narwhals (horns up!), for helping me develop into the writer I am today. Without our little slice of the writing community, I'd still be fumbling around in the dark. You helped me endlessly with critiques, story ideas, and title ideas. You trusted me with your words, and helped me learn how to be a better critique partner myself. You picked me up when I was in the dark depths of the query trenches and encouraged me to keep going. Most of all, you made it so I wasn't alone on this long, wild ride. My fellow MG PitchWars classmates. We went through something together a lot of people will never understand. The highs and lows of the experience wouldn't have been the same if we didn't have each other.

My agent, Emily S. Keyes, for taking a chance on me and my story. From the very first time we spoke, I could tell how passionate you were and knew you were the best partner for me and my career. My editor, Anna Parsons, for making my dream come true. You helped me elevate this book with such amazing, insightful feedback. You took a chance on me too, and I'll forever be grateful.

The random woman on my college tour whose pessimism caused me to change my major from liberal arts to interior design because "no one makes it as a writer." I don't remember your name, or your face, but I remember those words and the sinking feeling in my stomach as I let go of my dream. It wasn't what I wanted at the time, but maybe it was what I needed. It led me down a different path in life, and I wouldn't change a single minute of it.

All the authors whose books pulled me in as a child and gave me an escape from a hard and often sad childhood. The power you had. Thank you. I wouldn't be here without you. All my friends out there still chasing your dreams. Don't give up. And, finally, Avery for being the inspiration that led me to pick up the pen again. I lost that part of myself for a long time, and our time together reading inspired me to create again. Someday I hope you'll look back at this and be proud of your old mom.

About the Author

Damara Allen was born and raised in Syracuse, New York. She loves everything spooky and creepy. When she's not writing, she's spending time with her husband and daughter. Visit her at DSAllenAuthor.com.